THE MERCHANTS OF NATIONS

ALEXANDROS PAPADIAMANTIS in his own words (translated into English for the reader's benefit):

"I was born in Skiathos on the 4th of March 1851. I completed elementary school in 1863, but not until 1867 was I sent to high school in Halkida, where I attended grades A and B. Grade C I took in Piraeus, then interrupted my studies and stayed in the homeland. During July of 1872, I visited Mount Athos for pilgrimage, where I remained for a few months. In 1873, I arrived in Athens and studied grade D in the Varvakeio School. In 1874, I registered in the School of Philosophy, where I audited a few philology classes of my choice, while privately I occupied myself with foreign languages.

When I was little I used to paint the Saints, or write verses, and tried to compose comedies. In 1868, I attempted to write a novel. In 1879, my work *The Emigrant* was published in the newspaper "Neologos" of Constantinople; in 1881, a religious poem in the magazine "Sotira". In 1882, *The Merchants of Nations* was published in "Mi Hanesai". Afterwards, I wrote around one hundred short stories, which appeared in various magazines and newspapers."

After achieving popular success with serialized historical novels such as *The Merchants of Nations*, Alexandros Papadiamantis—today known as the "Saint of Greek literature"—received critical recognition for his short stories and became one of the most revered authors in modern Greece.

MICHAIL TZOUFRAS was born in Sweden and raised in Greece. He received his diploma from the National Technical University of Athens before earning a Ph.D. from the University of California, Los Angeles. A physicist with numerous academic honors and scientific articles published in scholarly journals, he has worked at the University of Oxford (UK) and in Silicon Valley. Since his childhood spent in Athens, he has been an avid reader of Greek literature—both the classics and the literary works of modern Greece. He currently resides in California.

The Merchants of Nations

ALEXANDROS PAPADIAMANTIS

translated by Michail Tzoufras

Sunstep Publishing • Sunnyvale, CA • www.sunstepbooks.com

First Edition: June 2016

Translated from the Greek.
Papadiamantes, Alexandros, 1851-1911, author.
[Oi Emporoi ton Ethnon. English]
The Merchants of Nations / by Alexandros Papadiamantis ;
translated with an introduction and notes by Michail Tzoufras.

Library of Congress Control Number: 2016944332

ISBN-13: 978-0-9976679-1-2

DEDICATION

To my brother Jason

CONTENTS

Part B

TRANSLATOR'S INTRODUCTION

I discovered the novel *The Merchants of Nations* in an old volume containing the collected works of Alexandros Papadiamantis in Greek at a university library in California. Having been one of his earliest writings (1882), it never received the critical acclaim that would be bestowed on his later works, especially his short stories and the novella *The Murderess*. Yet it is with this novel that Papadiamantis came to be loved by readers around Greece in the early 1880s. Papadiamantis himself did not heed the opinions of highbrow critics; his writings and life were guided by both his deep devotion to the Orthodox Christian faith and his affection for the genuine ethos of everyday Greeks.

The Merchants of Nations exemplifies his worldview by contrasting the devout medieval society of the Greek islands with the predatory vanity of the crusaders who arrived to subjugate them. Tasked with personifying the culture of the invaders, Marco Sanudo, one of the novel's main characters—and a historical figure who eventually established the Duchy of Naxos—sends the lives of Yiannis Mouchras and his wife Augusta into a tailspin. The plot takes the heroes and the reader across the Eastern

Mediterranean and reanimates the world of the foundering thousand-year-old Byzantine Empire during a time period (1199-1207 AD) that includes one of the most pivotal events in Greek history: the Sack of Constantinople (1204 AD), which arguably marked the end of the dominance of Orthodox Christianity. The fall of the Byzantine capital, which had previously withstood a dozen sieges by massive forces, to a comparatively small army of Catholic crusaders and the unparalleled rampage and looting they unleashed, left an irremediable trauma for which in 2001 Pope John Paul II offered an apology to Orthodox Christians. The event is only indirectly addressed by Papadiamantis who seems less interested in indicting the invaders than in shedding light on the conditions that prevail during such times of crisis, especially in the human heart.

Despite its ostensibly ethological nature, the story is anything but a dry study; it is a vivid account of the passionate pursuit of love, conquest, and revenge. And when in the latter part of the novel, we find the author and his heroes compelled to philosophize, they often do so with humor and witticisms to balance the otherwise-weighted topics of life and death. The result is endlessly quotable passages that possess strikingly sharp insight.

It is also at this part of the novel when Papadiamantis evokes the complicated relationship between the West and Greece—not only during the late Byzantine Empire but also in his contemporary Greece of the nineteenth century. This issue has hounded modern Greece since its independence in the early nineteenth century, when the first political parties were the English Party, the French Party, and the Russian Party. Throughout the twentieth century and even today, the question continues to arise: Where does Greece belong? In *The Merchants of Nations*, Papadiamantis indicates that such a question presents itself when a society does not stand on its own feet: "It seems slavery is always preferable to anarchy, just like leprosy is preferable to the plague." But here I must refrain from presenting any other sentences of Papadiamantis' out of their original context and instead allow the reader to draw her or his own conclusions.

Immersing myself in the world of this novel and revisiting its pages time and again in the process of translating it has been an exceptionally rewarding experience. For years, as I worked through the text, I had the story in the back of my mind, constantly contemplating ways to improve on troublesome sentences or concepts that seemed difficult to convey—and I must thank my wife and editor Lizzy for her guidance during this period. The reader does not have the time to dwell on each phrase or research every aspect of the story, so some context might prove useful. I have introduced a limited number of notes where it seemed essential and would not disrupt one's reading. For example, I employed notes to define character names that would have been obvious to a native Greek speaker; moreover, I have presented as Italian (rather than Greek) character names that sound Italian in the Greek text, that were derived from an Italian word, or that refer to Venetians. However, given that the original work contained no notes, I resisted adding too much information regarding the historical and geographical settings. Throughout, I aimed to match the tone and intent of the original.

Papadiamantis is particularly famous for the uniqueness of his prose and as such, his work is notoriously difficult to translate. Notwithstanding, ideas and the vehicle that carries them—the language—are inextricably linked; therefore, I aspired to translate both as faithfully as possible. There are also some minor logical inconsistencies and historical inaccuracies in the original, which I have preserved. These "mistakes" do not prevent the reader from enjoying the text, and their presence signifies another intriguing feature of the *The Merchants of Nations*: that initially it was not published as a self-contained book but as a weekly serial in the magazine "Mi Hanesai". Hence, the reader may notice that Papadiamantis regularly recaps the plot to accommodate those who may have missed earlier parts of the story. One could even start reading from near the halfway point (Part B) and still be able to follow along. Nevertheless, it is worthwhile reading the entire text from the very first page, not only because it is a pleasure to do so, but also to see chapter by chapter, Papadiamantis, the "Dostoyevsky of Greece", the "Saint of Greek literature", come into his own.

Michail Tzoufras
California
2016

The Merchants of Nations

AUTHOR'S NOTE

In one of the chapels of the Monastery of … there was a box, old and decrepit, full of shabby books. None of the wise travelers, who from time to time visited the Monastery library, had deigned to take a look at the forgotten box. Not until my friend, Mr. B., distinguished for his affection for neglected things, went through the box, despite only having visited these parts for sponge trading, and found amidst many liturgical books the scattered pages of an old membrane manuscript. After collecting and arranging them diligently, he managed to read almost the entire biography of a 13th century anchorite, who had led a tempestuous life prior to entering the monastic order. This biography of his is closely connected to the history of the Cyclades. Only a few pages were missing from the book, the contents of which were readily recovered from other sources.

My friend decided to copy the entirety without adding a word. He only slightly altered the phrasing before handing the book over to the publisher, who is reproducing it for the enjoyment of the readers.

PROLOGUE

1. EXCURSION

In the year of Our Lord 1199, no man in all of the Aegean archipelago had a wife fairer than Yiannis Mouchras[1], the wealthy nobleman of Naxos. Yet this did not prevent him from embarking on adventurous expeditions against the Genoese pirates, who constantly harassed the Venetian invaders and the peaceable islanders.

Yiannis Mouchras resided at the edge of Neochorio, on a hillside by the sea. His villa, large and seemly, was fortified with three towers and high walls. It was considered a shelter in the area. He had inherited some prerogatives, granted to his ancestors by the Venetians, and he protected and asserted them vigorously. As for those Genoese pirates, they paradoxically respected his house. But because he couldn't properly repay this respect by staying put, he would lead the bravest of the islanders to campaign against them.

Aside from that, he was hospitable and courteous to everyone. His wife, fair and innocent like a dove, was the source of honor to the house. In charge of a dozen handmaidens, she ruled prudently over it. It was unheard of for a poor man to be dismissed from this house empty-handed, or for a stranger to be denied hospitality. And all of the servants, following their masters' example, were exceedingly kind to strangers. The warehouses were filled with wheat and food, and the stables with grass and barley. God seemed to have opened His hand to this household, and the landlord received the blessings with uncovered head. He was akin to a biblical patriarch extending his open arms to the human souls lying at his feet.

There was only one shadow cast in this picture: the lack of children, and it drove him to despair.

Once a week Yiannis Mouchras would depart from his house at night, to return twenty-four to thirty-six hours later, sleepless and exhausted. The landlady, his wife, had gotten used to seeing him off unperturbed in the evening and waiting patiently for him in the morning. She had unlearned grumbling and complaining to him after the first few months of the marriage.

Where would he go?

The many nearby islets were often, especially when the weather was stormy, refuges for pirates. Mouchras would board his galley and pursue them. And this galley was grand and strong. He had purchased it at half-price from a hapless Venetian maverick, who had gone bankrupt the second month after setting it afloat and whose sailors had mutinied because they had gone unfed for three days. The Venetian had urged them to pillage the Genoese and the islanders for food. But the men, having fasted for three days, had no desire to attack others who were well nourished, and instead threw the Venetian overboard. After swimming to the nearest port, where he knew the galley was going to dock, he sold it to Mouchras' agent, who had for a long time been assigned with purchasing a ship on his behalf.

Who could have foreseen, eleven months earlier, when this handsome ship was being built in the dockyard of Saint Mark, that it would fall into the hands of the nobleman of Naxos?

Still, Mouchras could boast that this was not the only tie he ever forged with Venice. Many doughty and gallant knights of the Republic had benefited from his hospitality and would gladly reciprocate, if he were ever summoned for trial in front of the mighty Council of Ten.

Besides, the beautiful Augusta[2], Mouchras' wife, although born in Naxos, had half of her lineage hailing from Venice. She loved her husband and had deep affection for the beautiful island, where she had first seen the light of day. Not only was she welcoming to strangers and beneficent to the poor, but she was also a pious woman, and Mother Filikiti[3], the abbess of St. Kosmas, along with abbots Marthon and Vicentios, shared the fruits of her reverence.

The reason behind Mouchras' eagerness to pursue pirates was that he had received a special edict from Venice. His goal was to luck into, as promised, the title of admiral and nobleman of Venice.

One evening in the middle of March, he hastened as usual to board the galley. His crew, knowing to expect him at the usual time, was awake on board. A skiff with two raftsmen was waiting for him at the waterfront.

"Are you here, Minas?" called the approaching Yiannis Mouchras.

"I am here, chief," replied one of the raftsmen.

Mouchras boarded the skiff. The two raftsmen sat on the thwarts and started rowing.

"They haven't been showing their faces, chief, these heroes," said Minas, emboldened by his master's favor. "For five months we have been on our usual route every week, but neither a Genoese nor a Berber has appeared."

"Something tells me we will be busy tonight," said the other raftsman.

"What makes you think so, Old Pirachtis[4]?" asked the chief.

"My left eye is twitching, chief, and my right hand is itching."

"So be it. Whatever man's luck is, he wrestles with it," said Minas, who was in his twenties and philosophized prematurely.

"I was hoping for different words from your mouth, Minas," said Mouchras. "You spoke like an old man just now."

"Chief, don't doubt my courage. I will show it in action. Those who talk too much prove gutless, and their words are fat and round, like zeroes."

They had already reached the galley. Mouchras jumped on the deck with youthful briskness. The skiff was raised to the side. They detached the anchor and cast off.

As midnight approached, a gentle offshore breeze blew. The topsail bulged modestly and the ship moved noticeably. After a two-hour sail, they arrived at the islets of Makaras.

The moon had risen and was glowing palely on the sea and the bare rocks. When they passed the first islet, Minas was called by the barrelman to awaken the chief who had just fallen asleep.

"What is going on, Minas?" he asked.

"Chief, it seems there is a ship moored at Large Makaras."

Thus was the largest of the islets called.

Mouchras jumped up immediately.

"Where is it, Minas?" he asked opening his eyes.

"There it is, chief."

And he pointed at the stern of a ship by the coast. Mouchras stood for a few moments watching carefully.

"Sound the signal," he said turning to the barrelman.

Something was heard, like a sob, wailing through the air.

2. SKIRMISH

It was from Minas' bow, which he had extended and aimed at the ship in the distance, about a quarter of a mile away. The arrow didn't reach it but sank into the waves. Minas shot a second and a third one.

Meanwhile, movement was observed on the foreign ship. A skiff detached from it and reached the coast, then it immediately returned. After that, the ship seemed to budge. It was apparently stationed in a canal between the two islets, not anchored, just tied to the shore. It was already moving visibly. No doubt it was hostile.

Those on the galley felt the usual thrill that precedes every important deed. The arteries of Old Pirachtis pulsated, like in the time of his youth, and Minas felt his blood throbbing.

"What are the chief's commands?" asked the boatswain.

"Assume defensive position," said Mouchras. "Everyone with your arrows and your axes."

In a few moments the foreign ship had approached.

The galley had turned its stern to Large Makaras, like a warrior securing his back against the wall. In contrast, the pirate ship seemed to be looking for free passage. But

Mouchras had already blocked it. There wasn't sufficient space between the three islets, and Mouchras knew that the shallow waters and reefs on the opposite side made an escape in the dark difficult.

"Who are you?" yelled Mouchras loudly.

"Warriors!" answered a gruff voice from the pirate ship.

Simultaneously, arrows were heard whistling though the rigging and the masts. Those on the galley responded again and again to the enemy shots.

For a while, amidst confusion and noise, shots were constantly being exchanged. Minas' arm got injured, and the chief received two arrows, one to his cheek and one to his chest. But the pain excited him and called him ceaselessly to battle.

It was hard to determine the size of the enemy crew. Mouchras' crew consisted of twenty-five men.

"Ah, this is why my hand was itching," said Old Pirachtis.

"What happened, Old Pirachtis?" asked the boatswain.

"A sting on my right hand; my wife hasn't stung me this bad for a long time."

"Are you wounded?" asked the chief.

"Stung, I'm telling you, stung!"

And the battle continued and was not to be decided quickly. Worried, Mouchras summoned the barrelman and ordered him to signal retreat. But at the same time, he spoke in the boatswain's ear and told him to prepare for onslaught.

The deep and weary sound of the trumpet was heard thrice. Immediately, the boatswain, Minas, and a third sailor grabbed the boat hooks and tried to arrest the gunwale of the pirate ship. But they could not reach it. Finally, the barrelman took his grapnel and hurled it to the mast. He managed to catch and pull the ship, and then Minas and the boatswain with their boat hooks finished the job. The pirate ship had been violently tugged to the galley, before the Genoese had time to prevent it.

"Let's go, lads!" shouted the chief. "Today we see who counts!"

He was the first to climb the side of the pirate ship. Behind him charged the rest of them. A severe axe paralyzed Mouchras' left hand as soon as he put it on the enemy gunwale. Minas and two other young sailors hurried from behind and responded with fierce strikes to the defending pirates. The chief almost fell sideways into the sea, but he grasped the gunwale tightly with his sound hand and the others supported him from behind. In a remarkable moment of determination and persistence he defeated the pain, rushed and set foot on the enemy deck. The rest followed.

In a few moments, haphazard, fierce strikes of axes, oars, and swords, mingled with terrible curses and insults, could be heard on the deck. Two or three heads fell; hands, arms, and shins were pulverized. The exasperation on both sides was indescribable. It was impossible to distinguish who was striking from who was being hit, who was shrieking from pain and who was screaming from rage.

If instinct had been absent, this magic beyond cognition, which in the midst of agitation and darkness and in complete deafness and blindness survives to the very end, they wouldn't have been able to tell friend from foe.

The pirates outnumbered the attackers. Mouchras alone, despite the overwhelming pain from his pulverized hand, was able to notice it. Yet his courage remained unwavering.

And it seemed that eventually the islanders would succumb to their enemies' superior numbers. But at the moment when the first frost of fear sneaked into Mouchras' heart, a strange crash was heard on the deck. The hopes of this leader of the attackers were revived, and he turned in that direction.

"Open these hatchways at all cost!" a man's voice called brilliantly, and it seemed to possess something prophetic.

The man was pointing at his companions in the hull of the ship.

But those to whom this call was addressed, had no time to understand, or follow it. Because in an instant, five to six men emerged from the captain's cabin, armed to the teeth and very threatening.

"Curse! Thunder! Hell!" the pirate captain was heard screaming.

"We are on your side, Greeks!" hailed the first of the newcomers approaching Mouchras. "Let's throw these dogs into the sea!"

In the blink of an eye, in the course of the terrible battle against those pirates who hadn't yet lost their courage, the first of these men, a tall and majestic youth, threw himself into the struggle with redoubtable force.

"Your last hour has come, dog!" he yelled at the pirate captain. "Come face me!"

And the pirate captain, as if awaiting the invitation, flung himself in front of him and started to duel. The unknown man, who was holding a large and heavy cutlass and swinging it like a toy, fended him off. The attention of the exhausted men on both sides concentrated on these two fighters. The duel was quickly over. As brave as the pirate captain was, he couldn't compete with the rage and fury of this man, who had emerged from the depths of the ship, like a demon from the underworld, to take the soul of the pirate captain after the expiration of his signed-in-blood contract. With a final strike he pierced the pirate's neck, chopped his head off, and threw it into the sea.

And he shouted at the pirate crew:

"Surrender! Or you are doomed."

3. THE CAPTIVES

When the onslaught on the pirate ship had started, someone from the pirate crew had managed to make his absence from the deck go unnoticed. This man was a young black Ethiopian, named Mirchan. His color and features were most distinctly of the African race; his eyes and teeth shone brightly in the dark. Carefully avoiding the surrounding eyes, softening his footsteps, and holding his breath, he descended into the captain's cabin in the stern, lit a candle, opened a box, removed a large key, and fitted it onto a trapdoor. After opening it, he descended into the hull and lit the faces of eight men lying on straw mats with their hands and feet in chains.

"You are here, Mirchan!" said one of the men sitting up with effort. "What is happening on the deck?"

"Quiet, please, boss!" said Mirchan. "It seems to me that our troubles will be over tonight, my friends!"

"What is going on? Tell me."

"We have come under attack by a ship, and they are fighting well, not playing. An onslaught just started. And devil knows how they will get away this time."

"And us too!" groaned the man looking at his chains with eyes the color of blood.

"I think I can unchain you, boss."

Mirchan took a key from his pocket and unlocked the chains.

"Bravo, Mirchan!" said the man who seemed to be the leader. "You say little but do a lot. I give you my word that as soon as I arrive in Venice a free man I will proclaim you Bey of the Barbary Coast."

"Gaining the captain's trust was a good thing, boss!" said Mirchan. "If I hadn't gained this devil's trust, nothing good would have happened."

"Worry not, my friend; I will fix this devil well."

"Now, let me give you your weapons. Come along to the captain's cabin."

He opened an armory by the staircase, gave them swords, axes, and cutlasses, and fully armed, they rushed upstairs.

This is how the unknown men came to take part in the fight and how it turned against the pirates, who, after the death of their captain, put their weapons down.

Mouchras' fighters chained them, transferred them to the galley, and incarcerated them under the deck.

The chief ordered departure. It was already nearing daybreak. They tied the pirate ship from the stern, and because the wind was weak, the sailors used two skiffs to tug both ships.

The former captives were left on the galley with Mouchras, who welcomed their leader and shook his hand.

"I am not asking you how you ended up here, stranger. It's enough that you came to us as guardian angels."

"My name is Marco Sanudo, chief, and I am from Venice. Or rather I am from Constantinople, for I was born there."

"Marco Sanudo? You are, I think, a relative of Enrico Dandolo's."

"Certainly. I am his nephew."

"I have often heard of you as a brave and noble warrior."

"I am grateful, chief. But what you were not suspecting, when you referred to me as 'stranger', is that you are offering me your hospitality on my own ship. I mean, this ship that used to belong to me."

"I will offer you my hospitality in my villa, sir, for as long as you please to accept it. But, did you say this galley used to belong to you?"

"Yes, chief."

"Are you then the knight who sold it to my man?"

"It is me. And I recognized it as soon as I saw it. I sold it to a merchant who had been commissioned by a brave warrior. This is a handsome ship, chief."

"If you like it, it's yours, knight. Please take it; from this very moment it belongs to you."

"I am indebted to you, chief. Such generosity! I can pay for it."

"You have already paid for it. It is enough that you like it."

"Thank you."

They both fell silent. Sanudo thought that it would be best to talk about his circumstances before Mouchras reminded him.

"I still need to explain to you how I found myself on the pirate ship. Let me now tell you the story briefly."

"But are you not tired? Don't you want to rest, knight?"

"On the contrary, I need to keep myself busy. After the captivity I endured I need air, I need to move and work, chief. I think I can stay awake for a whole century to make up for this forced deathly slumber."

"As you wish."

"Two months ago," started Sanudo, "I received from my uncle Dandolo an order to campaign against pirates in the Adriatic. I had a fleet of four galleys with a crew of two hundred men under my command.

One night I managed to encircle the pirates. They had three ships moored in the Strofades straights. I sounded the signal. My men were full of bravery and my galleys mightily armed. Yet who could have thought?

I had never led a stronger fleet or a braver crew, and I had never been defeated by the Genoese before, until that night.

What I did not suspect," continued Sanudo in a trembling voice, "and to my detriment discovered that evening, was that the Genoese had a secret alliance with the Algerians and the Berbers. The Genoese were anchored windward, the Algerians leeward. As soon as the battle started, they used torches to signal to their allies, and I quickly found myself surrounded by two terrible enemies. My galleys sank, my men were slaughtered or enslaved, and I was taken prisoner and handed over to the Genoese leader, Carreccio. How happily I plunged my sword in his throat not too long ago! Remembering the battle, during which I killed the pirate captain an hour ago, I think his blood is like wine, rushing to my head and inebriating me, chief!"

"So the man you killed was Carreccio?" asked Mouchras.

"That was him, the snake!" said Sanudo.

Mouchras felt involuntary aversion.

"This ungodly man," continued Sanudo, "had chained my seven companions and myself and thrown us like dogs in the bottom of his ship. But glory be to Mavros[5] Mirchan—whom I want to introduce to you, chief—I was freed from my bondage and came to your aid."

"And I am grateful to you, knight."

Sanudo called:

"Mirchan! Mirchan! Are you here?"

Upon hearing his name, Mavros gamboled aft.

"Come here," said Sanudo.

"I am here, boss."

"Bow to the chief, Mirchan."

Mavros took Mouchras' hand and put it on his head.

"Describe, Mirchan, to the chief, how you fell in Carreccio's hands, why you hate him, and how you gained his trust."

"Aw, he, Carreccio," said Mavros in a tragicomic manner, "is now dead and eaten by a big dogfish. If only he would live once more, so I could slay him myself. Anyway, the boss did him justice and he won't be coming back."

"Had he harmed you?" asked Mouchras.

"He did not need to harm me! This Carreccio slit my mother's womb open and cut the baby she was carrying in four."

"Why?"

"My mother was a slave of this Carreccio, and she had had me before with another father, a black man, who was also slaughtered by Carreccio. This Carreccio slit her womb open because he claimed that the child she was carrying was someone else's."

"And why did this man trust you?"

"He thought that I hated my mother and that I was jealous, because she had had a child with him and the two of them used to spend nights together, after my father's death. And he thought that I enjoyed it when he cut her."

"How is that possible? It seems inconceivable," said Mouchras.

"Because I was dancing when my mother died. And I told him, 'Well done, she deserved it, master'. And I pretended to sing and dance. I was doing all this, so he would not kill me too."

"And Carreccio believed you?"

"He had no brain inside his skull. A black man can have more brains than a white man, if the white man is a fool and he drinks too much."

"Was he a drunkard then?"

"He would drink for five devils… ten devils. Even now he is drunk, and when the boss threw him down there he must have thought that the sea was raki."

Sanudo in the meantime, while Mavros was talking, had gotten up and sauntered with wide strides along the deck.

Mouchras dismissed Mavros and withdrew to sleep.

Due to unfavorable winds, the galley slowed and spent the whole day travelling. It called at the moorage around the second hour of the night. Mouchras and the stranger disembarked, knocked on the gate of the villa, and awakened the gatekeeper who recognized the master's voice and let them in. The absolute silence that reigned made it seem like everyone in the villa was asleep, so the host took Sanudo to a bedroom, wished him good night, and went to sleep.

4. THE COUNT'S TOWER

Mouchras' villa was situated by a majestic and picturesque beach. It had been built in the previous century and it was said that the count Pragotsis, who had established it, had irrigated its foundations with blood. Its towering battlement had been erected on a steep rocky coast. Beyond it, there was a terrible cliff, the sight of which overwhelmed the eyes and caused vertigo.

At the time of the present story, this battlement was called "the Tower of Pragotsis". Augusta, Mouchras' wife, was afraid to climb it by herself, yet she often did.

From its crown, it was said, one night Count Pragotsis had thrown his wife with her child because he had suspected her of unfaithfulness. Following this crime, he had gotten depressed to the point of mania, and had needed to find perversions in order to overcome his ghosts and pass the nights. Thus, he would snatch the wives and daughters of the islanders and drag them to the tower, where, after a night of nightmare and pleasure, he would throw them from the cliff as sacrificial lambs to the shadow of his wife.

It was also said, but these were perhaps fabrications of the credulous villagers and fisherman, that even forty years after the count's death, at the time of the present story, once in a while two shadows would appear atop the tower at midnight. They would clash and moan awfully, until at some point the splash of a body falling into the water would be heard. These were Count Pragotsis and his wife, returning to the scene to replay the gruesome tragedy.

There were a lot of people who swore oaths to having seen all that; especially old Mattheos the sponge diver would tell the whole story in detail to anyone curious.

But there were also those who doubted these rumors. The latter thought that the entire tale was nothing more than concoctions of foolish and superstitious people, whereas the former believed only the supernatural part of the tale, that indeed ghosts could be seen there, but regarding Count Pragotsis, they did not even believe he had ever existed.

These thoughts were scaring Augusta on that night, during which the aforementioned events took place. It was midnight, she had had no sleep, and she did not know when her husband might return. She had asked the gatekeeper to announce her husband's arrival no matter how late it may be. But because the gatekeeper was an old respectable woman who was terribly sleepy that night, as always, she figured that it would be cruel to disturb her lady's sleep in the middle of the night. And before finishing that thought, this blessed woman leaned her head to one side and fell asleep.

She used to foretaste sleep by sitting next to the fireplace with her distaff in her hands, while in the other corner, facing the fire, her husband, the old Manos, was snoring for five men and dreaming that his darling wife was standing watch.

But old Mano[6] had a clear conscience, and even though she was asleep she did not think any less of herself. Didn't she respond to the first sound of the knocker? Didn't she open the gate for her master and his guest? Didn't she close it again carefully? So what if she forgot to tell her master that his wife was waiting for him in her room? She also didn't happen to notice his arm hanging by his chest, as if it had been injured.

However, Augusta was awake, as we said above. She was sitting by a lantern supporting her head with her hand. The features of her face were symmetric; she had large dark eyes and a very lovely expression. She wore a white gown buttoned properly up to her neck. But what could be seen of her neck would cause one to make comparisons to lilies and milk and all the other known praises.

She opened a book and tried to read. In vain; her eyes were staring at the pages but she wasn't seeing the letters.

She called her lady's maid.

"Sentina, are you sleeping?"

"I can't be sleeping, if the madam is wakeful. What do you please?"

Sentina was a tall and bony woman of thirty-eight, sallow and objectionable. But she was devoted to her lady. She was taciturn and attended to Augusta's every nod and word. She could be used as a spy if needed. But she wasn't particularly fond of Mouchras, so she didn't have anybody to betray her lady to.

Because, in order to break two people up, they should, as far as Sentina was concerned, both be dear friends of hers.

"Do you want to go upstairs, Sentina?"

"Upstairs where, madam?"

"Upstairs… to Pragotsis'."

"The lady is excessively daring."

"Are you scared, Sentina?"

"I am not scared at all. But I advise the lady to moderate her queerness."

"Your master is absent, we will go gaze at the sea in case he is on his way back."

"I will follow the lady willingly, as is my duty. I am just saying that the lady has strange desires."

"But there is no better place for us to await my husband's return."

Sentina lighted a lamp. They crossed dark corridors, climbed stairways, and arrived at the Tower of Pragotsis.

They sat there and took in the sea breeze.

The rising moon was silver-plating the shimmering waves and the threatening rocks. The splash of the waves breaking on the steep coast could be heard. From time to time, the caws of the night crows resonated somberly and monotonously from the nearby forest.

Augusta's eyes wandered widely, flying over the sea as if to record this beautiful and mysterious picture in her heart.

But suddenly she fixed her eyes on one spot.

"Do you see, Sentina, the masts of that ship in the moorage?"

"I see, madam."

"Is this our ship that has returned?"

Indeed, over by the opposite coast that formed the moorage, the masts of a ship could be seen, rising over the sunken part of the isthmus. But it was unclear if they were two, three, or four, because the meager glow of the crescent-shaped moon could not illuminate them well. It was like a mockery of the darkness; the moon is the smile of the night, a sarcastic and very awful smile.

"I don't know, madam," replied Sentina.

"It's a pity that I can't recognize our galley."

"Who could recognize it this late at night!"

"But I forgot, Sentina, that you are nearsighted. Certainly you can hardly discern the thing I am pointing at."

"Discern what? The ship? I can see it clearly."

Sentina was lying. But she was conceited.

"Do you see the masts over there?"

"I see them," insisted Sentina.

Augusta fell silent. It would certainly be impossible to change her maid's mind, if she intended to insist that she could see.

Sentina feigned musing and getting sentimental.

"It is beautiful," she said, "but one gets frightened sitting up here."

"It is cold, Sentina. I was wrong not to bring my overcoat."

"I knew we were not staying here long, if the lady wishes. This is why I did not remind her to take her overcoat."

"I like it here. Could you do me a favor, Sentina, and get me my overcoat?"

"And the lady is not afraid to stay here by herself?"

"Not at all, Sentina. You won't be long. What do I have to be afraid of?"

"Strange things happen here, it is said."

"Don't believe, my friend, the foolish stories you hear."

"I have never believed them. But it is my duty to advise the lady."

"Go bring my overcoat then."

At the imperative tone of her lady's latest request, Sentina was unable to resist. She stood up, and taking the lamp with her, went downstairs.

Sentina's last step was heard as she walked away and then silence took over.

Augusta, having stayed alone on the tower, regretted her bravery and started to worry. The mysterious sense of the supernatural, which in defiance of all science and rational thought always affects the human heart, especially of the weaker sex, was, as is well known, even stronger with our ancestors. And there was something appealing in this fear, to the congenial soul of this woman.

Augusta involuntarily recollected and repeated to herself, like a teacher's lesson, the bizarre tales she had heard about this tower from her women. She pictured again the shape of the poor woman, the countess, who, if the stories were true, had one morning fallen from this tall battlement. And how she, with her child, had found death in the waves, which had become their final resting place.

She recalled the terrible bust of that ghastly count, who, after this crime, continued, according to the tradition, piling more crimes onto this place, throwing each of his victims from this tower, as if to build a waterfront of corpses.

She considered all that and shivered.

And there was another fear that had gotten hold of her; the fear that her visit to the tower, and Sentina's return without her, may be noticed and commented upon by some indiscreet maid. She knew what it meant to give cause for aspersion to the maids, for they were already gossiping about her every day without any reason.

In a few seconds she heard the steps of someone ascending.

"Sentina is returning too soon," whispered Augusta. "She is welcome, God bless."

However, the approaching steps were becoming heavy.

"Odd. These do not sound like Sentina's steps. Who is this?" said Augusta.

That moment, a strange man appeared in front of her, like a ghost; someone she had never seen before.

5. THE TEMPTATION

Augusta recoiled mechanically from the slab she was sitting on. She let out a scream and her body parts started trembling.

The stranger stepped back when he saw her, but did not seem startled.

"Who are you, madam?" he asked.

Augusta did not answer. Her tongue was paralyzed.

The stranger, noticing the terror he had caused this woman, recovered the readiness of his spirit.

"On my knees I ask for your forgiveness, madam," he said.

And he knelt down with one knee on the marble floor.

"I humbly ask for your forgiveness, madam," he repeated, "because I engendered terror involuntarily, and my recklessness is worthy of any reproach and any reprobation. You must, of course, be the wife of the noble landlord of this villa."

Augusta regained some of her composure but did not reply.

"I have no doubt that you are the lady of this house," repeated the stranger. "And I, madam, am your guest. Tonight, your husband has offered me his hospitality."

"My husband?" said Augusta.

"Yes, madam."

"He returned?"

"He returned with me."

"When?"

"Three hours ago."

"Where is he?"

"I think he is sleeping."

"And his men?"

"They stayed on the ship."

"Is he well?"

"He is well."

"Nothing bad happened in his excursion?"

"Fortunately not."

"And why did he not announce his arrival to me?"

"He thought you were asleep, madam."

"And you?"

This question put the stranger back in his place.

"You mean why did I improperly come up here at such a late hour? You are right, madam, I am guilty. I have abused the hospitality of your noble husband. But I had no sleep and was suffering greatly. I wanted to find the outdoors to breathe the open air. I humbly beg you to forgive me."

Augusta did not respond.

"Rest assured that this was my only reason and I had no other intentions. I insist on begging you and on asking you not just for your forgiveness, but that you excuse me to everybody else."

"I can excuse you," said Augusta. "But who will excuse me, sir?"

"I think, madam, that you are in no need of excuses; you are in your own house."

"But this very moment my lady's maid is coming here, sir. What will I tell her, what will you tell her...for she doesn't know you, for I don't know you, for you don't know me?"

"Aw, don't worry, madam. There must be a place around here where I can be invisible to her."

Augusta found the stranger's last suggestion rude. It seemed to her that this audacious climber of battlements and nocturnal visitor of rooftops was pushing her to share in his crime and guilt, when she was innocent. Rage got hold of her and blood rushed to her head.

"There is no place other than this cliff," she cried out, pointing at the entablature of the battlement.

And she really felt that at that moment it would be possible for the stranger to fall there, or that she may throw him.

With a concealed smile he straightened his posture; lightning darted from his eyes as he assumed a tragic pose and tone.

"Aw yes, I am willing to jump from this very cliff," he said, "as long as you say you forgive me."

And from the opposite corner of the terrace, where he was standing, he barrelled with steady step, as if to throw himself to the cliff.

The surprised Augusta hastened to prevent him.

"What are you doing, mister!" she called grabbing him by his arms. "Have you lost your mind?"

Her hands and voice were trembling. She felt that her touch was transmitting her terror to the arms of the stranger.

He stood for a moment observing her with a deep and admiring gaze. Dressed in white and illuminated by the dim glow of the moon, she possessed something fantastically charming.

Their glances met and she lowered her eyes.

She let go of his arms.

"Stay here, sir," she said, "and I will go downstairs to preempt my servant."

"But you haven't told me that you forgive me, madam."

"I forgive you. Stay."

She disappeared down the tall staircase. While on her way to her bedroom, and still thinking about the peculiar events of this night, she ran into Sentina, who was surprised to see her lady return from the tower before she had brought her overcoat. Augusta forbid her from talking about it and sent her to sleep.

Marco Sanudo (because this is who it was) had been honest about everything, except that he had come upon this outdoor space by coincidence just to catch a breath. The truth was that Sanudo was lying sleepless in bed unable to close his eyes when Augusta and her maid started heading to the tower. The windows in his room were facing the corridor, and from the light in Sentina's hands he saw through the glass the two women pass by. Struck by Augusta's beauty, he decided to follow them, for he was a man of many interests who was easily impressed. He rose and got dressed immediately, exited the room on his tiptoes, and followed the glow of the lamp until they suddenly turned to a staircase on the right and the daredevil found himself in the dark.

He waited, hoping that once the two sleepwalkers turned again he might see the light, but in vain. Confused, he fumbled around trying to get back to his room. But shortly, the glow of the lamp reappeared behind him. He heard footsteps approaching. He hid in a corner and saw Sentina pass in front of him. She did not notice him and continued on her way to the lady's chamber. Sanudo retraced his former path, and since the hallway Sentina was trudging down was straight—and if Sanudo had paid attention, he could have heard the following monologue between her teeth: "Your overcoat! But no… wait for half an hour… to get pleuritis"—it was, as I was saying, straight and very long, he sped up his footsteps and managed, guided by the last flicker of the departing lamp and by a ray of moonlight coming down from the skylight, to find the staircase to the right and make his way up the tower. The rest is known to us.

6. NUN

The next day, Mouchras, without suspecting the scene of the previous night, presented the guest to his wife.

Marco Sanudo, with compliments and bows, comported himself like a perfect knight and expressed his greetings to the lady most festively. Augusta was measured and solemn. A cloud had been cast on her countenance. Perhaps she was concerned about her husband's hand injury, which was not too serious and just needed to stay wrapped in gauze to heal.

After breakfast, her husband asked the stranger to tell the story of the skirmish two nights ago. But although Augusta was listening, she smiled sparingly to the narrator. During breaks, she looked at her husband empathetically, considering the dangers he had faced.

When they were left alone, she told him:

"Why did you not tell the story yourself, and instead asked the stranger to tell it?"

"Because the stranger was also sitting here with us, my dear."

"He does not make a good impression on me," she said.

"But why, my dear? He proved valuable to me, both he and the black man under his protection. If it hadn't been for them, we wouldn't have won the fight. And maybe I would not have returned."

"This is why I tell you," she said angrily and with tears in her eyes, "that I don't want you chasing pirates anymore! I cannot accept to owe your life to a man, but only to God, to whom we owe everything. This business of pursuing pirates is not for you anyway. Let the authorities persecute them."

"But there are no authorities, dearest. At this point, we cannot say whether we belong to the state of the Romans[7], to the authority of the Franks, or to the republic of the Venetians."

"To whom do we belong then?"

"To nobody. We ought to protect our honor, our life, and our property ourselves."

After all of these explanations Augusta remained pensive and glum until the evening. She declined to accompany her husband and the stranger on their excursion to the countryside, feigning a headache. When she was alone, she sent one of her servants to the nearby Monastery of St. Kosmas to ask the abbess to pay her a visit. Mother Filikiti abided immediately.

She entered the hall holding a rosary and wearing a vestment decorated with crosses.

Augusta latched the door of the hall and they both sat on a chaise. They would have been completely alone if Sentina, who always seemed to fly by the anteroom, hadn't been noticing her lady's glumness during the day, and hadn't attached her eye and ear to the keyhole.

"How are you then, dearest Mother?" asked Augusta. "It seems you have forgotten all about us for some time."

"It is rather you who has forgotten about me, my daughter," replied the nun. "Why don't you come to the monastery anymore?"

"You know, the housework, Mother, does not leave me time."

"But what is the matter with you? You seem to have cried," said the nun, squinting intently at Augusta's face.

She lowered her voice and approached the nun.

In vain Sentina stretched her ears. She couldn't hear anymore.

"I have a weight on my conscience today, Mother. I called you in order to tell you about it. I cannot suffer any longer; I am drowning."

"What happened? Tell me, my daughter."

"Last night I almost died from terror."

"Why?"

"It was midnight and I had climbed up to the Tower of Pragotsis."

"Alone?"

"With Sentina."

"For what purpose?"

"My husband had been gone with the galley. And because he was late, I was worried."

The nun shook her head.

"This is not the real reason, my dear child," she said. "Do you really believe that you went up there for your husband and only for him? These are incitements, nocturnal fantasies, provocations to temptation, carnal frolics. Avoid such things, like the married woman you are."

Augusta lowered her eyes.

"I don't mean to offend you," said the nun, "but we must be honest during confession. Continue, my child. What happened next?"

"It was cold and I sent Sentina to fetch my shawl."

And she talked about the appearance of the stranger on the tower and the rest.

"And is this man good-looking?" asked the nun.

"He seems quite good-looking, Mother. But let's leave that aside; tell me, am I right to be worried? Something is telling me that he did not climb there by coincidence."

"I concur. But do you think he would have really thrown himself off the cliff?"

"I don't know, Mother."

"He seems like a shrewd comedian."

"I want your opinion on whether I should talk about this to my husband," said Augusta.

The nun considered this for a few moments and said no.

"So I should say nothing?"

"Nothing good would come from telling. But you should convince him with other pretenses not to host the Venetian for a long time."

"Why? Is there any danger?"

"Who knows? I will pray for you. This I must do."

"Thank you, Mother."

"I have no doubt that this stranger has a devilish infatuation with you, my daughter. But I am concerned withal that you will be tempted and produce a combination of sin."

"Mother! What are you saying?"

"Saint Ephrem the Syrian urges us to guard our senses from temptation. It is prudent, when we walk, that we are careful not to fall. From all passions, carnal love is the most tyrannical. Because it has a trap to hold us in: our own body."

"Mother! Aw Mother!"

"And among all the fruits, the only one that doesn't need a lot of time, not a single hour, to mature, is devilish love, my child. The other fruits take hours and years to ripen. And this is the only fruit that does not need the warmth of the sun, but develops heat by itself. And in the dew and in the dark, and on the terrace or the roof, it always ripens in an instant. Those who are careless misstep, those who are prideful crash. The times are difficult. What goes up must come down; flight is followed by fall. This I said."

"Aw, God, pity me!"

The nun got up and raised her forehead; evidently satisfied with what she had said. But immediately suppressing her pride, she held Augusta's hand and kissed her forehead.

"Perhaps I judged you too harshly, my child. But a friend must have a sharp tongue. Be careful."

"I am indebted to you, Mother. I will protect myself from temptation with all my power."

"You will do well."

Meanwhile, Sentina, who had been stretching her ears for a long time and had still failed to hear anything, had gotten enraged. To compensate for the lack of a real story, she came up with another one, completely silly, that she rushed to share with the cook.

"Do you know anything, Aunt Ralou?" she asked her.

"Know what?"

"Something is wrong with the lady. She is unwell."

"What is wrong?"

"This is for the abbess to know, to whom she is confessing right now."

"Then why are you telling me?"

"If I tell you something, will you turn me in?"

"No. Why do I care!"

"So listen: The lady has given up and has no more hopes of bearing a child."

"So?"

"With her husband that is."

"And then?"

"This is taking a toll on her."

"So?"

"So she is looking for a way to get enlightened."

"Enlightened how?"

"Enlightened in other ways of bearing children."

"With medication?"

"Not with medication. The lady has exhausted all those in existence."

"Then how is she going to have children?"

"You are too innocent, Ralou!"

"What are you telling me? I don't understand."

"Of course you don't."

"How?"

"Without medication."

"How is it possible?"

"Just like all women."

"You are confusing me. I don't understand anything."

"Wait. Let's come up with an example."

"Let's."

"When Uncle Ralios was alive, rest in peace," said Sentina, "if you couldn't have children, Aunt Ralou, and you knew it was not your fault, but it was because of him, what would you do?"

"What would I do?"

"If you wanted to have children."

"Nothing."

"What nothing?"

"Nothing, I tell you."

"And if you had a large fortune, like the lady."

"Nothing."

"On the contrary, you would have called the abbess, to whom you like confessing, to tell her all of your thoughts."

"What thoughts?"

"Your desire for heirs."

"Eh, so what?"

"You would have liked to ask, if it is a sin…"

"What is a sin?!"

"To give birth to children…"

"Children?"

"Yes, children."

"But it is not a sin."

"With a man other than your own!"

"With another man?!" exclaimed Ralou. "Wow wow wow, what are you saying, Sentina?!"

Sentina guffawed and exited the room, leaving the poor woman stunned.

When she returned to her lady's chambers, Filikiti was on her way out. On her already solemn face she had put a mask of ice, and from the coldness pervading her disposition it was impossible to suspect what had been said a few minutes ago behind that door.

Mother Filikiti was fifty-four years old, yet still looked in her prime. When she had been young, she had gotten engaged to a handsome Venetian whom she had loved. After he was killed in a battle with the Franks in Monemvasia, Filikiti, acting prudently for the comfort of her flesh, got married to a middle-aged land-owner, with whom she lived peacefully for a few months. But he divorced her, alleging that she was excessively devout, spending several hours every day in the temple and neglecting her home. She was then forced to apply herself as a midwife, but because she was only successful at abortions and embryocide she was considered unsuitable to attend regular childbirth. Thence, she changed her art and became a matchmaker and a cerement-wrapper for the deceased. But because these two professions were contradictory, she soon lost her clients and had to find refuge in the nearby female monastery. There she managed to gain favor with the rulers of the island and on account of the services she promised to offer them in the future, she was promoted to abbess. And she was a virtuous nun, it was said, even though she forced the monastery vicar to mention during the ceremonies sometimes the Patriarch of Constantinople and others the Pope of Rome. This she considered masterful politics.

When Mother Filikiti left the villa, Augusta locked herself in her chamber and cried to comfort herself. Afterwards, as if an idea had occurred to her, she got up and exited. She took the same way she had walked the night before and climbed up to the same battlement of Count Pragotsis. She stayed there, observing the floor of the terrace, as if demanding an explanation from the cold stones. Then she bent over the entablature and gazed into the steepness of the cliff. What was she thinking? What was she studying? She walked back and forth for a long time, with her arms on her chest and facing the ground. She didn't lift her eyes once to look at the sea or the sky.

The view from that height was majestic: the tallness of the plunging cliff, the blue sea, smiling and occasionally playing with the rocks on the shore, yet mysterious, deep, and immeasurable in the offing; the steep and rugged coast spreading around the footing of the tower, overgrown grassy hills nearby and across. On one side the forest, on the other the mountains, in between the sea, on top the sky, infinity everywhere. Loftiness entangled with the graceful and the wild.

Yet Augusta had no eyes for such things anymore.

It was obvious that the impression of the previous night could not be expunged from her spirit.

She descended the stairs slowly and returned to her chamber.

She called Sentina and sent her to bring the gatekeeper.

Old Mano appeared hobbling and grumbling. She said addressing Augusta:

"What does my lady want from me? How can I, an old woman, climb the lady's staircase?"

"Old Mano," said Augusta very kindly, "I thought I told you yesterday evening that I wanted you to announce the return of your master to me, no matter what time he arrived, didn't I?"

"How could I have known what time the master would return?" said Old Mano. "And how could I have told the lady, if I myself didn't know. And why does everyone keep bothering me, an old woman, and I cannot find an hour's peace, and everything falls on my head, and I have the pleuritic Old Manos, who's gotten too old, who is not good for anything, and my Fate[8] has condemned me to have this pleuritic man…"

"What are you talking about, Old Mano?" called Augusta impatiently. "Do you know what you are saying? Did you plan all this babbling?"

"I don't know anything," said the old woman. "And I should be left alone, with my sins. My back cannot bear any more."

"I am telling you one thing, you are replying to another!" said Augusta. "I told you: you should have come to give me the news that my husband arrived, like I had asked you to, but you didn't come."

"Could I, an old woman, have brought the news to the lady? And how could I have known when the ship would arrive! And I have such confusion, such muddle in my head, and day or night I cannot find peace…"

"You are all over the place again! You are losing your mind, Old Mano! You are acting like you don't understand!"

"I don't understand! And I have my fill with the temptations I run into, and with the torments I endure!"

"Couldn't you at least have told my husband to come to my bedroom himself? I had explicitly asked you that no matter what time he came back, whether I was awake or asleep, I wanted to be informed of his return right away."

"I don't know anything; I have a great tumult and storm in my head, and God have mercy on me, for I am an old woman. And I have this pleuritic man of mine, who is not worth a penny, and eats prepared meals, and does not move from his place at all. And I need a crowbar to move him from his place."

Augusta figured that she was wasting her time trying to communicate with this woman. As such, she dismissed her and unburdened herself from her.

7. CONSPIRATORS

The following night, Augusta catechized her husband and he decided to dispatch the stranger, with the galley he had gifted him, the day after.

Sanudo had smelled it in the air before being told, and he went to meet Mavros on the ship.

"Do you know something, Mirchan?" he told him.

"What, boss?"

"People are nothing more than kids playing with marbles, and whoever wins has won well."

"Aw boss, this I figured out a long time ago."

"And that there is no justice, no prophet, no Allah."

"I've never believed in this nonsense," said Mirchan.

"They were made up by canny men to entrap the fools."

"Indeed."

"And if there is something a man can do to benefit himself, he should go ahead."

"Certainly."

"I am glad we agree. Still, two friends should help each other out."

"That is true."

"With proper compensation. Never for free."

"Goes without saying."

"So, I owe my life and freedom to you, and so far I have not paid you back in any way."

"You will certainly pay me back later, boss."

"Truly, it was no small thing that you gave me a chance to skewer that unsung and forgotten Carreccio. Did you see, Mirchan, how artfully I pierced his throat?"

"Nice skewering, boss."

"And you did not do it for nothing. You also wanted to get rid of the deceased."

"Very true."

"Nonetheless, I admit I am indebted to you. And if you want, this very moment I will sign a check for a thousand ducats, Mirchan."

"As the boss wishes."

"On top of that I will appoint you Khan of Africa, when I become doge of Venice."

"I wish."

"But checks are for the weak, those who don't have fingernails to rip them apart, Mirchan. And verbal promises are for the cunning and the flatterers."

"Of course."

"I am neither one nor the other, so I will neither sign anything nor give you any promises. But I am telling you, and this alone is the best guarantee for you, that I will have your need for a long time. I believe you have come to understand me with your devious instincts, Mavros. I have many plans, some honorable and some less so, and because I intend to use you as my associate I have to compensate you richly, like Satan his demons. Already today I am in need of your assistance."

"For what purpose, boss?"

Sanudo looked left and right, approached Mavros and lowered his voice.

"Listen, Mirchan. Mouchras gave this ship to me."

"He gave it to you?"

"Yes, it used to be mine."

Mavros shrugged.

"With this ship we are casting off tomorrow, Mirchan."

"Where to?"

"Everywhere. We'll see."

"So?"

"The men we will recruit today for the crew, I will recommend them to you, Mirchan."

"No worries, boss."

"You will take care of them, as is proper."

"With pleasure."

"And when I give you notice that the time to sail is approaching…"

Sanudo paused.

"Are you a trustworthy friend, Mirchan?"

"Does the boss have doubts about me?"

"Listen, Mirchan. The matter I will talk to you about I could have entrusted to one of my companions, with whom I had been taken captive. But I mistrust them, and although I have known them for a long time, I plan to leave them here. I will only take with me two of them. But I prefer you to those two as well. Am I safe with you, Mirchan?"

"Master," said Mavros, "I told you, I think, that while we have common interests, you can have faith in me."

"So listen."

Once again Sanudo examined all around, worried that he may be overheard. The seven former captives were on the ship, but they were all asleep, except for the sentinel, who was in the prow, far enough from Sanudo and Mirchan, and could not hear the low conversation (which was taking place in the Moorish language anyway).

"The men who will get hired as crew, can you get them drunk tomorrow, Mirchan?"

"Why, boss?"

"I want them all drunk, when we lift the anchor," said Sanudo.

"As long as I have enough wine, boss."

"I will give you notice two hours prior to our departure. The men will not know when we will cast off."

"Very well, boss."

"Mirchan, if you serve me, I will serve you."

"Have faith in me."

"When I give you notice, be prepared and be ready."

"Don't worry, boss. Anything else?"

"Nothing, that's all."

"I will get them soaked," said Mavros. "Do you want me to throw any of them in the sea?"

"No, that's not what I'm saying, Mirchan!"

"Just to make sure they are very drunk... But if you don't want me to, I won't do it."

"Do what you think best, Mirchan, as long as they are completely drunk."

"No worries, boss."

"Here. Take this."

Out of his pocket Sanudo revealed his seal, with his county's insignia and his name on it. He turned the handle until the seal split in two, and from a secret sheath at its base he uncovered a yellowish powder. He separated part of the powder and wrapped it in a piece of paper.

"What is this?" asked Mavros.

"This is bug-repellent powder, Mirchan."

"Bug-repellent? How?"

"Drop this in their wine; and when they drink it, they will sleep so well they won't have to worry about mosquitoes or bedbugs."

"Aha!"

"The small amount I gave you is enough to put ten to twelve men to sleep. It is a powerful drug, Mirchan."

"Nice, boss."

"If you mistakenly put all of this powder in the same glass, you will give someone a free ride to the other world."

"Really?"

"Don't you try, you trickster. Be careful. This is no time to play."

"No, boss. But I do hope this time will come."

"I believe it will come soon, Mirchan."

They exchanged terrible smiles.

"By the time you hear that I am ready to embark, all the anchors should have been lifted, all but the smallest one, and the dock ropes untied. After you are done with this job, have them drink to my health."

"Very well."

"And drop in their glasses this salutary powder."

"Very well."

"I will come aboard the galley with two or three friends. Don't be surprised no matter what happens, but be ready to obey my instructions."

"Very well, boss."

Sanudo, having conspired in this manner, bid Mavros farewell.

8. A PRESENT, A LOAN, AND A PLUNDER

Sanudo disembarked and went directly to Mouchras' to announce his intention of casting off on the following day. He borrowed from Mouchras one hundred gold ducats, hired sailors, and started preparations for departure.

What he must have neglected at first, but considered proposing later in the day, was that he wanted to celebrate his upcoming voyage, and he invited his host with his wife to join him on his ship for the occasion.

Yiannis Mouchras expressed qualms about whether his wife could accept this invitation, because, he said, she appeared to be very sick. But as far as he was concerned, he would gladly accept.

"I will be very saddened if your honorable wife does not grace me with her presence," said Sanudo.

"Me too, my guest."

Despite Mouchras' apprehensions, when Augusta entered the room and the stranger extended his invitation to her, she readily accepted.

"Why not, sir? If you are really leaving so soon."

"I am leaving, madam."

"Positively, sir, tomorrow?"

"Yes, forthwith, madam."

"Then we will be pleased to spend an hour with you on your ship and wish you safe travels."

"Thank you, madam."

Sanudo swallowed his triumph and his resentment for these prodding words like saliva. He was a man capable of changing masks at a moment's notice. And they all fit him, regardless of their shape and color.

He was among the noblemen and adventurers that Venice alone used to produce, whose slickness put to shame the uncouth and curmudgeonly chivalry of the sons of France. He was capable of suffering the worst calamities and persecutions and not be vanquished. He could carry out the most brutal savageries and not be shaken. His misfortunes were on par with his cruelty; his orgies commensurate with his boldness and his insolence.

He was a man of thirty-two years. He had already travelled ten times to the East and campaigned eleven; he had fought twenty, three times he had gotten injured seriously and eight times lightly, and he had been taken captive twice. His life was constant struggle. He wasn't malicious, but he was rabidly sensualistic and obsessively ambitious. These two characteristics were the sources of all of his actions and transgressions.

From the story of his latest imprisonment, which he told Mouchras, everything was true, except that Sanudo had been on campaign with a fleet, or an army, or on a mission whatsoever. The truth was he had left his home on an expedition with his galley, and after being closely besieged by the pirates he had been defeated and taken captive.

At the present time, Sanudo had found a victim and a daydream, and all the powers of his spirit were obsessed with it and committed to it. He imagined that everything had to assist him in the pursuit of his passion. Damned anyone who dared to stand in his way!

When night fell, Sanudo followed by Mouchras and his wife walked down to the beach. Mavros was waiting for the arrival of the skiff on the jetty.

"Is everything ready, Mirchan?" asked Sanudo.

"Everything is ready, boss."

"And the anchors?"

"Have been lifted, master."

"And the crew?"

"Sleeping, they are awaiting Your Excellency's command to wake up," said Mavros.

They got on the skiff. Mirchan and his companion, who had been among the captives with Sanudo, oared until they reached the ship.

"Come aboard, madam," said Sanudo, offering his hand to the woman.

Mouchras could not have suspected that he would remember for a long time the tone with which these simple words had been uttered: *"Come aboard, madam!"*

The woman stepped with her small feet on the ladder and climbed lightly on the deck.

The captain's cabin was brightly lit and a table had been set. Mouchras and his wife headed that way.

Sanudo quickly went downstairs to the sailors' quarters and inspected them with a handheld light. He listened to their breaths, felt their heartbeats, and shook their shoulders forcefully. These innocent men had fallen in a deep and shadowy slumber. The strong powder, which Sanudo had given to Mavros earlier, had knocked them unconscious.

Sanudo left them and returned to the cabin in the stern.

Mouchras and his wife were seated around the table.

"I am not worthy of entertaining you the way I ought to and the way I wish, sir," said Sanudo. "But remember that night when you welcomed me on this ship, following the fortunate occasion of your attack on the pirates that saved me from captivity. I told you then that you are hosting me on a ship that used to be mine. And now you too can tell me, sir, that I am hosting you on a ship that even now is yours."

"I am indebted to you, my guest," said Mouchras.

Mavros came downstairs and served some appetizers.

"Bring the good wine, Mirchan," said Sanudo. "This lady and this gentleman are honoring me doubly this evening, as benefactors and as friends."

Mavros went upstairs and returned two or three times bringing drinks and food.

Mouchras seemed to have a great appetite. Augusta barely touched anything.

"Drink from this wine, chief," said the Venetian. "Let me serve you some wine in your glasses. Who knows when we will meet again? Tonight, it is destiny for two of us to part from one."

Mouchras was far from suspecting the ambivalent, double-edged meaning of these words. He drank the wine and found it to be excellent.

"Drink to *our* safe travels, chief," said the Venetian, "I am serving you anew; who knows how far *we* will go."

"I am drinking to your safe travels, my guest," toasted Mouchras, thinking of course that plural was meant for Sanudo and his sailors.

The wine was strong indeed. Mouchras, after five or six glasses, which he drank unsuspectingly, could have gotten dizzy. But it was to his wife who had hardly wetted her lips that Sanudo turned and protested. She had been vexed by Sanudo's excessive eagerness, which she feared, and by her husband's exuberance. She felt a vague sense of threat looming over her head. She wanted to tell her husband to return ashore and bid the Venetian farewell, but she wouldn't dare. She had already voiced a certain dawning dark premonition in her heart; but now she was feeling her chest blocking the light like a screen and keeping darkness and fear in her soul. Twice or thrice she whispered to herself "Filikiti, Filikiti!" albeit so quietly that no words were uttered and no sound was heard; her chest became a gorge and buried them. Twice she told her husband using her hand and her elbow, even nodded to him, that she did not want him drinking wine. He was not listening to her. But as far as she was concerned, she had decided not to drink and she wasn't going to.

"You are not drinking, madam," said Sanudo. "But you are right. This is strong wine and may be a bit rough for you."

"I drank as much as I can, sir," said Augusta annoyed.

"And that inconsiderate Mirchan has not brought the wine from Cyprus. This is the only wine suitable for you."

The Venetian clapped his hands. Mavros appeared in an instant.

"Why aren't you bringing the wine from Cyprus, fair black man?" said Sanudo feigning anger.

"Why, I don't have wine from Cyprus, boss," said Mavros surprised.

"You don't have wine from Cyprus, my swan! But didn't I give it to you yesterday?"

"The master is wrong," whispered Mavros; "he did not give me wine from Cyprus."

"Then whom did I give it to?"

"I don't know."

For a few seconds Sanudo pretended to recollect.

"You are right, you white falcon," he said. "I put away the wine from Cyprus myself. I was afraid you would drink it, you trickster."

He stood up and with his eyes ordered Mavros to stay put, to keep an eye on Mouchras and his wife.

During his absence, the following conversation took place between the two spouses in lowered voices. Mavros' pupils looked elsewhere, but with the corner of his eyes he spied on the two interlocutors.

"Don't drink. I don't want you drinking," said Augusta.

"Why?"

"I am scared."

"Scared of what?"

"I don't know, but I am scared."

"Come on, don't be difficult! Do you realize you have been acting insultingly to this man? Why didn't you just ask to stay home? It would have been preferable to behaving like this. You see that he made an effort to find wine from Cyprus for you. He will feel snubbed if you don't at least have half a glass."

"I am afraid to drink."

"Absurd fear."

Sanudo returned bringing a certain bottle. He filled three glasses: for Mouchras, for the woman, and for himself.

"I demand, madam, that you drink this glass to my travels. Because up to now you have not deigned to wet your lips."

They clinked glasses…

The Venetian pretended to drink, the woman, having been forced to, drank a little bit, and Mouchras drank greedily…

In a few moments, the table, the bottles, the lights, and the people, everything was swirling like a whirlwind around Mouchras' head.

"What is happening to me, my friend?" he said to his wife. "I think I am getting dizzy."

The woman tilted her head and felt like she was sleepy and struggling to stay up…

"Yiannis, Yiannis! Save me! I'm suffering, I'm lost. Ah Filikiti, Filikiti!"

She leaned on the table and after a moment she wrestled her head upright again.

"Aw my God, my God!"

And with her hands she looked for her husband.

"I am sleepy," whispered Mouchras.

And he sank into a deep sleep.

"I will send you home to sleep peacefully, chief," said Sanudo with a strange smile.

Augusta made a last attempt. She stood on her legs, took two or three steps, and fell writhing on a chair. Sanudo offered her support.

"Aw traitors, traitors," she said bringing her hand to her head with her eyes closed. "Save me, God, save me!"

She coiled her body and crossed her arms tightly, as if to fortify herself from any treachery.

Marco Sanudo stood silent, motionless, steady, during the whole episode, observing the results of his drug. He had ordered Mavros to go upstairs and guard the entrance of the cabin.

But paradoxically, seeing this woman lean her head on her chest like an innocent carcass, and this man, so forthright and brave, surrender unsuspectingly to his hands, a reaction started roaring in the dark soul of this man. He was feeling regret for his actions.

He was alone and stood undecided between the two motionless bodies, almost corpses.

He smacked his head with his hand.

"What is going on?" he said; "what am I suffering from? What happened to you, Sanudo? Are you having regrets? Where is your steadfast resolve? What happened to your burning desire? Are you wavering like a woman? And now, what should I do? Bring these two people ashore and sail with my shame and without having achieved my goal? What will people say? That I got them drunk to rob them, to steal this ship from them and maybe their money. Should I let them sleep here peacefully until the morning and not cast off, but stay awake and guard their sleep? But what will they think? That I tried to poison them and failed. Should I keep both of them in the ship and cast off? But tomorrow I will have to duel with Mouchras, kill him and throw him in the sea in front of his wife's eyes, on his own ship and on my own ship. And is this not blackmail, wickedness, monstrosity?! Never, never! Should I return this man ashore and depart with the woman, as I had decided and planned? But my heart breaks, seeing this innocent man who helped me. Aw, one can easily conceive unholy plans, but how to carry them out! I never thought I could feel pangs of conscience. Am I losing my mind? Did I turn into a beast? No, no! It is not possible. I will return them both ashore. I will accompany them both to their home. And let them say what they want. As long as I don't do evil. But what will Mavros say! That I trusted him and spoke so mysteriously to him in vain; that I gave him that narcotic powder as a joke, for him to get the sailors drunk. The powder that I made using opium and other substances, and which few people knew how to make before me. Of course, when he finds out, he will think of me as crazy or silly. Certainly Mavros will hold me in contempt. Scorned by a black man! Aren't the gallows preferable? All the Venetians to the gallows, and all the noblemen to the gallows, if it is ever heard that a Venetian nobleman made his mind, then changed it, and a black man scorned him. This is no time for thinking. Onwards, onwards! I can't take the time to regret."

He clapped his hands impatiently.

"Mavros! Mavros!"

Mirchan appeared.

"Take this man, put him on the skiff and drop him ashore. I will take care of the lady."

Mavros obeyed faithfully: took Mouchras with his strong arms, carried him like a baby to the skiff, and oared to the beach.

Sanudo took Augusta, who was sleeping with certain fear and with trembling arms, and he put her on the bed prepared by Mavros, where the unfortunate Mouchras used to sleep during his many excursions on this ship.

And as antidote to the moral fatigue that had taken hold of him, the Venetian used physical fatigue. He went to the bow and with nervous efficiency and the power of three men started lifting the anchor, the only one that held the galley. He did not care to ask for the help of his former companions in captivity, who were the only ones sleeping natural sleep without having been drugged.

Mavros returned.

"I left him on the sand, master," he told Sanudo.

"Is he safe, Mavros?"

"He has nothing to fear, master."

"Beware; your head is at stake, Mavros. I don't want anything happening to him."

"I assure you he will wake up in the morning light as a bird."

"Good!"

"But as of today you owe me, master," said Mavros.

Sanudo sighed and did not answer.

They lifted the anchor, woke up the two sailors, opened the sails, and cast off to the open sea.

A nocturnal land breeze had started blowing and the Venetian thought this was sent to him from his benign protector Fate.

But like the voice of a ventriloquist, Yiannis Mouchras' voice reverberated in Sanudo's ears, whispering:

"We will meet again."

PART A

1. THE PROCLAMATION

In 1207, one morning after the sun had risen, a man in a black uniform with a sharp steel-edged whip in his hands exited the large gate of the Palace of Saint Mark and read aloud, albeit to no audience, the following proclamation:

"I, Pietro Ziani, by divine right the highest authority and Doge of the mighty and magnificent Republic of Saint Mark, of Venice, the Adriatic, the Islands etc. etc., call upon, declare, and permit the noblemen of this republic, those with ships and men under their command, to subjugate, using their own expenses and armies, the islands of the Aegean archipelago; and to rule over them as cordial friends of the mighty Republic. Signed by myself Pietro Ziani with the consent of the venerable Council of Ten. In the Palace of Saint Mark, March 21st, 1207."

Nobody was present to hear the reading of this important document. But the clerk, after reading it, posted it on a board hanging on the wall, and because he was freezing entered the palace to get breakfast.

Not a soul could be seen in the long shoal waterways of the city that morning. Venice seemed deserted. It was the day after the carnival and nothing is heavier and sharper than sleep after debauchery. Only around noon some gondolas started making their appearance, oared by indolent, sluggish ferrymen. Around sundown, the large bell of Saint Mark rang and the monks chanted the evening prayers. After the end of the liturgy, a man dressed in a long cloak exited the temple followed by a black man in a red uniform.

"Nothing entertains me anymore, Mavros," said this man. "If I am entering churches to listen to evening prayers, it means I'm desperate."

"Is Your Excellency suffering greatly?" asked Mavros.

"I am tormented, like the devil. I am not good for anything anymore."

"I am very sorry, master," said Mavros, and the tips of his lips flashed an insidious smile.

"The only thing left to do is to decide to hang you some day, to find a moment's delight. But even this would not be amusement enough."

"As Your Excellency pleases," said Mavros grimacing.

"Imagine, Mavros, if you can imagine with your African head, to be Venetian, a citizen of the mightiest republic, to be rich, a nobleman, powerful, gallant, prominent; to have traveled around the world a thousand times, to be feared and envied! Are you listening, Mavros? And afterwards not to be able to find happiness in your own house, nor a moment of rest in your conscience. Isn't this a curse?"

"But the boss cannot be happy because he banished happiness himself," braved Mavros.

"I banished happiness! Myself?"

"Yes, boss; not only did you banish it, you are not looking for it anymore, even though she could come back to you."

"What do you mean?"

"I mean that woman, whom the boss allowed to abandon him."

"Do you think that I am in love with her, scoundrel?"

"The day the boss was separated from that woman was when his melancholy started."

"How could I have kept her with me? By force?"

"The boss could have been loved by that woman, had he wanted to. And I believe that she had almost fallen in love with him."

"How do you know this, monster?"

"I know that that woman had a very tender heart, and if the boss had treated her with care and not incited her jealousy, she would have been his to this day."

"You have eyes then, Mavros?"

"The boss should let me speak freely, for I have already learned the Italian language," said Mavros. "Had the boss hidden his shortcomings from her, just like that she would have been his slave for life."

"But she was still remembering her husband, fool."

"I understand the feelings of black and white women. There has never been a woman who remembers her husband for very long."

The Venetian frowned. Undeterred, Mavros continued:

"I bet that even before my master kidnapped her, this woman had already forgotten her husband completely. But my master knows this better than me. None of them remember for very long, unless they have no other means of entertainment."

"You are blathering, deaf man."

"Believe me, master. It would not be bad to set in action the plan I proposed to you some time ago. To campaign to the East and search all the female monasteries. There is no doubt you will find her again."

At that moment, a handsome nobleman approached smiling. He extended his arm to the cloaked man.

"Marco!"

"Geremia!"

And they kissed each other.

"We haven't seen each other in a while," said the newly arrived.

"You must have just returned from the East, Geremia."

"Yes, and I am on my way there again."

"Again?"

"Yes."

"Why?"

"But you really don't know?"

"What?"

"Today's proclamation by the Doge."

"What proclamation?"

"A proclamation to the noblemen of Venice."

"Regarding?"

"He invites them to campaign to the East."

"For what purpose?

"What is the purpose of military campaigns?"

"There can be many."

"Enough. We have no other way of understanding our campaigns but one: conquest."

"I agree. And what will you conquer?"

"Are you absentminded then? What is to be conquered? Lands."

"Which lands?"

"He invites them to conquer the Cycladic Islands."

"The noblemen in general?"

"Yes."

"Under whose leadership?"

"No leadership."

"This is unheard of."

"Yet possible."

"How so?"

"Each for his own sake."

"How?"

"Paying his own way."

"Ah!"

"Are you not coming?"

"Me? No."

"No? You, with both ships and money? Shame!"

Marco's face sulked.

"But I have neither ships nor money," he said.

"You are joking."

"One has nothing when one is unhappy."

"So what happened to you?"

"I am suffering from a beastly disease, my friend."

"A beastly disease!"

"Yes!"

"What is it called?"

"I don't know… boredom, sloth, stupor, stupefaction; no, plain stupidity."

"That's too bad."

"It is what it is!"

"All the more reason to participate, my friend Marco. This occupation by itself will save you from that beastly disease."

"If it weren't incurable."

"I don't think any disease is incurable."

"Not for you, indeed, you are young, you are strong."

"And you aren't?"

"Me? I've gotten old before my time, dear Geremia."

He sighed.

"You are amusing," said Geremia. "So, what is it with you then?"

"I bid you farewell and a profitable campaign," said Marco abruptly.

And he left, followed by Mavros.

Geremia stood there perplexed watching the two men walk away.

2. THE COUNT'S HEARINGS

Marco went to his residence, one of the richest mansions in Venice, located at the Piazza San Marco.

Upon entering his chamber, he found on a table a letter addressed to him. He opened it and read the following:

"Dearest and honorable Count Sanudo,

I entreat you to appear today in the Palace of Saint Mark around the third hour of the night. H. S. wishes to notify you of something.

Marino Dorzini,
Secretary of H. S."

"What do they want from me?" said Sanudo after reading this letter. "I am in no mood for anything."

And he lay down on a chaise moaning. He turned from one side to the other, yawned for a long time, then finally got up and clapped his hands.

A servant entered.

"Isn't my doctor here yet, Lorenzo?" said Marco.

"He has been waiting in the antechamber for a while, boss."

"Tell him to come in."

"There is also a veiled lady who has asked for a hearing from Y. E."

"Then let the lady come in first."

"And there is a young sailor too, carrying a letter for Y. E., but he wants to deliver it in person."

"Let the lady come in first; he and the doctor can wait."

"As you wish, Your Excellency."

The servant exited.

After a few moments, a lady entered with her face covered. She was tall, thin, blonde, and clad in black. Once she had entered she raised her veil.

"So it is you, Olympia?" said Sanudo. "Must you come to my home covered?"

"The servants are nosy, Sir Count, and I don't like that."

"What news are you bringing me?"

"I received a letter from my sister today."

She handed an envelope to Sanudo who opened it and read:

"My dear sister,

... Tell the count that in all of the islands I've been to with my husband, whom he kindly bestowed on me, I have visited all of the female monasteries. But nowhere have I managed to find any information regarding the person in whom the count seems so very interested. I have not given up and intend to continue my search. If I discover anything, I will inform him without delay.

But is it worthy and fitting for someone of the stature of Count Sanudo to be looking so persistently and stubbornly for a nun?

Your sister Cecilia"

"Thank you, Olympia," said the count folding the letter. "Convey my kind gratitude to your sister."

"Your kindness, Sir Count."

"Go to my bedroom to rest, and after my hearings I will come visit you if you allow me."

Olympia opened a secret door, which she seemed to be very familiar with, and entered the bedroom.

The count called the servant and ordered him to bring the young man with the letter.

A young man entered wearing a sailor's hat and clothes, sunburned with a cheeky face.

"I've seen you before," noted the count. "Who are you?"

"I am Cartacci," said the young man. "Eight years ago, I served under the command of the Sir Count, and had the opportunity to greatly enjoy myself."

"On what occasion?"

"When, after escaping from the hands of the Genoese, the Sir Count abandoned us on the island of Naxos, myself and my companions."

"And why are you telling me this, beast? Is it not enough for you that you were saved from the pirates? You owe me the ransom money, which you could never repay me."

"I did not intend to enrage the Sir Count."

"Then you are very foolish indeed."

"I apologize."

"You talk too much. Give me the letter you are carrying and get out of here."

"I have no letter for the Sir Count."

"Then what did you tell my servant?"

"I told your servant a lie because otherwise he would not have let me in. You probably would not have allowed me in either."

"So you deceived me, insolent?"

"I did not deceive you; suppose I am a letter myself. Besides, I could have come up with a letter and could easily have borrowed a couple of white pages and paid a writer to compose it. But I didn't do it because I wanted to tell you the truth. I have no letter, but I have important information to give you."

"What information?"

"The Sir Count will have to pay for my fare and my meals from Naxos to Venice, for my idling, and for the interest of six years. And then I will provide the information."

"Do you prefer the prison or the gallows?" said the count sending a grim glance to this claimant.

"I knew very well what you are capable of. But you do not realize what desperation means. Believe me, you will benefit me greatly with incarceration and save me with the gallows."

"You are a crafty funnyman," said Sanudo. "I remember you now. You made the others mutiny against me."

"Because I always had one complaint in this world: that my services had not been appreciated. That's why I want the Sir Count to value them for the first time."

"And how much do you want me to value them?"

"Twenty gold ducats will suffice."

"I will give you your twenty ducats; but if your information is not worth it, I will hang you."

"Agreed," said the sailor.

The count sat by the table, signed a check for twenty ducats, and gave it to the man.

"Now speak and be brief."

"Sir Count, Mouchras is in Venice."

The count paled.

"Mouchras who?"

"The man whose wife the Sir Count kidnapped eight years ago."

"And who told you?"

"I saw him."

"And what is he doing here?"

"I don't know. But I will find out, if the Sir Count commissions me to."

"I couldn't care less. But if you do find something out, tell me."

"Very well."

"Has he been here long?"

"A few days."

"What is his purpose?"

"Something is telling me that it has to do with Your Excellency. But he is hiding carefully."

"Where is he staying?"

"He doesn't seem to be staying in any specific place. But if he has a lair, I will discover it."

"Go and make sure," said the count, accompanying his words with a motion of his hand.

The sailor bowed deeply and exited pressing the twenty-ducat check in his pocket.

"Lorenzo," said Sanudo, "don't let the doctor in yet. Bring me here my friend Augustos. I want to see him and entertain myself a little."

Having said that, he opened the secret door and entered for a few moments to stand next to Olympia who was sitting idly on a seat by the bed.

He offered her friendly smiles, caressed her, and said:

"Are you getting lonely sitting here by yourself? I will bring you my friend Augustos right away to keep you company and entertain you."

And he returned to his chamber where he found his friend Augustos.

He was an oversized black dog with curly hair and red lightning darting from his eyes. When he saw the count, he snarled hollowly, showed his teeth, and started wagging his tail.

The count petted him, grabbed him by the ear, and took him to Olympia.

"Enjoy yourselves, the two of you," he said.

And he closed the bedroom door.

"Lorenzo," he called the servant, "let the doctor in now."

Immediately, a crooked middle-aged man entered bowing over and over. The count motioned for him to sit.

"How are you, Sir Count?" asked the doctor. "Did you take the medication I prescribed for you?"

"I haven't taken anything," said Sanudo.

"You are neglecting your health. Yet the nervous condition you are suffering from could turn for the worse."

The count did not respond. Silence reigned for a while and the doctor was thinking that he could not understand why he had come and that it would have been better if he had stayed in the antechamber even after Augustos had been brought forth.

"Tell me, Doctor," said the count, breaking his silence. "What kind of diet would you find suitable for me, given my constitution?"

"Regarding the issue of dieting," said the doctor in a pompous tone, "this is an approach accepted by Galenus and Hippocrates, but modern medicine is of completely different opinion. It recommends pills, enema, and laxatives in general. Because if it was all about dieting, medicine would be redundant."

"So modern medicine wants to make itself useful by force?" said the count.

"You spoke well; 'force' is the right word. Because every conquest, be it in politics or science, cannot come about without force."

"Is medicine a conquest then?"

"A conquest, precisely, that's the word, Sir Count."

"And what has medicine conquered thus far? Laxatives and enema perhaps, as you were saying earlier."

"Indeed, Sir Count; and above all, it has conquered nature, the human."

"The human?..."

"Indeed. Because both nature and the human would be incomplete without laxatives and enema."

"It follows then that in order for someone to be perfected..."

"He must take laxatives and enema often. Indeed, Sir Count. And because man has one way in and one way out, medicine has invented these two powerful levers for these two doors."

The count got up and started walking around the chamber. He was getting bored.

"Tell me finally, Doctor, would it be helpful in my current condition if I were to travel and lead an active life, like I used to?"

"Traveling? For Your Excellency? An active life? Never! On the contrary, this would kill you."

"Then what should I do?"

"Continue following my prescription, Sir Count. This and only this is my recommendation to Your Excellency."

"You can go, Doctor. Thank you. Please do not return until I call for you. Do you have a prescription to give me today?"

"I will send it to your pharmacist."

The doctor exited with some suspicions and the count went to find Olympia and Augustos.

3. THE DOGE

Around the third hour of the night, in accordance with the letter he had received, Sanudo left his home and headed for the Doge's Palace.

For all the deathly silence that had reigned over the palace and its surroundings during the day, it was notably noisy and busy at nighttime. The halls were alight and the hallways packed with people. Everywhere talking, voices, conversations. The Doge seemed to be celebrating the end of the carnival.

It would take long to present an account of all the babbling and quips amongst the many noblemen. Besides, these discussions of the middle ages have often been memorialized. It is known how 13th century Venetians used to converse, especially in the halls of the Doge's Palace.

A sample discussion, for example, would include the following:

"The lion of Saint Mark is bulimic."

"It is sharpening its teeth."

"Gold, gold! Venice alone has found the philosopher's stone."

"The insects fly for the chicken, the chicken for the hawk."

"And the nations for Venice."

"But the nations can't fly."

"Because Venice has clipped their wings."

"Venice sells Christ and buys Muhammad."

"It would be best to sell them both."

"As long as the price is good."

"And to make the Caliph kiss the Pope."

"And share his harem with him."

This would have been a political crowd; elsewhere, the following could be heard:

"Count, I think you've been saving that brunette."

"This is why he keeps traveling to the East, so that he doesn't get bored."

"Have you ever gone hunting at night?"

"In how many positions, Count, have you conquered her?"

"Cyprus wine goes straight to one's head."

"One is then forced to change head."

"And what is your opinion about monastic life, my friend?"

"Really? Inside a gondola? Did the ferryman not see you?"

"He was looking toward the bow."

"This is too stressful an entertainment. You must have been holding your breath like a thief, to make sure he didn't hear you."

"I like novelty. Another time I did it in the street."

"In the street how?"

"In a poorly lit street corner, there was a stone buttress which served as a standing wedding bed."

"Are there any actual standing wedding beds?"

"This is small potatoes. We are being left behind. A Hungarian friend of mine told me better stories."

"Like what?"

"She was a shepherd girl guarding her flock by a beach. As soon as she saw his skiff approach the coast, in order to save herself, because her beauty and the poor opinion she had of sailors gave her reason to worry, she betook herself to a tall tree, a fig tree I think, where she thought she would be safe."

"And then?"

"Well, he had crooked nails, with which he could easily climb. So he got to her and they chitchatted on the tree."

"Really, on the tree?"

"Indeed. With one hand holding a branch."

"How about the other hand?"

Sanudo, followed as usual by Mavros, passed through these rambunctious groups without addressing anyone and headed straight for the Doge's antechambers.

"I have been invited to a hearing this evening," he told one of the officers of the guard.

"Is your invitation in writing, Sir Count?"

"Certainly. Here it is."

The officer did not read the letter and let him in.

"Talk to His Serenity's valet, Sir Count."

The valet was familiar with the count and aware of the scheduled hearing.

"His Serenity is expecting you inside," he said. "Come in, Sir Count."

Pietro Ziani was a 55-year-old man, florid and able-bodied. His mustache and beard were shaved. He was sitting on a chaise and next to him was the old Carlo Mandrozini, a member of the Council of Ten.

"Welcome, Count Sanudo," he said extending his arm. "We were talking about you just now, myself and my friend Mandrozini."

"Your Serenity is honoring me," said the count, "for taking the time to concern yourself with me."

"Aren't you wondering what we were talking about?"

"I am aware of Your Serenity's favor, and that you always say good things."

"Do you read minds, Count?"

"Is Your Serenity flattering me or deriding me?"

"Not at all, Count; and I will prove it to you right away."

"His Serenity speaks highly of you," said the old Mandrozini.

"Count, do you have ships and sailors?" asked the Doge.

"If I am to offer something to the Republic, I always do, Your Serenity."

"You are not to offer anything to the Republic, but campaign for yourself."

"Me, Your Serenity?"

"Yes, Count."

"And where to? If Your Serenity pleases."

"To the Aegean archipelago."

"Is the Republic sending me?"

"No, Count."

"Then who?"

"You will go on your own."

"I don't understand, Your Serenity."

"Were you not informed then of the Republic's decision?"

"No, Your Serenity; I have not been engaged in politics for some time."

"That's a shame, Count. A nobleman like you!"

"I have been of ill health, Your Serenity."

"This is no excuse. The will of the Republic is that all of the noblemen not otherwise occupied take part in this venture. Thus, I assume you will go as well."

"If Your Serenity commands me."

"I am not commanding you. You will go by yourself, Count."

"In the name of the Republic?"

"In your own name."

"How do you mean in my own name?"

"Today's proclamation, of which all the noblemen other than you are aware, says word for word: 'I invite all the noblemen to occupy at their own expense the islands of the Aegean archipelago.' You have ships and you will participate in this campaign. And if you don't, the Republic will loan you some of its own ships."

"Aw, I don't accept loans."

"Why not, Count? This sounds exceedingly haughty and it is offensive to your homeland."

"I would accept buying ships from the Republic. I want to be free to burn them if I so choose."

"Would you be capable of such a thing, Count?"

"Easily. That's why I don't want loans."

"Are you convinced then?"

"It would be great if Your Serenity were willing to grant me some time to think about it."

"You can give your commitment now and think about it tomorrow, Count."

"With your actions, Your Serenity has already wrestled my commitment, before I could decide for myself and express it confidently."

"I think I have the right to behave this way, Count, in the name of the Republic."

"Then without having to promise, I am obligated to comply, Your Serenity."

"Celebrate your last feast, Count, at your mansion, and prepare for this campaign as soon as possible."

"I will hold multiple feasts, Your Serenity."

"One for each of your lovers?"

The old Mandrozini smiled.

"Once in a while you remember your youth, my friend?" the Doge told him.

And he stood up and followed by Sanudo he entered the adjacent hall, where men and women mingled.

4. BLOOD FOR TEARS

It was around midnight when Sanudo exited the Doge's Palace. He was sullen, silent, and Mavros, who had been waiting for him in the antechamber for many hours and was now following him, would not dare speak to him.

When they reached the square, he stood for a few moments contemplative.

"Go find a gondola then, Mavros!" he said. "We need to get home."

Mavros rushed to abide. Shortly, he returned on a gondola with two ferrymen.

Sanudo boarded and sat in the back.

"Where does the boss order us to go?" asked one of the ferrymen.

"On the other side of the Piazza San Marco," replied the count. "And hurry up."

Upon hearing his voice, the other ferryman looked at Sanudo insidiously and pulled his cap down to his eyes. He seemed to be considering something suspicious and gloomy.

Soon after the gondola left the jetty, this man started shouting to his companion in a language Sanudo knew well. It was Greek.

"This favor, only this favor I ask of you, my friend," he said. "Give this man over to me; leave him in my hands. It is him! For long I've been looking for him. I've been looking for him in Hell and I find him here! Either he takes me out or I spill his blood and then I can die."

The other ferryman did not answer and did not seem to understand. Hearing this voice Sanudo sprung agitated, without comprehending the exact meaning of these words, but rather instinctively, reaching for the dagger in his belt.

Mavros jumped, opened his eyes widely and grinned, baring his teeth in the dark.

In the meantime, the man who had uttered these words in Greek, put the oar aside and with a rapid move seized Sanudo by his beard, threw him on the wooden beams of the gondola, and pushed his knee against his chest.

Everything happened in an instant. Sanudo did not have time to put up a defense.

The other ferryman, nonplussed, observed the struggle. But Mavros attacked Sanudo's aggressor vehemently from behind. Grabbing him from the neck, and gripping the yataghan, which he carried in his belt, he stabbed the man in the right thigh.

The man felt the edge of the blade and brought one hand to his thigh, but with the other he still held the count pinched on the beams with the head on the gunwale.

"Courage, master, courage," yelled Mavros. "I will throw him in the sea now."

But the second ferryman considered it prudent to get involved, and he locked Mavros' head in his underarm and struck him repeatedly with the tholepin. Mavros fell unconscious face down on the bow.

Sanudo, struggling and defending himself tirelessly, managed to rise halfway despite the pressure of his opponent, who seemed to be holding back because he could have plunged the dagger he was holding into Sanudo's chest.

Perhaps this delay was due to the diversion caused by the injury he had received from Mavros.

Sanudo rose, and finding himself on equal footing with his opponent drew his dagger. But his opponent grabbed him by the throat this time, gripped the hand that bore the dagger, and twisted it twice or thrice with his sturdy arms.

Once again Sanudo recovered. He got up, and seizing the man violently from his hair and arm tried to topple him. Then, as the two men were entangled on the floor with their heads on the gunwale, the other ferryman, who was probably trying to help his companion, due to clumsiness benefited Sanudo by forcefully pushing him away and separating them. This gave Sanudo time for a renewed attack, fiercer than any of the previous ones.

But then this ferryman pushed Sanudo, who was standing on the beams, with so much force that he involuntarily threw him into the sea.

"All the better," he said. "Go to Hell, rabid cat."

But defying all expectations, his companion, as soon as he saw Sanudo disappear in the waves, threw himself into the sea behind him.

"I don't understand a thing!" exclaimed the second ferryman. "Did my damned companion go mad? Poor man! It's a shame. He was a good drunk; we never argued during our drunkenness. But what happened to him tonight anyway? I saw it coming: he was losing his mind. That must be why he was speaking Greek to me! A clear sign of madness."

And he stood there, carefully observing the waves. After some time, somewhere in the sea far from the gondola, two shadows appeared clashing and struggling like sea monsters. It was Sanudo and his adversary, emerging from the water.

"Aw, there they are!" said the ferryman. "Still with their bathing and their games."

He took a second to consider. Then he saw one of the two sinking anew.

"But I guess it is time for me to get out of here. Visiting the underground chambers of the Hall of the Ten is not very pleasant."

He started oaring.

At that moment, Mavros regained consciousness, moaned, and moved slightly.

"Aw, you just reminded me of your presence, my friend," said the ferryman. "You must be delighted that I am not sending you to meet your boss." And leaving the oars, he approached Mavros.

"How are you doing, my friend?" he told him as he struck his shoulder. "Do you have a weight in your stomach perhaps?"

And he went through his pockets looking for any coins.

Soon after, the gondola reached the waterfront. The ferryman covered Mavros with a piece of old sail and disappeared.

5. A CORPSE FOR A CORPSE

The following night, a man with a big turban on his head and dressed with a long cape entered a tavern on a disreputable street in Venice. He was black in his color all the way to his nails. He eyed the customers carefully as he headed over to the taverner.

"Can you tell me, madam," he asked her, "if it is here where the notorious Skiachti[9] the aquatic frequents?"

"What do you want from him?" replied the woman looking at Mavros suspiciously.

She was a woman whose eyes always looked sharply at any strangers who walked into her tavern by luck, unlike regulars. Such strangers aside, most of the patrons were spies, crooks, and ferrymen of dubious distinction.

Old Kokkinou[10] (that was her name) was more of an intermediary than a taverner. This is whom the newcomers would go to if they were looking for a service that was otherwise hard to come by.

"I want him so I can give him some money," said Mavros.

"Is this for some business arrangement?"

"Exactly."

"Tell me what it is and I will let him know."

"Is he not here in person?"

"He is here, but I doubt he will leave his drinking party to come and talk to you."

"Please call him over. Tell him that he will make a lot of money."

Kokkinou shouted:

"Skiachti! Come here."

A man in sailor's clothes with herculean shoulders and a massive head rose from a table.

"What do you want from me, Kokkinou?" he asked.

"This black man wants to talk to you."

Skiachti approached looking at Mavros suspiciously.

"What do you want to tell me?"

"Let's sit aside somewhere, if you please. Bring us wine, Old Kokkinou," said Mavros.

They sat at a table. Kokkinou set down a wine bottle and two glasses.

"My master sent me to assign you a job, my friend," said Mavros.

"Who is your master?"

"It is Count Sanudo."

"And how come you reveal it so easily?"

"Because he won't be exposed in any way. We only need your skills. We aren't asking you to commit any crimes."

"Neither do I commit crimes."

"I have no doubt it is so."

"Well then, what do I have to do?"

"Last night, a friend of my master's, a foreigner, fell in the sea and drowned."

"By himself?"

"Yes. He was crazy."

"So?"

"This morning, you are to search the entire coast, in case he's washed up somewhere. Because my master wants to bury him with all honors."

"And if I don't find him?"

"Is it not true that you are an expert diver?"

"That is what they tell me," said Skiachti modestly.

"Do you have any companions in this trade of yours?"

"I have many."

"Any of them present?"

"In this tavern?"

"Yes."

"There is one."

"Call him."

Skiachti shouted:

"Morozzi[11]! Morozzi! Come here."

A tall man rose from his chair and approached the two conversing men.

"What do you want?" he asked.

"This black man wants you."

"Sit down, Morozzi."

Morozzi sat.

"This morning," said Mavros, "the two of you will take your skiff and search the entire coast of the Gulf of Venice, in case you find somewhere the corpse of a drowned man. And if you can't find it, then you will look for it on the sea floor, in case it is stuck there."

"And why would we do that?" asked Morozzi.

"To make fifty gold ducats, paid in total to you by my boss."

Morozzi, upon hearing about the ducats, did not even bother to ask who this boss was, as Skiachti had done.

"But success will be difficult," said Skiachti shaking his head.

"Why?" asked Morozzi. "I don't see any difficulty."

"How are we going to find the corpse of a drowned man on the sea floor? We need to dive the entire sea of Venice. And devil knows if it hasn't been devoured by some seal."

"We will do our best," said Morozzi.

"And if we don't find it?" Skiachti asked Mavros. "Will your boss not give us the fifty ducats?"

"Of course not," said Mavros. "Only the advance, which I will give you today."

Taking a wallet out of his belt, he tossed its contents on the table.

"Here are ten ducats," he said. "Five for you, Skiachti, and five for Morozzi. And here is one more ducat for you to drink. But don't drink too much tonight because you have work to do in the morning."

"I cannot go diving in the sea without having drunk enough," said Skiachti.

"Me neither," said Morozzi.

"As you wish, but I think one ducat should be enough for tonight."

"It certainly is," replied Skiachti.

Mavros stood.

"So, do as you think is best. If you find the drowned man, that's good. You will make fifty ducats. If you don't, you should still be happy. I promise another treat from my boss."

"But how in the devil can your boss profit from a drowned man?" asked Skiachti.

"That's for him to know; to me it seems crazy," said Mavros.

"You are not fooling me," replied Skiachti.

"I assure you, I know nothing," insisted Mavros.

And he exited, leaving the two divers behind. As Skiachti tortured his imagination trying to guess the motive behind this bizarre request, Morozzi counted the eleven ducats over and over.

"Bring wine, Kokkinou!" bellowed Skiachti.

Kokkinou obliged.

"What did this black man want from you?" she asked.

"Stay out of my business, Old Kokkinou," said Skiachti. "Your job is to sell wine. Bring another bottle. Come over, friends, let us treat you," he called to a group of patrons.

Two or three of them got up from their chairs and joined the two divers.

The glasses clanked.

They drank heavily that evening. The eleventh ducat of Mavros' barely sufficed.

After midnight had passed, and the two divers were completely drunk, Skiachti asked Morozzi:

"How about a sea bath?"

"No," answered Morozzi.

"I'd like to take a dive now."

"This late?"

"With the fishing lamp, it's nice."

"But I prefer Kokkinou's wine bath."

"This is fun too, but it's expensive."

"Not that expensive," said Morozzi.

"To do it properly, we need more than the ten ducats Mavros gave us."

"How do you mean?"

"For Kokkinou to pour ten barrels of wine into a cistern, and for the two of us to dive in there!"

"Wow!"

"Do you want to do it?"

"I feel sorry for my five ducats."

"So, we can do the other one then," said Skiachti.

"Which other one?"

"To go and dive the way we know to."

"But with such drunkenness!"

"All the better! Get up!" said Skiachti, pushing Morozzi to stand.

"You are acting strangely, but so be it," said Morozzi.

"We will light the fishing lamp and go look for that drowned man," said Skiachti. "We will find him and go haggle."

"With whom?"

"With Mavros and the man who sent him. You really think I will turn him over for fifty ducats?" asked Skiachti, trying to strike a chord with Morozzi's avarice.

"You are right. For this kind of job we can."

They left the tavern and headed to a small dockyard in the nearby jetty. Skiachti took a key out of his pocket and opened the door. The strong smell of tar and asphalt overwhelmed their noses.

Morozzi lit a candle and took two oars, enough torches, and a convex iron rack with a long curved handle, which the fishermen call a "fishing lamp".

They dragged a skiff, which was docked in the jetty, boarded it, attached the oars to the tholepins, and rowed away.

Morozzi was very cheerful, even though his participation in this excursion had been both rushed and involuntary.

However, Skiachti was glum and murmuring ceaselessly.

"Fifty ducats!" Morozzi would say from time to time.

"A corpse!" Skiachti would mutter between his teeth. "Where should I find a corpse? Can I steal one from the cemetery?"

"What are you mumbling, my friend?" asked Morozzi.

"Nothing."

But he soon continued his imperceptible monologue.

"Fifty ducats!" said Morozzi again.

"Fifty ducats," muttered Skiachti. "Isn't it silly to murder your mate for fifty ducats? But how is one to survive? One can't borrow fifty ducats from the devil himself. For thirty years I have lived underwater, like a seal, and I have never made fifty ducats."

"What are you talking to yourself about Skiachti, mate?" said Morozzi.

"Nothing, my friend, devil take us," replied Skiachti.

And he continued pulling the oars.

"Old Kokkinou has some strong wine," said Morozzi. "It's a shame we didn't take a bottle with us."

Skiachti leaned to the skiff's bow and revealed a wooden flask.

"Drink, my friend Morozzi, from the flask," he said. "There is some leftover wine from a couple of nights ago."

Morozzi took the flask and drank.

"Well done, my friend Skiachti; it's even better than Kokkinou's."

"Better than Kokkinou's!" repeated Skiachti in a lowered voice. "But where the hell is one to find a drowned man? And would the seals and the dogfish leave a drowned man for Skiachti to find? But to become worse than a dogfish! To eat one's own friend!"

"What are you saying again, muttering to yourself, Skiachti?" asked Morozzi.

"Not saying anything," answered Skiachti.

Morozzi gulped wine again and again, then he started singing.

After they had distanced themselves sufficiently from the jetty and reached a cove, Skiachti took the torch and lit the fishing lamp. The skiff, the sea, and the coast were illuminated brilliantly.

Morozzi rubbed his eyes and looked at his companion in awe.

"Your face looks very terrifying, Skiachti," he told him. "This is not your usual look."

"You shouldn't have drunk so much, Morozzi. It won't be long before I seem like the Gorgon[12] of the sea to you."

"Aw, Saint Mark, help us," said Morozzi crossing himself.

"And you too are going to look like a vampire, mate."

"Why?"

"Because this year the dead turn into vampires."

"And am I dead?" asked Morozzi.

"I forgot; I thought I was talking to the drowned man, the one we are looking for."

"Are you just being weird or have you gone mad?"

"I got drunk and don't know what I am talking about," said Skiachti.

"But since you want to chat with the drowned, undress and dive," said Morozzi.

"No, you dive first."

"Is it my turn?"

"Yes, for tonight."

"And are you not diving at all?"

"When you hold the lamp, I will."

"I am getting hot anyway. I will jump in the water to cool down."

Morozzi quickly disrobed and jumped into the sea. He submerged himself and disappeared under the skiff.

Skiachti remained holding the oars.

"They are looking for a drowned man," he soliloquized. "Are you sure you are not mistaken, Mavros? Are you sure you didn't mean to say a dead man? Where can I find a drowned man for you? With a single stab I could serve you. But a drowned man? Where can I find him?"

He was getting frantic; the oars fell from his hands.

"A drowned man!" he repeated. "And is it not sad if one is forced to choke his best friend with his own hands? For fifty ducats!"

Meanwhile, Morozzi had visited the sea floor twice and had come back to the surface twice. And he dove again.

"Fifty ducats!" repeated Skiachti. "With fifty ducats I could get my own trawl; live like a man; get away from the nails of Old Kokkinou, who buries all of my efforts in the bottom of her barrels. But with twenty-five ducats I can do nothing, other than stay drunk for an entire week. Onwards; time for a decision!"

Skiachti stood up and got undressed instantly. He pulled a yataghan from a secret sheath at the skiff's stern.

Then, changing his mind he dropped it.

"Aw, no! It's better with my hands," he said.

But he regretted again and grabbed it.

"With my hands? With my hands I can finish it; but I must start with the yataghan."

He held it upside down to hide it under his arm and stood on the stern before diving headlong into the water.

Morozzi, who at that time was on the sea floor, saw Skiachti dive and suspected nothing, until Skiachti seized him by the scruff and plunged the yataghan into his chest…

Then Skiachti grabbed his neck and strangled him.

The poor Morozzi, fighting hopelessly and with terrible convulsions of agony, expired as he rose to the surface.

Skiachti took the still-gasping body, lifted it to the skiff's side, tied a rock that was used as ballast to its neck, and sent it to the bottom of the sea, after marking the location well to ensure that he would remember it.

Having finished this job in complete apathy, he now seemed inebriated, as if from the fumes of must.

"Eh, my pal Morozzi, have patience; we all suffer a lot from our friends. But who is really at fault? Does it seem easy to you to find a drowned man? But you were right; for you it was easy. Because to get murdered, one needs to make no effort. The difficulty is in committing the crime."

He considered turning off the torch and leaving. Somehow this torch radiated a sinister light. Shining on this man, naked, blood-drenched, horrible, and bent over a sea that had just swallowed a corpse.

Suddenly it occurred to Skiachti.

"And what if the seals eat it?" he said. "It will have been all for naught."

He dove anew into the water.

Shortly he emerged carrying Morozzi's corpse. He put it on the skiff.

"I will take him to a safe place," he said. "I have my own underwater lair, where he has nothing to fear."

He started rowing forcefully and soon reached an outlying inlet.

He threw Morozzi into the sea, jumped in, and laid him in a shallow place under a rock that jutted out like a boat's aplustre over the coast. Underneath it, a secret sandy cavern in the shape of a child's bed had formed. This was his underwater lair, as Skiachti called it, and it was to serve as the deathbed for the unfortunate Morozzi.

6. FEAST

One week after the events detailed above, the sound of songs, madrigals, and musical instruments could be heard throughout the night from Count Sanudo's mansion.

Passersby, before continuing on their way, would ask one another:

"What happened? Has the count overcome his melancholy?"

"The count is departing and he is rejoicing with his friends."

Around the first hour of the night, Count Sanudo had gotten up from his bed and called Mavros.

"Come, I want to get dressed," he told him. "Lorenzo can't see my condition."

"I was lucky to make it out alive, boss," said Mavros. "The companion of this rabid man struck me five times, I think, with an oar to the head. He thought me dead and left me snoring, boss."

"If you were snoring, how could he have thought you dead?"

"Because I was snoring on purpose to trick him, boss."

"He would have been right to think you crazy."

The count took two or three steps. His legs were numb; he was hobbling.

He took his shirt off to reveal his chest and rib cage covered in bruises and injuries. Three bandages were wrapped around his underarms.

He winced, turned pale, and bit his lip. Mavros supported him to keep him from falling.

"How will my boss manage to host his friends tonight?" asked Mavros.

"I have to. Nobody can suspect that unfortunate event."

"But why is Your Excellency in a rush to hold this celebration today at home?"

"Because I am in a hurry to campaign. And I cannot depart without a feast. But the circumstance of that devil, that terrible night, ruined me, Mavros!"

"It is enough that Your Excellency emerged victorious."

"That was a poor victory, my friend Mirchan."

"Why boss?"

"Because… Devil take you, and don't mention it again. Ah! I am hurting! I am hurting!"

Sanudo's teeth chattered.

"Courage, boss!"

"It's nothing. And you know I have courage. We have spent days upon days together, you and I, as patients, surgeons, and nurses to each other. Damned wound! How awful to be in pain and to have to pretend you are fine!"

"But how beautiful it is though, to have the heart for it!" said Mavros.

"Yes, to suffer martyrdom without expecting laurels."

Sanudo got dressed and prepared to go to the hall.

"Have you seen either of these two divers?" he asked hesitating at the doorstep.

"This morning I found one of them," answered Mavros. "But he hadn't discovered anything yet, he told me."

"They should try harder," said Sanudo. "I am very interested in finding this corpse."

"Why master? Do you want to embalm it perhaps?" dared Mavros.

"I want to know with certainty, Mavros, that he is dead."

"But he is a corpse!"

"Who knows if he didn't find his legs and his way to some beach."

"Him? Unless he turned into a vampire."

"He's bad news for me if he is still alive."

"And for me."

"So they should be diligent! And they need to get me a corpse already."

Mavros muttered: "If that is the case, they should turn a living man into a corpse and offer him to Your Excellency."

"What are you murmuring, Mavros?" asked Sanudo.

"I am thinking, master, that if I were in their place, I would fish out a seal and bring it to you."

Sanudo shrugged.

"This night you are free to revel, Mavros. Drink as much as you can."

"I will do my best, master."

"Act as befits your nature, like the black man and the beast you are."

"I will try not to surpass my boss."

Sanudo grimaced. But Mavros had been taking liberties with him for a long time.

The count's hall was alight and glittering throughout. A large table had been set. Around the table sat eleven women and three to four men. They were the count's guests for that evening.

Sanudo entered, kissed the women on the forehead, shook hands with the men, and took a seat.

The women, in a variety of gowns that revealed their shoulders and chests, and some of whom with shadow-like black masks on their faces, were beautiful with light blue circles drawn around their eyes and pellucid paleness around their temples. It would be impossible to think of more pleasant company.

These young faces were adorned with smiles that evoked desire and pleasure. From time to time, sounds that ranged from teasing laughter to sensual sighs could be heard.

"Thank you, my friends, for honoring me," said the count. "If you hadn't come, I wouldn't have been able to entertain these ladies by myself."

"You invited us for the ladies then?" asked one of the men.

"Of course; is this offensive to you, my friend Geremia?"

He was the same nobleman whom Sanudo had met a few days ago on Piazza San Marco and with whom he had had a long conversation.

"Don't pay attention to Ghizi, Count," said another man. "I consider it a double honor that you invited me for the benefit of these ladies."

"You consider everything to be an honor to you, Quirini," said Geremia. "But in the end all these honors will become a burden for your back."

"Don't start fighting, noblemen," said a blonde young woman, "because you will force us to split you."

"I would gladly fight, if I knew that you wanted to stop me, my little Cloelia," said Quirini.

"Get into a fight then and I will," said Cloelia.

"With pleasure."

And he got up and addressed Geremia.

"Sir Count Ghizi, not long ago you uttered improper words against me. Will you take them back?"

"No," said Ghizi.

"Will you duel?"

"I will."

Immediately the two noblemen drew swords.

"Gentlemen, if this is nothing but a joke, I will not forgive you in my own house," said Sanudo.

"Have you ever seen me joking, Sanudo?" asked Ghizi.

"So please go in another room and figure things out between yourselves."

"No, here! Here!" exclaimed some female voices.

"I will not allow it," said the count.

"Here, here," repeated the women.

"But I did not invite you here to duel."

"Count, you are acting strange," said Ghizi. "Did you become sensitive all of a sudden?"

"Fine, go ahead! Tear each other apart, if you like, gentlemen, and devil take you all!" shouted Sanudo.

Quirini and Ghizi stood across from one another. The guests, motionless, turned their attention to them.

Ghizi attacked first with a triple strike. Quirini repelled him readily. But Ghizi, getting nervously excited, rapidly brought multiple complex strikes on his opponent, who barely managed to repel them. After a few more strikes the arm of the latter of the two adversaries seemed to tire.

Sanudo saw this moment coming but continued to stare. Stopping the two opponents did not cross his mind.

However, one of the women took it upon herself to plead for Quirini.

"Count Sanudo," she said. "Stop them. Ghizi is overreacting."

"It was their choice," said Sanudo.

But at the same time the blonde Cloelia remembered her promise and rushed to intervene. She stood up, approached the battlefield, and extended her two arms to the two swords.

Ghizi tried to scare her by brandishing his blade, but she darted and grabbed Ghizi's scabbard with one hand and his arm with the other.

"You are my prisoner," she told him. "I was the cause of the fight and I apologize to both of you. Put your sword down, Quirini. Come and embrace me."

Quirini obliged to a tee.

"Well then! Are we not eating after all, Sanudo?" demanded some other woman. "Or did you bring us here to fast, like Saint Mary of the Desert?"

"God forbid that your beautiful teeth would ever have to fast, dearest Provvidenza!" said Sanudo.

"Then should Fortuna perhaps fast?" asked Provvidenza.

"Fortuna must drink eternally to my health," said Sanudo.

The two women called Fortuna and Provvidenza were to the right and left of the host. They were his favorites that evening.

"What? Provvidenza will be eating by herself and Fortuna drinking by herself?" asked Cloelia.

"Precisely."

"And what about the rest of us?"

"You admire."

The meal was served. The waiters went in and out bringing delicacies and bottles.

Cloelia, Olympia (who is already known to us and was also present), Fortuna, Hestia, Prudencia, and all the rest of that swarm of wasps were competing for who would be the first to toast the host.

"I drink to the success of your campaign, dearest Count."

"I drink to your beautiful eyes, Count."

"I drink to the feathers of your helmet, Marco."

"I drink to your brave mustache, my friend!"

"And I drink to your white underskirt, my dear."

It's impossible to transcribe here all the babbling of that night. Suffice it to say that the food was delectable, with spices tantalizing to the larynx, and that eventually all of their heads were deluged with wine.

Around midnight, Mavros appeared in the hall and whispered a couple of words in Sanudo's ear.

He exploded from his chair.

"Where is he?" he asked.

"Outside."

And they both exited.

7. THE DESSERT

A man in a mariner's outfit, with a hat lowered to his eyes, had arrived at Sanudo's mansion not long ago and asked for Mavros.

Upon seeing him, Mavros recognized Skiachti the aquatic.

"Aw, is it you?" he said. "Any news?"

"I fished him out," said Skiachti, staring at Mavros.

"You fished him out? Whom?"

"The man you asked me for."

"When did you fish him out?"

"Today."

"Where?"

"In a place far removed from the one you indicated," said Skiachti.

"I did not indicate anything."

"You did not indicate, but I understood where he had sunk."

"And?"

"So he was far from there. He had been carried by the waves. This is why it took me so long to find him."

"And where is your companion, the other guy?"

"Who? Morozzi?"

"Yes."

"He caught a cold. Tough job, Mr. Mavros, and your master should pay me well."

"Only you? How about Morozzi?"

"Morozzi does not get a share," said Skiachti assuming a brazen tone and stance.

"Why?"

"He decided not to participate in this job."

"But didn't you just say he caught a cold?"

"He caught it in Kokkinou's cellar."

"Did you then do all the work yourself?"

"Myself. Every day I spent nine hours in the water. By devil! I almost turned into a water snake!"

"And you found a corpse?"

"I did."

"And are you certain that it is the man we are looking for?"

"Excuse me, I am not certain about anything," said Skiachti boldly. "Our agreement was that I bring the body of a drowned man."

Mavros examined him suspiciously and probingly, but Skiachti braved his gaze like a fearless patient about to undergo surgery.

"And where is the drowned man now?" asked Mavros. "You must still have him in your skiff, right?"

"No. I brought him here."

"You brought him here!"

"Yes."

"Here, where?"

"Right outside of this mansion, in front of the garden gate of the noble count."

"Why?"

"Because I did not have a safe place to put him, and I figured that the Sir Count would like to see his acquaintance as soon as possible."

"In the name of God… I mean in the name of the devil! I suppose this is fine," said Mavros. "My master often has queer ideas himself. He may even be happy that you brought him here. I will go and inform him. But how will he react amidst his drunkenness?!... If he takes it the wrong way, try to sense it, take your find, and run, run!"

Mavros entered the hall, as was said earlier, and announced the aforementioned to Sanudo.

"So, did you find anything?" asked Sanudo as soon as he exited.

"Yes, boss, today I fished him out," replied Skiachti.

"And is it him?"

"The Sir Count will judge."

"Where have you put him?"

"I brought him up to the gates of the palace of the Sir Count because I assumed that the Sir Count would like to see with his own eyes."

"Bring him! Bring him over!"

Skiachti and Mavros descended the stairs for a moment and returned carrying something long, around five feet, covered with a linen sheet.

They laid it on the floor and made the revelation…

It was a human corpse, deformed, unrecognizable, and putrid…

From the swollen and fissured face, one could tell it had been extracted from the sea, where it had been partially devoured by fish.

The count bent over and examined it carefully…

Although he might have recognized the man when he had been alive, it was impossible to identify this corpse, so deformed…

"It's him! It's him!" exclaimed the count. "These are the wounds I made on his chest."

Mavros shook his head. He noticed that Sanudo in his drunkenness had betrayed his secret to this vile man, in whom Mavros had no faith whatsoever.

However, Skiachti's eyes immediately lit up, showing that he understood what Sanudo had said.

"At least I," he thought to himself, "can recognize my own stabs and can't get fooled. But I am glad to be your accomplice, Mr. Goldfool, and I will greatly profit from you in the future."

"It seems like my boss has lost his mind," thought Mavros. "The devil himself couldn't recognize whose corpse this is."

"It is him," said the count, "and now I can sleep in peace. You will get your reward, my friend," he told the diver. "Because you have offered me a great service."

"Devil knows," reckoned Mavros at that moment, "if this degenerate did not drown a man on purpose in order to offer you this service."

Having conceived this idea, he leaned toward the corpse, searched it and paid special attention to its right thigh, as if eager to observe a certain feature.

"It is not him," he whispered as he got up.

"What are you muttering, Mavros?" asked Sanudo.

"Nothing, my master. I was just saying that from this husk, we can't tell what kind of fruit this was. But it must be him if you think so."

"How dare you question, you fool?"

"I have no doubts that this was a man before he was killed, boss."

Two women from Sanudo's company had exited the hall and were coming to see what the count was up to, since he had mysteriously disappeared with Mavros without saying a word.

"What are you doing here, Count?" called one of them. "Are the women in your hall not enough for you that you have to receive others in the hallways?"

"Take it away! Take this thing away quickly!" said Sanudo to Skiachti and Mavros.

"Right away, boss."

They lifted the corpse by its arms.

But the two women were not too far and there was plenty of light in the hallway. They saw the two men carrying something.

"What is this!" cried one of them.

"Nothing, my friend Fortuna!" said Sanudo.

"Why are you two leaving? Wait! Let us see what it is."

"It is the devil, dearest," said the count, standing between the door and the two women.

"And what is the devil doing here?"

"The devil is everywhere."

Fortuna hastened her step and pushed Sanudo aside in time to discover that terrible thing.

"Horrible! Aw, my God," she cried turning pale.

"I told you not to see it," said the count.

"What is it? What is it?" called the other woman rushing to see as well.

"Back away, Satan!" shouted Sanudo.

And he grabbed her shoulder to stop her advance.

The two men exited and Sanudo closed the door behind them.

But all of a sudden, Geremia Ghizi, one of the guests, appeared on the scene. He had observed how Sanudo had departed from the hall after the secretive exchange with Mavros and how the two women had slipped away as well. Spurred by jealousy, he had imagined hallway kisses and scheming and had gotten offended. So he came out to see what was going on.

"What are you ladies doing here? What is going on, my friend, Count?"

Sanudo pursed his lips and remained silent.

"What happened to you, madam?" asked Ghizi, seeing Fortuna's agitation. "What just happened here?"

He had barely caught a glimpse of the door closing and the two men carrying the corpse before disappearing like shadows. Ghizi went to the door, opened it, and before the count could prevent him, descended the stairs.

He found the two men in the gateway laying the dead body on a carriage.

Sanudo, regaining his composure, ran after him. But Mavros, seeing Ghizi descend the stairs, reached the staircase with two or three leaps and seized Ghizi's arm.

"Your Grace cannot leave my boss's house without your hat and sword," he said amicably and peaceably.

"What is this fool talking about?" cried Ghizi. "Is he playing dumb?"

"The feast is not yet over," insisted Mavros.

But Ghizi, with sturdy arms, pushed him vehemently, almost throwing him down the stone stairs.

"Leave the gentleman alone, Mavros!" ordered the arriving Sanudo. "Don't mind this night-crow, Ghizi. Talk to me if you like. What is it that you want? Tell me."

"I want to see what mystery is being concealed here," said the inebriated Ghizi.

"I am not so drunk to be afraid of mysteries," said Sanudo, without really knowing what he was talking about. "Fortunately I still have some sense left and I will bring this present to the main hall, so that everyone can see."

And he addressed Skiachti and Mavros:

"Take this log and bring it quickly to my hall, workmen!"

"Which log?" asked Mavros.

"The corpse, you idiot, not yourself," said Sanudo. "Lend a hand to your companion and bring it to the hall."

At first Skiachti was surprised to hear this command; but then he was satisfied because he sensed he was about to be rid of both worries and danger. Besides, he had understood for some time that Sanudo was not looking for the body to provide a burial, as Mavros had claimed in Kokkinou's tavern. Yet he had continued to pretend that he believed this story and used it as pretext to deliver the corpse to the count's residence.

Skiachti and Mavros lifted the corpse.

"Well done, Count! Now, this is the man I know!" said Ghizi clapping his hands.

They headed for the main hall, with those carrying the corpse in front, followed by Sanudo and Ghizi.

Fortuna and her friend had disappeared.

It is impossible to describe the shock and terror of the women in the hall, who had been singing and dancing before the half-eaten, malodorous corpse arrived. Their first reaction was like the spasmodic spring of a snake when stepped on; the second, a muffled cry; the third, an attempt to flee; the fourth, petrification that forced them to the chaises. Then, all of a sudden, by some miracle, they recovered from their drunkenness.

The men on the other hand, had gotten up, and the hair on their heads was standing. Quirini spoke first.

"What is going on, Count Sanudo?" he squawked. "This is an ugly joke."

"This is no joke," said Sanudo. "Ask Ghizi. He shamed me just now, saying that I house unseemly secrets in my mansion. I will prove him wrong, but he has no more right than the rest of you to see this secret."

While the count was gloating, the women's terror gradually abated. A few of them had gotten up and approached the dead body. Others headed for the door in hopes of leaving. But Mavros, for no reason other than to relish in the terror of these sad creatures, stood motionless with his hands on his waist, blocking the exit.

However, he couldn't block the entrance of a visitor who had a very acute sense of smell. The dog Augustos, who had smelled, wherever he may have been (in the kitchen probably), the appetizing scent of rotting flesh, arrived running and frisking. He crossed under Mavros' legs to reach and snatch the corpse by its neck...

In vain Quirini tried to detach him. Augustos grunted, crackled his teeth, barked, threatened, beat the ground with his feet and shrieked; but he wouldn't let go. He dragged the body with his teeth and tried to take ownership of it.

"Let him, Quirini," said Sanudo. "Augustos has the right."

"More so than all of us, it seems," said Quirini.

"But it's a wretched sight!" screeched Provvidenza.

"Horrible!" said Hestia.

"I see you are disgusted, ladies," said Sanudo. "Augustos, my friend Augustos, leave it here and go play."

The dog did not obey.

"Mavros," said Sanudo, "get him out of here."

Mavros grabbed Augustos by his ear, threw him squealing out of the hall, and closed the door behind him. But for a long time, Augustos could be heard barking impatiently and scratching the door with his nails trying to break in.

"But finally, what is this corpse?" asked Quirini. "Will you tell us, Count?"

"I will tell you, Quirini. But please, be seated, be quiet, and don't worry."

Sanudo sat comfortably on a chaise.

"Be seated, ladies," he said, "and don't be afraid. It's nothing. By God you will laugh at this story."

And to validate these words he guffawed in a forced and macabre manner.

"Don't you love contradictions, ladies?" he asked. "Here, this evening I have offered you everything in my power: food, wine, songs, music, games, caresses, a corpse, and a story. What else could you ask for?"

"Clearly he has lost his mind," said Quirini.

"On the contrary," said Ghizi.

"But for the love of God!" cried Olympia, finding the courage to speak, "if you want to tell us the story, have them take this dreadful thing away from here."

"No, my lady," said Sanudo. "I like having the corpse here."

"Then let's go to another room."

"Why should we leave our table and our wine?"

"Come on, Count," said Quirini, "tell us your story."

"It's easy, my friend Quirini. Here it goes: Seven years ago, if I remember correctly, I abducted the wife of this corpse."

"Aw, aw!" exclaimed several voices simultaneously.

"And was it really such a big deal, my ladies? Devil! Can't a man fish a single Greek woman out of the whole Aegean sea?"

"Aw, was she Greek?"

"Yes. And this corpse, her husband, had hosted me in his home."

"Horrible!"

"Awful!"

"Unspeakable!"

"Impossible."

"Unbelievable."

"So, as you can see," continued the drunk Sanudo, undeterred by his companions' exclamations, "today I am returning his hospitality in my own home. That's all."

"But we have understood nothing."

"But your story lacks both head and legs."

"No names, no locations."

"Unlikely."

"Untrue."

"Horrible."

"For you to understand, this dead man should, devil willing, recover his breath and voice this instant. Then he could tell the rest."

And Sanudo let out an awful laugh. But, alas, he couldn't convince his audience to mimic him. He was looking for a way to transmit his cheerfulness to them, but he was breaking his head and exhausting his body in vain. It was indeed a thoroughly terrible and repelling sight, which I would have preferred not to have shared with the readers of this book. Unfortunately the chronicles of that era confirm it as factual, and naturally its depiction couldn't be absent from 13th century Venetian art collections.

"Isn't it, I think, time to dance, my ladies!" blurted Sanudo as he rose. "My lovely Olympia, will you accept my arm?"

And he offered his arm to Olympia who winced in utter revulsion and pushed him away.

"You don't love me, my friend?"

But Olympia's hand had touched Sanudo's chest. He felt pain, turned pale, gritted his teeth and let out a sonorous scream. He lost his balance, slipped, and was about to fall down. Quirini supported him.

"What is it? Are you injured?"

"It is nothing. I will lie down; I am hurting; it is from the wine; I am dizzy; oh I am hurting, hurting!" he said, as he reached for his chest. "I am feeling a flame here. Mavros, Mavros, where are you? Aw, cursed Mavros, why did you bring this hideous monster here? It's your fault! You have nothing inside! You are godless!"

Hearing these words, Mavros left his station at the door and approached the chaise where they had laid the count. He opened his mouth widely, pricked up his ears, and listened:

"Mavros! You are godless! You are revolting!" repeated Sanudo tossing and turning. "I will hang you, you idiot… because I dislike impalement."

A yellowish bilious look flashed in Mavros' eyes, and he bit his lip. He seemed to be getting ready to attack Sanudo.

At that moment, a man clad in a gold-plated uniform with a sword at his side appeared at the door, entered, and greeted the company.

"Count Sanudo," he said, "I come on behalf of His Serenity the Doge to give you this order."

And he placed an envelope sealed with the lion of Saint Mark on the table.

He turned, and despite noticing the corpse lying on the floor, neither did his eyes reveal any surprise, nor did his mouth utter a word.

8. THE NURSE

That very night, in an impoverished shack in Venice, an acutely feverish man lay on a bed. An old woman sat on a low footstool by a fireplace, where a feeble flame burned, and a sleepily glowing lantern hung over her headscarf. This woman did not seem to be paying attention to the delirious man, either because she was deaf or because she had gotten used to his condition over several days.

"Once, only once, I wanted to kill him," raved the patient, "but he managed to kill me first!"

And after a little while he repeated, in a hoarse, half-muffled voice:

"He murdered me twice! Once in my home and once more in Venice."

"Certainly," whispered the old woman to herself, having apparently heard these words, even though she wasn't paying attention. "Certainly, what this patient is saying seems absurd. But who knows if he is telling the truth? For the truth is always absurd, which is why it is never professed by the sensible and the elderly, but only by the drunkards, the crazy, the sick, and the very young."

She stoked the fire.

"I wanted to drive my dagger into his heart," repeated the feverish man. "But he plunged his yataghan into my chest, my head, my body, and into my soul. He murdered me on dry land and in the sea, in the East and in the West, in the sky and on earth. He murdered me in the present century and in the next!"

He sighed from the bottom of his heart.

"Aw, this man! This man is a monster with eight heads and ten horns! For eight years, eight long years, I had been looking for him from Venice to Constantinople. I had been looking for him in his nest and in his burrow, in his pen and in his slaughterhouse! But I couldn't find him, couldn't find him to slay him. Then I found him, but he killed me. He killed me and the injuries he inflicted have torn my chest apart. Aw, but his stab does not hurt half as much as his cursed betrayal did. He robbed my treasure, my honor, my happiness! Damned the night I offered this Venetian my hospitality. Cursed the roof that housed him, cursed the table on which he dined, cursed the fireplace that kept him warm. Where will I find him again? How will I take my revenge? He eludes me like a shadow, like a dream, like a ghost. Here, here he is! He's come back. He's come back to mock me. He's baring his teeth in laughter. Here, he is escaping again! But I will catch you, Venetian!"

And with an abrupt, violent movement he bounced on the mattress, set his feet on the floor and extended his arms, as if to arrest a shadow. The old woman crossed herself and shrunk in her corner.

"Jesus, Mary, help us. Saint Mark, save us. Lie down, my friend, on your bed. There is nobody there. Why, this has been written for me too!"

She got up and helped him lie down. As the paroxysm of his fever passed, he lay on his back and fell asleep.

The woman returned to her footstool by the fireplace. She didn't seem frightened by the patient's outburst, but lamented that her destiny had condemned her to be a nurse, not allowing for some other profession.

"It seems," she said, "that destiny had no other skill left to give me. Others become madams, abbesses, prostitutes, ladies, or thieves. Was there nothing else for me, but a nurse for the sick? Couldn't I at least have been a nurse for the healthy! Why, it has been written for this to fall on my head too!"

She trimmed the lamp's wick and started preparing gauze for the patient.

"I am doing this for you, my son," she said addressing the patient, who couldn't hear her. "Calm down and keep your heart strong. I cannot stand seeing the sick struggle and shout at crows like you do."

The neighbors called this woman—perhaps as a taunt—Old Forkina[13] and she was seventy years old. She maintained, as if by revelational dogma, that she was invulnerable to disease. Twenty times, in the long rosary of her life's years, she had faced injury, plague, and smallpox, and she had tended to typhus, cholera, and scarlet fever patients. In her youth, she had been a key-reader, foretelling the fortunes of passersby, and from time to time she had partaken in witchcraft. She had arrived in Italy and had started selling this product of hers, until one day the commissioner of the city of Padova had her arrested and thrown in jail. This is where she spent those years of her youth during which she could have hoped to perfect her art. Instead, her talent was condemned to death and buried in the ashes of her incarceration. Upon exiting that correctional facility, she was forced to switch professions and became a nurse. She was not happy with it, but it was too late to make another choice.

Old Forkina (who was sometimes called Aunt Written because of the phrase she used to exclaim: *this is written too!*) harbored an aversion toward all healthy men. It was said that she could not stand rosy cheeks, that she wanted the entire human race, if possible, sick and bedridden, in order to be tended to by her. But all of this was obviously feverish talk by someone she had never treated.

Meanwhile, the sick man seemed to be sleeping. The night was advancing and Aunt Written, who sat on her footstool holding the gauze in her hands, was getting sleepy too and had started bobbing her head like a boat amidst turbulent waves.

She dreamt that she was in a huge hospital room, with one thousand beds and one thousand patients with various illnesses, who, upon seeing her, extended their arms from their beds and asked her to tell their fortune. Aunt Written was pleased by this and prepared to satisfy their reasonable request, when somehow the relentless commissioner and ruler of Padova appeared and immediately forbid Aunt Written from practicing that profession. He threatened that if she were caught telling anyone's fortune illegally, he would send her directly to the executioner, specifically the impaler because the state did not have the means to feed her in prison.

Aunt Written woke up terrified.

At that moment, there were knocks on the door of the shack.

Old Forkina got up and searched for a place to hide, worried that the commissioner or even the executioner of Padova was looking for her. She thought it prudent to squeeze under the patient's bed.

The knocks were heard again repeatedly.

Forkina moved her eyes around trying to shake off the dream's shadow that lingered in her imagination.

"It may not be the executioner," she said. "And what is the executioner doing here anyway? Who would harm an honest woman? But who is it then?"

She approached the door on her tiptoes and toenails and listened. She put her eye on the keyhole but could discern nothing in the darkness.

"Open, Old Forkina," yelled someone outside.

"Who is it?"

"It's me."

"Who are you?"

"Me, Minas."

"Minas who?"

"Minas, the friend of Yiannis Vendikis."

"Who is Yiannis Vendikis?"

"Yiannis Vendikis, the one who is the patient in your house."

The old woman considered for a moment. She summoned her memories and said:

"He could be right. This injured man must indeed be called Yiannis Vendikis. I have known him for a long time and this must be his name. And he, the man shouting outside, must be called Minas. I recognize his voice. I remember he used to be called Minas; this was his name when I met him. This means that Minas is looking for Yiannis Vendikis."

"So, are you going to open?" bellowed the voice.

"Are you Minas then?" replied the old woman.

"I told you I am Minas."

"And are you looking for Yiannis Vendikis?"

"Yes, this is who I am looking for."

"But who told you that Yiannis Vendikis is here?"

"A friend told me."

"Which friend?"

"Cartacci."

"Cartacci who?"

"Cartacci, who frequents the nearby tavern."

"Which tavern?"

"Kokkinou's tavern."

"Aw aw, impressive acquaintance!"

"Regardless, open; I need to see Yiannis Vendikis."

"But what do you want him for?"

"I can only tell him that."

"He is sick."

"I must see him, even if he is dead."

"Has it been long since you saw him last?"

"Very long."

"And where are you coming from?"

"From a distant journey."

"From which place?"

"From the East."

Aunt Forkina murmured: "This has been written for me too… to fall on my head." She crossed herself thrice, invoked Saint Mark, Saint Lorenzo, and Saint Perpetua, and finally decided to open the door.

A young man in his thirties, with the rugged and kind mien of a sailor, entered. He headed calmly for the bed where the sick man was lying.

He bent over the bed and observed the patient carefully.

"Is he sleeping?" he asked.

"Sleeping?" replied Old Forkina. "Why don't you ask if he has slept at all these eight days? He screams, struggles, punches, gets killed, and then he faints."

"Is he injured?" asked Minas.

"All of his chest and his body is a big wound. He has no parts injury-free."

"And have you been taking good care of him?"

"For the devil! If he escapes, it will be a miracle."

"Who brought him here?"

"One of my neighbors asked me for an act of charity."

Minas sighed.

"My poor and kind master," he said. "You were destined to suffer unfairly in this world."

"This has been written for me too," interjected Old Forkina.

"Does he ever talk?" asked Minas.

"He talks to himself. He tells stories, which I don't know if they ever happened."

"They must be coming from his fever."

"Where else do you want them to come from? I have been a nurse for forty years and I am well acquainted with typhus, meningitis, scarlet fever, the plague; and all of these are my good friends."

"Does he ever talk to you?"

"To me? Never."

"And does he not understand you if you address him?"

"Who knows if he understands?"

"Is he not, after all, of sound mind?"

"Of sound mind? But what do you expect? I have encountered, I told you, typhus, the plague, cholera, pestilence…"

"But what do all these have to do with an injured man?"

"He has all of them at the same time."

"Are you perhaps crazy, good old woman?"

"Me crazy? Bite your tongue! Back away, Satan! This has been written for me too. It is my fault, for opening the door to you."

"Forgive me, old woman. I did not mean to insult you. But my unfortunate master must be saved. Do your best, dear Old Forkina, and you will be paid handsomely for your efforts. Have you brought a doctor here?"

"I brought doctors, but don't believe them. They are all crooks, my child."

"Call doctors, old woman, and do everything in your power. You will be paid. We are rich. Tomorrow morning I will give you plenty of money. Aw, my poor master, and if you knew how I want to talk to you! If you knew where I am coming from and whom I have unearthed."

At that moment, the sick man moved. Oddly, Minas' last phrase had restored his faculties and his sense.

"Whom have you unearthed?" he uttered in a muffled voice. "Is this not Minas talking here?"

"It is me, master!" exclaimed Minas jubilantly, as he approached the bed.

"What were you saying just now?" asked the patient.

Minas bent, kissed his hand, and whispered something in his ear.

The sick man jumped up.

"Really? You found her?" he said. "And is she well? Minas, Minas! Did you see her? Were you not mistaken? Truly she lives? Aw Minas, thank you."

And he sat up on the bed.

"Aw yes, yes, master," said the crying Minas, "I saw her and she lives."

"Did you talk to her? What did she say?"

"I didn't want her to recognize me."

"Why?"

"Because I was afraid she may insist on staying in the monastery and disappear from our eyes again."

"So be it. Too bad! At least she lives."

"She lives, master."

"Aw, how I've been reborn. Come, come, old woman," he said addressing Forkina, "come and change my bandages. I am departing tomorrow."

"It's not the right time, master. You are still sick and you should protect yourself," said Minas.

"No, we are departing, Minas. I have nothing to fear anymore. It is enough that she is alive."

"As you wish."

"If only I can see her, Minas. I can die after."

"We are on our way, master."

Old Forkina was in shock. She searched for gauze and bandages, to change the wounds of her patient, and could find neither. She had been taken aback by the sudden turn of his illness. She asked herself whether the injured man had finally gone mad. The facts in front of her eyes overturned all clinical and nursing notions and all of her own views.

"Come, hurry up, good old woman," repeated the patient. "Change my bandages and prepare a broth of some kind for breakfast."

"Good idea, master," said Minas, rubbing his hands. "If only this good old woman had a bottle of wine! I am so thirsty!"

"Do you have wine, old woman?"

"No, my child, where would I find it?"

"Nevermind," said Minas. "We will wake your neighbor, Kokkinou, and she will give us some."

"Wine! Wine! Bring wine, old woman," said the injured man.

And he stood up and sat by the fireplace, on the meager chair where Forkina had been sitting not that long ago.

PART B

1. THE EXORCISMS

On a Sunday in April, as the rising sun absorbed the dew from tree leaves, and the swallows flew from roof to roof to bring food to their twittering chicks who opened their beaks at the edge of the nests to reveal red tongues, monks, with their cowls lowered to their eyes, were slowly exiting the main temple of the Monastery of Saint John the Theologian in Patmos.

The last one to exit was an old humpback monk, who, leaning on a crutch, headed for his cell. He had a warm drink, prepared for him by his subordinate, and lay on his modest mattress to rest.

A few moments passed, and while the old man was still awake, another monk appeared in the corridor in front of the cell and knocked on the second of a set of twin doors.

"Brother Simon!" the monk called.

"Bless you," said the voice of the old monk's subordinate.

"Is your elder asleep?"

"If he is not praying," said the subordinate opening the door.

"He is needed to confess a sister."

"Which sister?"

"Sister Aghapi[14]."

The old monk, hearing the conversation from his room, stood up, went to the door, and opened it.

"Is Sister Aghapi in danger, Brother Nehemiah?" he asked.

"I don't know, but she is asking to confess without delay."

"I am coming straight away."

He threw his cassock over his shoulders, exited, and followed Brother Nehemiah.

They crossed the threshold of the monastery gate and passed by a cavern in the form of a cross, where, according to tradition, Saint John the Evangelist had been inspired to write *In the beginning was the Word*, and an earthquake had followed that had split the boulder apart. They climbed a rocky and narrow mountain path, Nehemiah breathing loudly with his strong lungs and Abbot Amun stooping under the weight of his old age and his hump, holding his knees with one hand and his stick with the other. They reached a cave with a built-in entrance that faced the sea and the monastery on the foothill.

Nehemiah opened the door to let Amun go through, closed it behind him, and stayed out.

This meager dwelling comprised a room with walls carved in the boulder and a dirt floor. There was a bed in a corner and a woman was lying on it. Amun took the sole footstool in the room and sat by the bed.

"What is it, my child Aghapi?" asked the old monk.

The suffering woman opened her eyes and observed him with a sympathetic look. Her tunic was pitch-black as were her bedcovers. But her obstinately beautiful face radiated amidst these sorrowful colors.

She was a woman of no more than thirty-five years. She might have only been thirty. There was something pale and sickly about her beauty, suggesting torment and agony. Her forehead was like a halo, pale and blue-veined around her temples. Her eyes shone with secret rays and quixotic dawns.

It would be difficult to guess whether such a countenance and comportment were due to physical suffering or pangs of conscience. The black headscarf around her head could not completely conceal her gold blonde hair.

Do some women resort to monasteries from satiety and do others embrace the monastic life to avoid starvation? Perhaps. But to which category did she belong?

"I want to confess, Father," said the woman.

"Are you suffering?"

"Who knows if I'll live? I don't want to take secrets to my grave."

"You will do well, my child. The secrets that the sinners hide during confession devour them while they live, just like the worms will devour us when we die."

The nun sat up on her bed in a way that revealed her forearms, which were exceedingly beauteous for a nun.

She let out a short inscrutable sigh, rested her head on her right hand, and started in a calm voice:

"I have often told you my life, Father. But the outward appearance of the facts does not reflect the internal condition of my soul; those who talk about their lives at length, reciting their suffering and sins, are lying because this amounts to bragging. What I—exactly because of my compunction—have never dared to tell you, and to my disgrace I will admit for the first time, is this: Although it was with force and deceit that the Venetian nobleman abducted me from my husband's house, no later than the very first day did I consider it a stroke of luck to live with him and be his lover. For there was something overwhelming and satanic that overturned and subdued my conscience. I had never loved my husband with youthful passion. He had seemed gloomy and bothersome to me, even though he loved me. And in the eyes of the Lord it is me who is probably guilty, for it was I who followed the Venetian rather than he who kidnapped me. Because he acted in the throes of a temporary inebriation, in a passion violent and tyrannical. Whereas I—alas!—was deceiving myself and everybody else because I was feigning deep sadness while my heart was secretly rejoicing, intoxicated with amorous elation."

"This is a mistake of course, my daughter," said the holy man looking at her with confusion, "but it suffices that you repented for this a long time ago."

"I have never honestly repented," replied the nun sighing. "And if I abandoned the count, I only did it from spite and fervent jealousy, not from the desire to save my soul."

"It does not matter, my child, and if you didn't repent long ago, you are certainly repenting now."

"There is no repentance, Father."

"What are you saying? Blasphemy! Aw, women!"

"I don't believe this is true repentance, Father, except if hypocrisy and pretense of repentance can be called that."

Father Amun rose convulsively from his footstool, crossed himself, and fell in bewilderment.

"Why did you call me here then?" he asked. "What good is the doctor for an incurable disease?"

"To confess, my Father."

"To confess without repentance?"

"And to ask you to teach me how to repent, if possible."

"But repentance cannot be taught. It is spontaneous, my daughter."

"Then, I am telling you, it is impossible."

"You have the evil spirit of blasphemy inside your body."

"Listen to me, my confessor, carefully, and forgive a sick woman. Consider me drunk and raving. I admit that there are moments when my soul is devout and cries silently or mourns ardently in front of God, which is the loftiest thought of any mind. But these moments pass, as all moments do, and the flesh revolts and makes its demands. Forgive me, Father, and don't condemn me. For a long time, on this bed, I have suffered the tortures of Aidos[15].

My heart drips blood and my head is in the dark. Ungodly thoughts descend to my lips and painful desires arise. My sighs translate both of them into the fiery language of passion and desperation. Blasphemy is the natural result of distress, not of impiety. I don't believe there is another woman in this world more damned than I am. Like a convict tied to a stake, where he is to serve his sentence, my soul is tied to this passion, my curse for this century and the next. I love him, who destroyed my marital bliss and mangled my husband's heart. I love him so passionately and manically that this love is like a demon living in my flesh, an entire legion of demons extending like an octopus with its tentacles in my veins, sucking my blood and absorbing my breath. I have never repented for this crime of mine, Father, and I don't think I can repent. I wonder, Father, how come God allows on his watch the existence of a feeling more powerful than faith, and another deity above all godly might? In vain, my Father, I have performed lengthy fasts; in vain, I have genuflected a thousand times per day. My lips whisper mechanically the formal prayers I memorized as a child, but my heart reverberates his name..."

Father Amun listened to these words in some sort of trance, having been transported to another universe, wholly incomprehensible. It seemed to him that in the desert of Thebes, where he had pilgrimaged in his youth, the sunless caverns were opening and demons were swarming to penetrate his flesh. Her dialect was unknown to him. Various confused and labyrinthian thoughts were ramifying in his mind. First of all, was this a confession? If it was, it was nothing like the usual confessions he had been hearing every day for the past forty years of his vocation. Either then the confession of this woman was not such, or those of the other ones weren't.

"I have listened to the confessions of many women in my life," said Father Amun to himself. "And what do they divulge? Aspersions, lies, arguments with their husbands, sometimes envy, never theft; they often talk pompously about their virtues, or malign their neighbors and their friends in the pretext of confession; never do they reveal their wicked thoughts of adultery or the act itself; they mention that they drank water prior to receiving the holy bread, that they were chatting in church, that they have this or that habit, and so on. These they confess. But what about the dreadful unthinkable confessions of this woman?"

Father Amun proceeded with these thoughts, wondering if men are more honest than women during confession. He wondered whether he, Father Amun, had himself ever confessed honestly, with true and unfeigned candor to his spiritual father. Eventually he reached a conclusion in the form of a question: What is the point of confession and why does this ordinance exist?

But he couldn't share these notions aloud with his spiritual daughter because he did not want to switch positions with her and devolve to confessing to her.

Since he had no other means available to put an end to this suffocating line of thought, he resorted to that which he had refrained from thus far: He proclaimed that this woman had been evidently and manifestly possessed, as she herself had admitted, by an evil spirit.

"Demon, you are possessed by a demon, poor woman," he said. "You spoke the truth yourself, or rather the demon itself professed its presence."

He stood up, took the book of prayers out of his pocket, and started reading on top of her head the exorcism prayers of Saint Basil the Great: *"The Lord rebukes you, aw devil, that you depart this creature… Yes, Lord, expel from her any evil and impure spirit nestled in her heart: spirit of deceit, spirit of pride, unbelief, acedia, idolatry, spirit of fornication, adultery, lust, prodigality, salaciousness, and all impureness…"*

These powerful and mysterious words resonated in Aghapi's ears like the buzz that often accompanies acute fever. She could feel the "evil and impure spirit" writhing and shuddering inside her. She wanted to protest but couldn't. Sometimes she wanted to kiss the hand of the old monk, yet other times she wanted to seize him by the beard and throw him out of her cell. She felt two powers pulling and pushing her over a gaping abyss under her feet. Occasionally she leaned toward the abyss, but then she flew high into the ether. Religion, life, love, deception, sins, sorrows, dreams, everything appeared in her imagination as a blurred comingled picture. She extended her arms to catch the vision, but it eluded her like a shadow and vanished from her eyes.

The priest, meanwhile, continued reading the exorcisms. *"And make her renounce Satan, and all of his angels, and all of his worship, and all of his works… and not to harbor dark spirits in her heart or be possessed by them…"*

Aghapi burst into tears. They ran from her eyes like waterfalls. The monk took pity on her and stopped reading the exorcisms.

"Continue, Father," said Aghapi, wiping her tears.

Amun repeated: *"I exorcise you in the name of God to deliver this creature to the Lord… spirit of darkness, spirit of rage and resentment and murder, spirit of lust, spirit of disagreement… come out of this servant of God…"*

At that moment, a timid and hesitant knock was heard from the door of the cell.

"What is it?" said the monk.

"It is me, holy Father," replied the voice of Brother Nehemiah.

"What do you want?"

"They are asking for Sister Aghapi."

"Who?"

"Two strangers, a man and a woman, who just arrived."

"Don't you know that I am performing a holy service right now? How can you interrupt this confession?"

"I know, my Father. I beg your holiness to forgive me."

"Then why are you knocking?"

"The strangers insist on entering."

"Let them wait."

"They are unhappy waiting for too long."

"You are irreverent, Brother Nehemiah."

"I beg your holiness for forgiveness."

Meanwhile, Aghapi, upon hearing that she was being sought after, awakened, as if from a nightmare, and felt hope and excitement. Her heart started beating the harmonious warm pulse that produces sweet agitation, one she had forgotten a long time ago. She thought she should intervene.

"Excuse me, my Father," she said to Abbot Amun. "You will return as soon as possible to read these exorcisms anew. But who knows if they are not my relations or friends, those looking for me, fretting and worrying, as it sounds, for my health. Allow me to accept these strangers."

"I don't disagree, my daughter," said the abbot, restoring the book of prayers to his pocket and signalling the resolution of the exorcisms.

And he opened the door of the cell.

2. THE SCOUT

A young, sufficiently beautiful woman entered, followed by a man who was tall, malformed, invidious, and awkward. He seemed such a curmudgeon that he could neither trust the ground under his feet nor the roof over his head, looking up and down with his eyes wide open and his nose jutting out straight like an exclamation mark. Upon seeing this couple, one could tell that the woman, who looked fair and intelligent, must despise the man from the bottom of her heart if he happened to be her husband.

The young woman glanced quickly at Abbot Amun and averted her eyes immediately, in a manner that clearly revealed what she was thinking: "Eh, a monk, why do I care?" Then her gaze fell deep, probing, and sharp on the lying nun. She looked at her as if she did not just intend to photograph her image, but to measure her conscience and read life's imprints on her pale forehead.

Aghapi was perturbed and surprised by this predatory gaze. She could not remember having seen this woman before.

"What does she want from me?" she asked herself. "Why is she looking at me like that? Who is she?"

"Is it her?" the other woman asked herself. "She is beautiful and she has suffered plenty. Her eyes recount mysteries. She hides passion inside. It *is* her! I think I can see traces of the count's kisses on her lips. Aw, he knows how to pick his victims."

However, the stranger assumed an apathetic pose, lowered her eyes sheepishly, and addressed the nun first.

"Forgive our boldness, madam," she said. "We are pilgrims, coming from far away. We left our beasts of burden with our belongings down there, and because we were thirsty and couldn't find water, we dared to stop by for a moment and ask for your hospitality. I humbly beg you to forgive me."

"You are forgiven, madam," replied the nun, "but I am afraid I cannot entertain you the way I want in this modest abode of mine. Be seated and rest. Brother Nehemiah will offer you water."

While Aghapi was saying these words, Brother Nehemiah had already offered water to the strangers. Abbot Amun had disappeared.

The woman sat on the footstool and the man accompanying her on a stone. The conversation commenced again.

"This man is my husband, madam," said the stranger. "My name is Cecilia Viamini and I am from Venice."

"I did not ask you, madam; you are a stranger, and as such you are always respected by me, with your name or anonymously."

"You did not ask me because of your politeness, but I owe it to you and I am gladly telling you. My husband is perambulating the islands in his capacity as an officer of Venice, madam. We have visited almost twice or thrice all of the islands in the Aegean. I have met many people."

"Very well, madam."

"I really enjoy travelling; it is the best way to live, I think, on this earth."

The nun responded with a nod of her head.

"I can never tolerate confinement. I love meeting people."

"You do well, madam."

"I am not saying this to sadden you," repeated the stranger. "Because one never knows the other's private business. I don't like intruding. Besides, how do I know if you haven't seen the world more than I, and if you haven't been very happy in the past, or if you are not content today?"

The nun strained a smile.

"You are not saddening me, madam," she said.

"Then I can tell you honestly that I would never agree to become a nun," said Cecilia. "Someone with such beauty and youth, as yourself, to go and get buried! To become an ascetic, a hermit, a bat, an owl! Not to see people, not to hear life! To condemn oneself to a lifetime of agony, to slow soul-wrenching anguish, to a frantic death? Aw God! And for what? I assure you, it is better to suffer from jaundice, or to have a nervous breakdown, or to wither little by little from tuberculosis!"

Hearing all this, Aghapi did not show the slightest change in her expression; she observed the stranger peacefully, waiting for her to finish. Then she said:

"Forgive me, but it seems you are saying these things as a traveller, madam."

"What does 'as a traveller' mean?" asked the stranger.

"It means that you are a pilgrim, and you don't have much time to think through what you say. As you already confessed just now, you love travelling. Your words are then the words of a traveller, and forgive me for saying it."

The stranger bit her lip.

"It is me who should apologize," she said.

"You are forgiven, madam."

"I certainly did not come to your cell to tempt you, madam; rest assured that I respect you more than anybody in this world."

"Thank you."

"However, I have formed firm opinions on everything I say. I am not speaking as a traveller."

"Are you then applying these generic observations to me?"

"Perhaps."

The nun shrugged.

"Do you mean to say then," rejoined the stranger, "that you are not a person to whom I can apply them?"

"And how do I know?"

"I see that we have wandered off, madam. Believe me, it was not my intention to offend you or to intrude."

"I believe you, madam."

"Forgive me then."

"Don't worry about it, madam."

The stranger rose. She took a few steps to the entrance of the cell and stood for a few moments surveying the wildness of this location, surrounded by canyons, forests, and steep rocks, and ending at the eternally blue and infinite sea. Beyond, immeasurably far, there were cloudy and hazy islands, and even farther the towering mountains of Asia Minor obstructed the view.

Cecilia's husband, not having anything better to do, followed her with his eyes, without understanding what she was up to.

"What are you doing? Shouldn't we get going, Cecilia?" he asked her. "The dark will find us here, and where are we going to find a place to overnight?"

"Don't worry, it is not your business," answered Cecilia without turning to him.

If the nun had wanted to get even, she could have certainly told the stranger "Aha, so this is married life then?" But woe! She did not wish for revenge; it did not even cross her mind. After a few moments, Cecilia returned and sat on the footstool.

"Stay here, madam," said Aghapi, "if you have no other place to go. From the Monastery of Saint John the Theologian, which you can see down there, the Fathers can send us bedding."

"Aw! No need, madam. We have our luggage. I told you, our mules are waiting for us down the road."

"As you wish."

"Is there any danger here if one is to sleep in the countryside?"

"Why sleep in the countryside, madam? You can sleep in this cell. But even in the countryside there is no danger, other than being cold."

"Ah! I forgot," said the stranger snidely. "This is the holy republic of the monks. Should I guess that there are no thieves around here?"

"I don't think there are."

"And how is this island governed then, if you please? I am truly curious."

"I am not well informed about this. I don't know if Brother Nehemiah is around to advise you."

"Eh, I can't be talking to monks!" said the stranger with deliberate aversion.

"I am sorry. But I don't know how to inform you."

"So are these monks autonomous?"

"Yes."

"And they are themselves the civil authorities on this island?"

"It seems so."

"Do these monks then exercise all the civil functions here? That is, are they lords, dukes, commissioners, advisors, generals, elders, and even executioners?"

"In the West, madam," said Aghapi embittered, "it may be possible to have executioner monks. Here such a thing is unheard of."

"Don't get upset. I don't mean to say that they literally act as executioners."

"What do you mean to say then?"

"You know that if the executioner deserves our contempt, the judge who hides behind him is his accomplice, and indeed responsible for the crime of the executioner and deserving of even more contempt."

"So?"

"So aren't there monks who are judges here?"

"There are."

"Don't they issue the death penalty?"

Aghapi gave an uncertain nod.

"Therefore, the monks are executioners," said Cecilia, interpreting the nod as agreement.

"But I am not sure they issue the death penalty," objected Aghapi.

"Then what do they do? What are these judges good for?"

"So, wherever there are judges, they are needed to condemn people to death?"

"Certainly."

"I thought that the work of judges is to bestow justice."

"And how can justice exist without the ultimate penalty?"

"Is this what you believe?"

"Yes."

"Why?"

"Because if the slightest misdemeanors receive the corresponding sentences, it follows that the worst crimes must be punished with the maximum penalty."

"I don't know, madam," said Aghapi. "I am not wise enough to resolve such matters. It seems to me we are both babbling and we know nothing of what we speak."

"Haven't you read the New Constitutions of your kings[16]?" asked Cecilia with mild derision.

"I haven't read them," replied Aghapi.

"Then I understand why you became a nun. You were born from your mother's womb destined for this life."

Aghapi went silent and was getting rather displeased. She couldn't follow the stranger in her ostensibly pointless meandering, but she vaguely suspected that there was a specific purpose to it. But what could it be? Sinful hopes arrested the mind of the wretched nun, and she sunk into her usual daydream, which, as we discussed, arrived persistently every day and clouded her head. And this was the only delight, and at the same time the ultimate torment, of her soul. It was the final stop at the gates of Hell, where she hesitated for a moment to recall for the last time the ambrosial fruit of the tree of knowledge, whose flavor lingered in her pharynx—a magical oasis in the middle of the infinite and suffocating desert of eternity.

Finally, Cecilia, noticing Aghapi's musing, launched her long premeditated attack:

"You must have met many colleagues over the years, madam," she said. "Because in this path you have chosen, you can't have made any acquaintances other than monks and nuns."

"Not that many," muttered Aghapi.

"And each of your acquaintances certainly had her own sorrows, her own suffering, isn't that so? As you must have your own."

"I don't know what you mean, madam."

"Have you met many young nuns like yourself?"

"I don't remember."

"And who does? Young and beautiful perhaps. Imagine a young girl or woman, blonde or brunette, cosmopolitan, ambitious, unchaste… who is forced, by God's grace, to join the monastic order. So, madam?"

Aghapi remained silent.

"She is young and beautiful, soft-hearted, alluring, a joy and a delight, a delight and a dream. And she is victimized by love."

Aghapi lowered her eyes in sorrow. These words were torture.

The Venetian, however, sneakily fixed her eyes on Aghapi's face and seemed satisfied by the discoveries she was making with this tactic.

"A victim of love! Forced to become a nun! How many such women must there be! And how much secret torment, passion, desire, and mystery is shrouded by the cassock! The devil alone may know what can reside in the conscience of a girl or a woman, especially a woman. A girl can make a reckless mistake and decide to become a nun! But a woman? A married woman? Who knows what mighty passion seduced her, and what dire need drove her to the monastery?"

"Why are you telling me all this, madam?" asked Aghapi anxiously.

"Yes," continued Cecilia, ignoring her question. "There are many such mysteries. How I wish I had the spirit of Python[17] that is mentioned in the Bible, to know how to read the hearts of people. I have never envied any profession, other than that of the confessor. But unfortunately, women have been ignored and the Church has not accepted this dogma yet. Otherwise I may be pleased to be a nun. What more could one desire than to know how to read the hearts of others? With this tool, one can convert all the devout to followers. To be declared a saint while still alive. Has any young nun ever confessed to you, madam?"

"No, madam."

"Too bad! This would have been good entertainment. Especially if the confessant is naïve and she admits all of her errors, or those she considers as such. Some women have their souls and hearts at the edge of their tongues. But this may be very rare. In general, women have tongues to rattle and flap the air, like churches have bells. But they never reveal what is in their minds. Because the astute woman judges for herself and guesses what others think. While the gullible is deluded into believing that everything around her exudes sanctity."

Aghapi felt as if she were drowning in this flood of words. Realizing this, the Venetian kindly decided to shorten her suffering and land the final strike.

"Did you ever happen to meet," she said, "among the nuns, a young and beautiful woman by the name of Augusta?"

She said this staring into Aghapi's eyes. Upon hearing this name, the wretched Aghapi felt an electric shock, turned red, then pale, and nearly fainted.

"No…" she said with a muffled voice. "Why are you asking me about her?"

"You haven't met her?" insisted Cecilia.

"No … I don't know… I don't remember."

Cecilia was telling herself: "I know. It is you! I am holding you and you cannot escape me. It is up to me to decide whether to keep you, if you are of any use to me." Considering this, she smiled, thereby bringing forth the inmost darkness of her conscience.

Aghapi, on the other hand, seemed like a writhing fish caught on the hook of a deft fisherman. She beheld the woman standing before her with fear and bewilderment, wondering if it was an angel or a demon disguised as a beautiful animated wax doll, and if she was on a special mission to pry her from this land and transport her on winged and hollowly beating words to the land of dreams.

"So you haven't met her?" repeated Cecilia.

"But why are you asking me?" replied the nun.

"Don't worry. I am asking if you ever happened to meet her by chance. There is interest in her."

"Someone is interested?"

"Yes. But it is none of our business. It is pointless to talk about it, if you don't know her," said Cecilia slyly.

"But… I am not sure… I don't have all of my memories handy… It is possible that I did meet her and just can't recollect it."

"Perhaps. Try to remember."

"But who is it that is interested in her?" asked the nun directly.

"A friend of mine."

"A friend of yours?"

"Yes, a rich Venetian nobleman."

"A rich Venetian nobleman?" said Aghapi blushing.

"Yes."

"And what connection could there be between her and a Venetian nobleman?"

"So, have you remembered her then, this Augusta?" asked Cecilia with extreme sheepishness.

"I think so. If it is her that I met."

"What kind of woman was she?"

"A nun."

"A nun, I know. But what kind of woman did she seem?"

"A lost soul she seemed," said Aghapi. "But we shouldn't reproach. I don't know if she is still alive or if she died."

"Why? Was she sick?"

"Man is always sick."

"Did this Augusta seem to suffer from misfortunes and regrets?"

"Innumerable misfortunes and regrets," said Aghapi with a sigh.

"And what was the source of her regrets?"

"I don't know… perhaps her misfortunes."

"You are funny," said the stranger, "with your monastic reasoning."

"But you haven't told me after all," dared Aghapi, "who it is that is interested in her."

"You."

"Me?"

"Yes."

"Why?"

"Because you keep asking."

"Suppose I am the third interested party," said Aghapi, determined to finally find the courage because there was no place to retreat anymore. "But there is another, whom I am asking about. Your friend."

"I told you: a Venetian nobleman, a friend of mine."

"What is his name?"

"What good is his name for you? Besides, why are we even talking about the dead?"

"About the dead?" said Aghapi trembling. "So your friend…"

"No, my friend is fine, I think," replied Cecilia, "but your friend Augusta, you said she is dead."

"Dead, of course, poor soul."

"Does it not seem like we are disturbing, as it is said, the remains of the dead by talking about her and my friend? Does it not seem to you that the bones are standing upright, getting animated, and starting to walk in this doleful place you call home?"

"You are pious, madam."

"Certainly. Since I came here, in the state of the monks, let me purchase some piety that I can afterward sell when I return to the world."

"But why don't you want to talk to me about the deceased and your friend?"

"Because I think my friend had wronged her and wanted to make up, and this is why he was looking for her. Indeed, he intended to hold a memorial service for the resting of her soul."

"Ah, this was what he was concerned with!" said Aghapi with a deeply hurt voice, replete with bitterness and despair, such that Cecilia was almost moved. "It seems your friend is a sullen fellow who loves funeral services."

"Him? Aw, no, on the contrary, he is very jovial," said the Venetian harshly.

"Aw, he is jovial. I am glad to know."

"Why do you bother to be glad? Why do you care?"

"I wish all of your friends are jovial and happy."

"This is your duty, as a nun, to pray for peace in this world."

"Exactly. Is your friend married?"

"Married?... No… he doesn't have time."

"Doesn't have time for what?"

"Doesn't have time to get married."

"Why?"

"He has many… preoccupations."

"Does your friend always stay in Venice?"

"I believe he has already arrived in the Aegean."

"In the Aegean?"

"Yes. I heard he was preparing for a campaign."

"A campaign?"

"Indeed. My friend has never stopped his campaigns."

"And whom is he campaigning against this time?"

"Against the Greco-Romans[18], of course."

Augusta fell silent.

"Very well then, if I happen to meet my friend sometime soon, what should I tell him about Augusta? That she died?"

"Tell him whatever you want."

"Is she alive then?"

"Who knows?"

"In the end, how would you rather have it? That she is alive or that she died?"

"Tell him that she died."

"Did Augusta entrust you with a message by any chance?"

"No, madam."

Cecilia rose and circumambulated the four walls and the entrance two or three times, encircling the nun's bed. Then, she settled again on the footstool, took a stylus and some paper out of her pocket, and started writing on her knee.

"What are you writing, madam?" asked Aghapi impatiently.

"I am writing to my friend," replied Cecilia.

"And what are you writing him?"

"I will read you my letter when I am done. Be patient."

For a short time, she continued writing.

"Do you want me to read you what I wrote?" she asked the nun.

"I am afraid I am too nosy, madam. But it seems nuns can have curiosity."

"So listen."

And she read the following:

"My dear Count,

Today, on the island of Patmos, I discovered Sister Aghapi, who used to be a friend of the person we are looking for. She informed me that her friend may be dead or alive, or in-between, if such a thing exists, that she hasn't left a message for you, and that she does not require a memorial service, etc. This is the ultimate conclusion of all of my expeditions and efforts.

As a result, my dear Count, you are free to marry, if you will, etc.

Kisses,
Your friend,
CECILIA"

Aghapi listened greedily to the reading of this letter.

"What do you think?" asked Cecilia.

"You write well," replied the nun.

"I believe I do. Would you like me to include your kisses to the count?"

"What for? I don't know him."

"Well… in case you want to meet him."

"What do I, a nun, have to do with the business of the world?"

Cecilia sealed the letter and put it in her pocket.

"I will send it urgently with my men," she said. "I have two ships in the harbor waiting for me."

"Ships of your own?"

"Of Venice, but under my command. Would you like to travel anywhere? I can grant you the ship that will carry this letter."

This time the heart of the young nun skipped a beat, and even though Cecilia seemed to have mentioned the above jokingly, Aghapi had the burning desire to say *yes*. But modesty and prudence prevailed, and she said *no*.

Alas, she did not foresee that for many days and nights, she would burn and agonize with bitter regrets for having turned down this suggestion by the stranger.

Then, the Venetian, as if to leave her last phrase "I can grant you the ship" buzzing in the nun's head, saluted Aghapi abruptly and nodded to her husband to follow her outside.

Aghapi got up and approached the door.

"Spend the night here," she called. "Where are you going?"

The Venetian replied by gesturing with a repeated motion of her hand: "We are going far, far away."

"Stay!" insisted Aghapi, feeling her hopes fly away with the stranger.

But the stranger remained adamant and she departed with her husband.

3. THE ENCOUNTER

One morning, from a boat docked in the port of Patmos, two strangers disembarked. They seemed to have come from afar. One of them was very young; the other appeared to have grown old before his time.

"We have finally arrived, Minas," he said. "How emotional I am to set foot on this ground!"

"And how hopeful, master!" said Minas.

"Yet I have a bad premonition, my friend. It seems to me this ground is nothing more than a grave."

"Stay hopeful, my master; our premonitions deceive us," objected Minas, who, from the tone of his voice, seemed to have gotten tired of repeating this argument every day.

The older of the two men walked heavily and with slow steps, dragging, as it is said, his feet. He climbed to the top of a boulder, the roots of which stretched out to the sea, and lowered himself onto it. Minas mimicked him.

"We just set foot on solid ground, my master," he said, "and we are already sitting down, as if we were tired from a long trek."

"Minas," said he, without directly addressing his companion's observation, "are you sure that she is here, in Patmos?"

"I am sure, my master," replied Minas. "I saw her with my own eyes."

"It seems to me, Minas, that I am not meant to see her again, or that an accident will happen to her because of me. I wish I had not come here. What do I hope to gain from this trip? My place is there, where my revenge is. Revenge is the last refuge to a man betrayed, abandoned, and old. Can I hope to recover my youth, love, and domestic bliss? Impossible. And if she lives, can she come back to me innocent, as she once was? And who knows if she did not fall in love with the Venetian, and if she is not still in love with him? He is a charmer. He is an enchanter and a demonolater. How can she return to me? How can a woman, having tasted the libertine pleasures of dissolute life, return to her husband's hearth? Don't believe it. No matter how virtuous the poor woman had been, her willpower would have been overturned and her heart hardened after communion with the Venetian. Who knows what orgies he taught her! He treated her to the glass of whoredom, as described in the Book of Revelation. She cannot be in her right mind anymore, and even if she has retained a grain of reason, she will desire to dedicate her life to God. I fear finding this wretched woman tottering and raving the nonsense of salaciousness. Aw, if only she were capable of at least devoting herself to God! How could one be jealous of such a rival? But I am terrified that one day I will hear that the Venetian has found her again, or, God have mercy, that she went to look for him herself! This is what Written, the witch, foretold me one night, and I wish her mouth had been shut for good before she had said those things. I had never conceived, nor could I have conceived, suspicions against my wife. I had thought that she hadn't loved the Venetian, that she had been his victim.

But that unsightly old woman, Forkina, turned me upside down. And I did not believe her then—not even heard her words. But today, for the first time, her words are coming to me and they seem to have flesh and bones, and they turn into bogeymen that make me cower. Can you imagine, my friend? Do you know what it means? To be a man honest, kind, blameless; to love a woman passionately, the one who is your wife, to consider her your happiness, your jewel, your treasure, your refuge, your hope in this world! And to have a stranger arrive at your house, whom you willingly host, and to have him kidnap this woman and escape with her! Aw, hell! To wake up one morning, abandoned, betrayed, humiliated, cursed! And for a very long time I believed like a fool, like a child, that she was a victim and that she had followed him involuntarily. But today, as I am gathering my thoughts, I am convinced that she loves him… and this word tears my heart to pieces, like a thousand swords. Aw, that witch, the awful Old Forkina, was right. Of course she loves him! She loves him! But what is my crime that I should be tormented like this? Or am I being punished alive because of my excessive credulity? … Is there a hell before Hell then? …"

Minas had no counter to this torrent of thoughts. He sat, listening quietly, barely managing to follow the words.

"This is why, Minas," continued the man, "now that we have finally arrived on this island, what's been done cannot be undone, and it is time to think before we act. Listen to my plan: I will stay in this village and wait for you. You will go by yourself to the Monastery of Saint John to find out where this woman resides. When you confirm definitively that she is alive, Minas, and where her residence is, you will return to me. And we will have to think again, if it is better for me to come with you to see her, or if you should go alone with me waiting here, which seems preferable to me."

"As you wish, my master."

"So, today, you will prepare for this road. You will go to the monastery as a pilgrim and at the same time, you will look for the residence of that unfortunate woman."

"I will go, my master."

At that moment, at the foot of the boulder on which the two men were sitting and discussing, a raftsman approached the coast in his skiff. And on the beach under the rock, where the main jetty of that harbor was (and approximately eight to ten boats were berthed there), a woman appeared in nun's clothes, followed by a monk carrying a bundle. With the help of the nun, he set the bundle down on a stone jutting out of the sand.

"May God repay you in multiples, Nehemiah," said the woman. "Take care and ask Father Amun to pray for me."

Hearing the sound of that voice, the older of the two men sitting atop the boulder jumped up and nearly fell headlong down the cliff.

"Minas! Minas! Did you hear that voice? Look at that nun. Look!"

"What is it, master?"

"Who is this woman?"

"I don't know."

The woman they were talking about was facing the coast where the aforementioned skiff had approached, with her back to the two strangers. But the reader has by now figured that this was the nun Aghapi. After the departure of her Venetian visitor, her cell had oddly turned into a suffocating prison for her. It had seemed to her that the four walls were clamping together and becoming one, and that the roof was collapsing to the floor, such that it could no longer shelter her. Her bed had turned into a red-hot iron grill, like the one on which Saint Lorenzo had been roasted alive; and her pillow was not comforting her head, but burned both sides of it, turning the redness of her cheeks into flames of fever, and instead of giving sleep, it bore dreams, dreams continuous, raving, and bizarre. The last word by the Venetian had become a chain enfolding her heart with a thousand links. She could feel her destiny thrusting her irrepressibly. She could no longer walk safely on such shaky ground.

She felt the need to escape but would not dare admit to herself that she was going to look for the "Venetian nobleman." Her excuse to her conscience was that she was going to look for peace elsewhere. And she was forgetting that no matter where she voyaged she was bound to carry her heart with her.

She had no way of defending herself, nor was she strong enough to fight this cruel enemy, who, despite Father Amun's exorcisms, continued to nestle in her body, and one morning, in a feverish fit, she called for Nehemiah to accompany her to the harbor. It had been that same morning when the two strangers had arrived, those who were squatting atop the boulder. Was it then destiny that had preordained this encounter?

I wish I could express my thoughts about this without lyricism. But who condemned the unfortunate human race to this utilitarian and beastly existence? Who condemned it to crawl on the ground and grovel in the mud; to consider it insane to attempt to extend a momentary flight with an ant's wings?

What ironic fortune had contrived this encounter by that boulder, between this man, crouching under the weight of his misery, and this woman, carried by the zeal of her vehement passion; two unfortunates who could not join to comprise one happiness? Would it not have been better for them to never see each other again? Would it not have been better if they had never met at all? Would it not have been more tolerable if they were already dead, or if they had never been born? This agonizing encounter, this shocking confrontation, could turn one's head into Medusa's and the other's body into a pillar of salt!

Who can face such sights without being dazzled? Who can touch such lava without burning his hands? The tongue of the narrator of such scenes runs the risk of paralysis and his shins of pulverization. It is better that such burning bullets pass by in silence, or that they are prevented from coming on the scene. This material is like living fire: it forms, gets incarnated and inspired, animated and roused, it finds voice, and as it escapes and vanishes, it scowls at whomever imprudently thought he had it under control: "Do not touch!" And to the brave and curious observers of those who unwisely struggle on a ground that shakes from explosions, it exclaims: "Untie the shoes from your feet!"

Aw, don't think that the narrator is like a cat playing with its victim, a mouse. In this case the victim becomes the slayer, and under his pressure the foolhardy hunter, who thought he made a catch when he had only heard the flapping of his own brash flight, writhes in agony.

Our goal is to cast these few lines like a veil, and slur over what we can get away with. Let them imply all the unspoken and unspeakable misfortunes. We wish to narrate nothing that does not provide us with the material to be described. Sky and despair speak with ellipses, a poet once said, and he went silent before his time, perhaps for this very reason…

Do not disturb these mysterious strings that you all can feel, but whose mechanism you don't understand. They are not guitar chords, and the hand that will stroke them and the key that will press them have not been discovered yet. They are not guitar chords, these chords of your hearts. I know that nobody dares to gaze into himself, into a bottomless borehole that causes vertigo. You prefer to mirror your own faults to your neighbors, and you do well. I advise hypocrisy to everyone, and my advice is unnecessary, because however much I may urge honesty, it is completely impossible in this world. But your dishonesty is so transparent that you can neither conceal it yourselves nor hide it by reflecting it off your co-sufferers.

You ask for moral books? But where can you find morality?... We are nothing but Echo[19]. Do you prefer healers, those who prepare you to be fed with your own malice, your own embellished passions? Do you prefer to romanticise the social hideousness and indecency or to satirize them? We should await your answer in vain because it would not be permanent. So we shall continue on our predestined, toilsome path.

But we have wandered in a vacuum long enough; let us walk on pavement already.

Yiannis Vendikis (this name was used by Minas, as the readers remember, for the wounded man in Old Forkina's care) assumed this name when he first arrived in Venice, a few months ago, with his loyal companion Minas. Some thought this name derived from Benedictus, *blessed*, while others from Vindict, *vengeful*. With this name he met the sailor Cartacci, the same one who was then compensated by Marco Sanudo for his "idling", after revealing the presence of Yiannis Mouchras in Venice.

This same Yiannis Vendikis was discovered one morning, injured and half-dead on a deserted beach not far from Venice by a kindhearted fisherman, who tended to him, and went and knocked on the door of his acquaintance, the palm reader and nurse Forkina, who then took care of the wounded man for several days.

It seems that this Yiannis Vendikis was the man who had fought Marco Sanudo that night in that terrible struggle, from which miraculously both had come out alive after exhibiting incredible endurance and strength. Apparently, when Yiannis Vendikis jumped into the sea after Marco Sanudo, his well-honed, sharp dagger slipped from his grip, and as a result, he was unable to kill his adversary. Sanudo himself must have lost his deadly weapon, the one he had kept under his clothes on the gondola.

This same Yiannis Vendikis had sent his retainer, Minas, to Patmos to look for a woman whose trace had been lost long ago. And he stayed in Venice in hiding, and because he had nothing specific to do, he would spend unsparingly for the pleasure of various mariners and low-ranking officials, patiently awaiting his enemy. Everyone considered him a peculiar character, but nobody dared to bother him because of his boundless generosity. He used to offer a helping hand to the fishermen and ferrymen of the city without accepting payment. Yet many among his acquaintances thought he was crazy; how else could his constant melancholy, his wilted countenance, his gloomy gaze, and his silent, almost muted, mouth be explained?

This same Yiannis Vendikis is the man whom we find this morning with Minas, disembarking in Patmos and finally explaining his feelings. Because he seemed to have roamed around the world, without having known what he was looking for…

4. THE VENETIAN

While the startled Yiannis Vendikis was watching that scene unfold from the top of the boulder, the nun Aghapi gave her bundle to the raftsman, who placed it inside the skiff. Then Aghapi stepped on the skiff, while Nehemiah kept crossing himself and wishing her farewell.

The raftsman sat down and gripped the oars.

The nun Aghapi wore a black headscarf down to her eyes and bent her face deeply. The way she was sitting, with her back to the two strangers, her face was completely invisible to them. But when the skiff took a turn, Minas, who had been on alert after his companion's pronouncement, managed to momentarily see the shape of that face. And he could not withhold a smothered cry:

"Mrs. Aug…"

That was the only syllable he was able to utter, because Yiannis Vendikis, who had other plans, immediately muzzled him by shutting his mouth with his hand.

"Silence, Minas," he told him.

"Why?"

"Silence, I'm telling you."

Minas didn't dare persist.

It is unclear if Minas' cry was heard by the nun, for the height of that boulder was significant and the wind in the opposite direction. She turned her head for an instant, but probably couldn't recognize the two men, because Minas was sitting with his side to the sea, and Vendikis had for a long time made every possible effort to become unrecognizable and had perfected his means for it. A thick black beard, with the occasional gray hair, covered his jaw line; and his hair, plentiful and wild, shadowed his forehead. Besides, when Minas gave off the aforementioned cry, Vendikis stooped instinctively and simultaneously turned sideways.

The skiff withdrew quickly until it reached a small boat.

Vendikis, who was holding his breath, and whose eyes and life were concentrated in the direction of the skiff, saw the raftsman carry the nun's luggage on the boat. Then, he saw her climb on the deck and the sailors prepare to lift the anchor and raise the sails. Minas kept moving his eyes from the boat to Vendikis and back.

"Minas, Minas," grumbled Vendikis eventually, and these words hardly sounded like they belonged to an articulate human voice.

"Tell me, master," said Minas.

"Minas, go. Why are you sitting here?"

"Where do you want me to go, my master? I await your command."

"Go, Minas, to the boat."

"Which boat, master? That one?" said Minas, pointing with his eyes and not daring to extend his arm.

"To our boat, Minas."

"The one we travelled with?"

"Yes."

"I will go right away, master. But to do what?"

"Tell the captain, Minas…"

And his voice broke off. It took effort for him to pronounce the words, and he could not express himself in full. His eyes had not left that boat, the one the nun had boarded.

"Tell me, master," said Minas. "Be brave and don't make me cry like a child."

Indeed, poor Minas was crying. The philosophy he had championed since childhood was of no use in the face of such silent and heart-wrenching emotion.

"Go, Minas. Find a raftsman!"

"A raftsman?"

"Yes."

"To do what with him?"

"To send him to that boat."

"To *that* boat?" asked Minas, with his eyes pointing straight at the boat the nun had boarded.

"Yes."

"And what should he do?"

"To say…"

Vendikis brought his hand to his chest. The words seemed to be drowning inside him, in the waves of his mental anguish.

"To say, master, to the… nun that we are here? Isn't this what you want to say?"

"No, Minas."

"But what, master?"

"To ask the captain where…"

"To ask him where he is going?"

"Yes."

"And to return and inform us."

"Yes."

"I am going straight away, master."

Minas, who had been standing for some time, leaped down the slope of the rocky hill and reached the wharf. At first, it occurred to him to untie the first skiff he saw, but he held back, considering that his orders did not extend that far. Eventually he found a raftsman in an inn and assigned him the task he had received, giving him a silver coin.

This good man, who was in need of exactly that piece of silver in order to spend his evening drinking, untied his skiff, and, pushing with a pole against the shallow seafloor, reached the indicated boat. After a few moments, he returned and informed Minas that the boat was about to sail, God willing, to Mykonos, Paros, Naxos, and perhaps to other Cycladic Islands. Minas gave him a second coin.

"Are there any passengers on it?" asked Minas, overstepping the orders he had received from Vendikis.

"By my faith, I saw no passenger, other than a nun," replied the man, moved by Minas' generosity. "And what a nun! Beautiful face, I swear, boss. Isn't it a shame that all the lovely fruits fall in the mouths of these wretched monks! They have the ceremonies, the charities, the sweet wines; they have the beautiful women! How did this terrible idea get in this land's head, to put these black crows up to darken it? Forgive me, Lord! And after a poor man has slaved all day, and his own soul has reached his teeth, he does not have a pound of wine to wet his lips in the evening! And instead of having a woman under his command, the woman herself tells him that he will sin if he lies with her and then she rushes to find the monk and bring him offerings, treats, and koliva[20]! This is what exhausts me!"

"And wasn't anybody else accompanying the nun?" asked Minas, grabbing the opportunity as soon as the raftsman stopped to take a breath.

"Nobody, I swear, by my faith. It seems she was unhappy in the monastery and managed to escape, to take her chances elsewhere, to make a fresh start. If she had needed a companion on her journey, I would have gone myself, I am telling you! But what a harsh punishment it is, to cringe here at the feet of the monks, to have no steady job, to make little money, and not to find a drop of wine to wet your throat in the evening before going to bed! And to have your wife run to the monks, complete fasts, vigils, prayers, and try to perform miracles! Here is a woman who does not care to learn about miracles. That one, who decided to escape from the grip of the monks."

"How about the captain of that boat?" asked Minas directly. "What kind of man is he? Do you know him?"

"The captain is a good man. It's Old Jacomo. I know him. I have shared his bread. An old sailor. We used to load salt from Phocaea. And Old Jacomo was obsessed with sailing straight against the wind. The water would rush in through the hatches, the salt would melt and return to the sea, and Old Jacomo would not seem to mind in the slightest. 'All the better!' he would cry, 'the sea to the sea. To multiply or melt.'"

"Is he a reckless mariner then?" asked Minas.

"He is stiff-necked. Everything whirls around him. The wind, the sea, the boat, the sailor with the winch handle, the sails, the masts, and the land appear to whirl and the sky too when one is afloat. The wheel whirls, the bow whirls, the stern whirls. Only Old Jacomo's mind stays put, always. Neither the winch handle nor the ship's wheel can change it. Five times he shipwrecked to avoid granting his sailors' wishes. 'Captain Jacomo, jump; we are lost.' 'Onwards! To Hell full force; get me some wind!' And he shipwrecked it. 'Captain Jacomo, windward or we'll sink' 'Jump, go to Hell; you are not getting what you want!' and he threw it on a reef."

"Really?" said Minas worried. "Is he that obstinate?"

"Devilish. He can drown people, and more people, and even more people. And if he has made it until now, he must have a guardian angel or devil. I am guessing devil because where would Old Jacomo find an angel?"

As the raftsman continued talking, Minas nodded goodbye and rushed off. The raftsman looked at him bemused.

"What happened to him?" he said. "Something must have happened. But let me go wet my tongue because I am out of spit…"

Minas went to Yiannis Vendikis and repeated what he had been told by the raftsman.

"According to him," he said, "the captain is excessively obstinate and there is danger of an accident."

Yiannis shook his head.

"I have no intention of becoming Providence myself, and people try in vain to prevent what is written."

"You believe, master, in destiny?"

"I believe in Divine Providence, and I will always believe, my friend Minas. This is why I have contempt for all human effort."

"Should we then leave ourselves to the whims of luck?"

"No, but we should follow the circumstances carefully and not try to get in their way."

"So, what are we going to do?"

"Exactly that; we will follow."

"How?"

"There, as you can see, that boat is already departing, my dear Minas."

"I see, master."

"So, go find the captain of a good schooner among the ones berthed here."

"And arrange what?"

"And arrange to board that schooner and follow this boat, the one currently departing."

"I understand."

"And wherever it goes, we go. This will be our agreement. Go!"

Minas got up and walked quickly to the beach. He wondered about the strange peacefulness and serenity that had taken hold of Yiannis Vendikis ever since Minas had returned from his previous mission. A mysterious comfort, like a gentle caressing breeze, seemed to have come to him. Was that pronouncement true then, the one that Byzantine painters used to include in certain icons on the pages of an open book: *"Come to me… and I will comfort you. Lift my yoke… and find comfort for your souls…"*?

Alas, these words, widely respected in those days, used to be engraved on icons by Byzantine painters with shortened symbolic characters. And this expression of devout simplicity and truth is today more incomprehensible than cuneiform.

What had happened to the emotional tempest in which Minas had left Yiannis Vendikis when he had been sent to discover the destination of the departing boat? It had been scattered like a cloud, and clarity had dawned on the forehead of this unfortunate man.

Minas quickly carried out his mission and returned to Yiannis Vendikis.

"Well, Minas?"

"It's done, my master."

"Did you find a boat?"

"I did."

"And you agreed?"

"Agreed."

"And are we casting off?"

"We are casting off."

"When?"

"Immediately."

"Let's go then."

"Let's go."

And they walked down to the seashore.

"What kind of man is the captain, Minas?" asked Yiannis on the way.

"A very good man he seemed, my master; middle-aged, handsome, cheerful, must be a good sailor."

"And his boat? Did you see it?"

"Here; this is it."

He pointed at a large schooner anchored four to five fathoms from the pier.

"Seems like a good schooner."

"Strong schooner; two-year-old keel."

They retrieved their baggage, which they had left in the inn after disembarking that morning, and handed it to the sailor who was waiting for them on a skiff at the pier.

"What? You are leaving, gentlemen, so soon?" asked the innkeeper. "But I thought you were going to spend a few days on our island. Don't you like my inn then? That is too bad because I happen to be losing two good guests who I had the pleasure of hosting for some time."

"I am afraid we have to leave, my friend," said Yiannis Vendikis, tipping the innkeeper with a few silver coins. "But how about a meal, Minas?"

"Indeed, I would like a meal, my master. I am very hungry," said Minas. "But won't you join me?"

"I have no appetite. I will take a walk on the seashore and wait for you."

"Are you in a rush, my master? Don't worry, we have time to catch up to the other boat; it won't get away."

"I am not worried, no; I know we will catch up."

"If you are worried that it will get away, I won't eat, and we can board immediately."

"No, eat, Minas, eat."

"I am not eating if you don't accompany me, my master."

Yiannis gave in and sat on a stool by a bandy-legged table. Minas sat on the opposite side of the same table.

"Bring us something then, and be quick," said Vendikis to the innkeeper.

The innkeeper, who could hardly hide his joy for the upcoming compensation, after the two passing strangers had conceded to staying for dinner, scurried to bring sea urchins, shellfish and appetizer fish, a favourite of Minas', whose voracious appetite was only moderated by the presence of his companion.

Vendikis, on the other hand, barely touched anything the whole time they were there.

In another corner of the inn, around a large table, five to six fishermen and raftsmen sat, smelling and sucking shellfish and sea urchins, and drinking wine. Among them was the garrulous raftsman, whom Minas had sent to the boat on which the nun Aghapi had departed.

As Vendikis and Minas were getting up to leave, a beautiful, opulently dressed woman appeared at the entrance of the inn, followed by a surly, unsightly man. She addressed the innkeeper with a foreign accent:

"Sir, can you please tell me if a young nun passed by this place, and whether she boarded a boat or is still around?"

"Why are you asking me, madam?" asked the innkeeper, who always seemed to be suspicious or looking for a way to profit. He also might have been completely in the dark.

"I noticed that your inn is so close to the pier that if she had boarded a boat, it would have been impossible for you to miss her. And that she came here today I am certain."

"I don't know, madam," said the innkeeper.

The young woman approached him and placed a silver coin on the kitchen tile.

"Do tell me, if you know, please."

"I don't know, I swear, madam," said the innkeeper grabbing the coin.

This time he was being honest, of course.

"But look, madam," he added lowering his voice. "Do you see these men over there, who are eating and drinking by that table? They are all sailors, seamen. Ask them, the fishermen and the raftsmen, and if a boat departed today, and if it had passengers, how many and who, they will know."

In the meantime, the raftsman who had learned of the nun's departure on the occasion of Minas' mission, heard the stranger asking about a nun, noticed the cling of the silver coin on the tile, and stood up and approached the stranger.

"What would you like to know, madam? I can inform you. What do you want? I would be glad to be of service."

"Do you know if a young nun boarded a boat today and if the boat has sailed?"

"I know. She got on. It sailed. She was a beautiful nun, madam. But it can't be too far. And if the lady wants, I can use my skiff with six rowers and we can catch up to her. I have a good skiff, madam; even with four rowers, I can catch up. And they won't ask for too much. Enough to drink. Would the lady like me to get the skiff ready?"

"No, thank you," said the stranger, giving him a silver coin. "I just want to know which direction that boat is headed."

"I can tell the lady; I know. The boat is going to the islands. To Naxos, to Paros, to Mykonos, and elsewhere. It can be an easy trip or a difficult one, depending on the weather. But Old Jacomo has a screw loose. I am not going with him again to get myself drowned. See, I was telling that gentleman over there…"

"Who?" asked the stranger.

"That one," said the raftsman pointing at Minas. "His master sent me, just about half an hour ago, or it could have been one. Who knows? He sent me to the boat, the one the nun boarded, to find out where it was headed."

The stranger stared Minas and his companion up and down, intently and suspiciously. She was trying to guess what these two strange men could possibly stand to gain from knowing the whereabouts of that young nun, the same one she was after.

As for Vendikis and Minas, their curiosity had of course been stirred as soon as the strange woman had appeared at the inn and uttered her first words. Yiannis Vendikis studied this woman puzzled. He did not know her. Had never seen her before. Why was she asking about the nun Aghapi? What business was it of hers? Had she been sent by anyone or had she come on her own? But why would she come on her own for that nun, an outcast of this world? Most likely she had come on someone else's behalf. But who had sent her? And in the depths of Yiannis' heart, like an elegiac murmur, one name rustled. Aw, that name again! Why was it always that name? Why did it persecute Yiannis everywhere like a ghost? A man can be terrifying or loathsome to another man, it makes sense; but a name, a whisper, a word, a shadow, a sound, an ear's pinch, a stroke of wind? Why, why does this gentle breeze ceaselessly reverberate, this hollow prick in Yiannis' soul? A prick? But this prick was agony for Yiannis' heart, a massacre, cruel venom, a long, sharp, and awful rapier. It was rooted in his body, inseparable from his existence, a companion for life.

This was what he told himself, and despite his agitation, he nevertheless thanked God for not voicing it aloud. His thoughts remained private, deep in a chasm at the bottom of his soul. But in his chest, foaming bile rose, poisoning his mouth. He asked himself for the millionth time, what did he do wrong to be punished so harshly, and for the millionth time, he answered: "It must be that my punishment is just, since I am being punished, but I fail to understand why."

The foreign woman did not hesitate any longer. She took a couple of steps toward the two men and said:

"Are you also familiar then with the nun Aghapi, whom I am looking for?"

5. AUTONOMOUS

Yiannis Vendikis replied nothing to this question, which had been curiously addressed to him when it should have probably been directed at Minas, for he was the one pointed at by the raftsman who had gone looking for information regarding the nun.

Minas, having nothing better to do, mimicked his companion's silence. Besides, he was plain confused; he was far from experiencing the multifarious swirling emotions in which Yiannis Vendikis floated.

The stranger was forced to repeat her question.

"Do you know, I asked, the two of you, the nun Aghapi, whom I am looking for?"

This second time her words had a deeper, drier tone, like a command.

Yiannis Vendikis was getting irritated.

"Why the question, madam?" he said.

"I would like to know what connects you to this woman," said the stranger, moderating the harshness of her voice. Yet even now there was something imperative in her tone.

"And by what right, madam?" repeated Yiannis Vendikis.

"Because this is what I want," said the stranger.

And she turned around to give a quick glance toward the door. Only then did Yiannis Vendikis, following her eyes, notice the unknown men standing on both sides of the door: men foreign, bearing no kinship to the islanders, looking like Venetians. They all wore long cloaks and there were about ten of them.

But this discovery hardly intimidated Yiannis.

"Let's go, Minas," he told his companion.

They headed for the door.

But as soon as they had taken two or three steps, the woman, cracking a whip she had previously held curled in her hand, called the Venetians standing just outside the door.

"In the name of the Republic! Arrest these men!"

"Which republic? The republic of bandits?" asked Yiannis Vendikis, understanding immediately his position.

And he brought his hand to his belt and reached for his dagger.

Minas followed suit.

The Venetians revealed their swords, which they had hidden under their cloaks, to execute the woman's command.

Yiannis and Minas assumed defensive positions and retreated a few steps to secure their backs.

The six or seven fisherman, who had finished consuming all of the shellfish and had drunk several glasses of wine, stood up, opened their mouths and extended their ears, but they could understand nothing.

The innkeeper's jaw dropped and his eyes opened, watching and watching. He was terrified. His ears drooped and he didn't know what to say or what to think.

At the door, the timid heads of many islanders had gathered because of the commotion, and they observed the happenings.

The words "In the name of the Republic! Arrest them!" had been spoken by the Venetian in her language.

On the other hand, Yiannis had replied "The republic of bandits?" in Greek. As a result, the armed men had not understood his words; but the Venetian, who was innately short-tempered and easily enraged by any kind of resistance, translated them.

"This man is insulting our homeland!" she yelled. "Arrest them both and bring them to my ship."

"Your ship? What ship?" whispered Yiannis. The Venetians attacked them with their swords and daggers, but the two friends defended themselves like lions.

"Don't fight, don't fight!" called the Venetian mockingly. "Surrender, brave Greeks, surrender."

None of the attending islanders dared to intervene, to protect or help the defending men. But they stared bewildered and with gaping mouths at this uneven battle.

Meanwhile, the innkeeper was cursing the moment that he had complimented these two passing strangers, forcing them to honor him by eating at his place. He regarded the bottles, the glasses, the dishes, the pots, the jars, and he was mourning and crying over all of them in advance.

Upon hearing that one of the two men had insulted their homeland, the Venetians intensified their charge, but the endurance with which Yiannis and Minas resisted defied belief. The daggers in their hands were palpitating manically, paroxysmally, tirelessly. Their faces drenched in sweat, anxiously panting, striking, struck, bloody. They looked more like demons than human beings. On the one hand, Yiannis thought he would be delighted if he at least managed to die honorably on this occasion. On the other, Minas, whose youthful bravery and hope were much more thriving, wanted to save his companion while saving himself, and he held the strong conviction that he was going to achieve it.

Eventually, an idea occurred to Yiannis, which he first dismissed as impractical, but was then forced to accept, since he could see no other way out of imprisonment and shackling—the heavy and rusty shackles of Venice. For he was not certain of death, but he thought it more likely that he would fall into the hands of the enemy alive.

"Brothers!" he said addressing the islanders, while his eyes were glued to his adversaries and his hand ceaselessly wielding the dagger. "Brothers, did you hear what this woman said? She said, 'In the name of the Republic!' And you are autonomous."

Hearing this appeal, the islanders were moved. It was the first time they had heard that they were autonomous, a word whose meaning they were unfamiliar with, but were flattered by, suspecting that it must mean something good.

"You are autonomous! And they are coming to arrest us on your free soil," repeated the panting voice of Yiannis. "Us, your compatriots and coreligionists. They are coming to arrest us in the name of the State of Venice! And you are tolerating it!"

From the circle of these baffled men, the peaceful fishermen and sailors, certain movement was heard. One of them cried:

"He is right, friends. We cannot allow them. It is dishonor and shame!"

And he rushed to take part in the scuffle. The rest of them had nothing better to do, so they joined him. The man who had spoken first grabbed an oar lying on the floor (because the inn also served as a boathouse and occasionally as a warehouse of tools for sailors and fishermen), the second took an old rusty adze, another a grapnel, another a harpoon, and they all attacked the Venetians from behind.

"Let these men go," they yelled. "Let them go."

They were striking, and they were enjoying this more than they had ever imagined. And other islanders, standing outside the door, intervened in the same way and joined the fight. In a few moments, the number of these auxiliaries had exceeded twenty.

Such help Yiannis Vendikis had never hoped for.

But neither had the Venetian ever anticipated that such a great number of impromptu assailants would come against her men. And seeing them ready to succumb to the overwhelming numbers, she pulled at her hair in a rage, screaming and shuddering.

"Animals! I would have never believed that these beasts could intimidate you. Ah, I did not bring you here to humiliate me. Traitors, dishonouring Venice! Ah, don't you ever dare do this, for the gallows await you. Betray Venice? You scoundrels, Venice shall never be dishonored! The proud queen of the seas; aw homeland, may you never have this happen from your own children. Cowards, it would be better and more pleasant for all of you to die with your swords in your hands and not to have a pound of flesh left for the vultures to devour. How can I show my face to the count again? How can I look at the flag of Saint Mark? Isn't it better for me to be murdered by your blades? Pierce me, cut me to a thousand pieces. Alas, alas, for the love of God, strike, strike; be brave my children; heart, valor, courage, courage!"

And the Venetian cried desperately, stomping on the ground with her feet and ripping at her cheeks with her fingernails.

But her appeals were lost in the midst of this turmoil, confusion, and riot. Blades, arms, oars, heads, harpoons, chests, bottles, tables, stools, clangs, thuds, screams, curses, profanities, damnations, cries of rage and agony. And among them one could only discern the words *autonomous!* and *fight!* This miraculous word that was almost accidentally and hopelessly sown by Yiannis Vendikis, had fructified that second word, which can be its only buttress.

The confluence of the crowd to the scene was, given the total population of the small port, huge. Fifty men were in and around the inn pushing each other. The Venetians, although armed, realized that they could not persist in confronting such a crowd. But their leader was neither discouraged nor ready to retreat.

"Strike," she cried in a rage. "Arrest them! The two of them! Just these two! Scatter the rest of them."

Nobody could hear her. Only the innkeeper, who this whole time had been clasping his hands in a grill-shape, noticed her blustering and spoke to her.

"What is it, madam? Why are you acting like this? At least compensate me for the glassware your men have broken."

She gave him no reply.

Thus, the Venetians gave up. They dropped the swords from their hands and the scuffle ended. Nevertheless, some of the islanders, holding oars and grapnels, seemed intent on continuing the game.

"We surrender," said one of the Venetians to Yiannis Vendikis.

"Calm down, lads. Stop fighting," he told the crowd. "They have surrendered."

The men did not understand the meaning of the word "surrender", and wondered why they were supposed to stop, once they had started. But they respected Yiannis' desire, for he had gained a high degree of rapport with the crowd.

The queer woman shuddered.

"What did you say, cowards?" she screamed biting her hands and darting feral glances from her eyes. "'Surrender' you said? Ah, before that word came out of your mouths it should have cut your throats, become a knife's blade, and killed you. 'Surrender…' Don't you know that your grave has already been dug and that I will send you to forced labor? Don't you know that I will hang you from the masts of my galley?"

This time, since the battle had stopped, the outrage of the Venetian was visible to everyone. The entire crowd of these simple people lingered for some time, observing with deep curiosity this perplexing specimen of a woman.

"Should we arrest her, boss?" said a fisherman to Yiannis.

He considered it for a few moments.

He was trying to figure out the possible motives this woman had for looking for the nun Aghapi and for ordering her companions to arrest him. He thought to himself that perhaps she could inform him about it, if forced. He acquiesced to the idea for a moment but changed his mind.

"No," he said.

And as if addressing Minas, who was looking at him in wonderment, he repeated:

"We should not outrun Providence, but follow it."

6. LETTER

One morning of May, a few days before the events in the previous chapter, a Venetian fleet of twenty galleys had anchored at the island of Thera[21].

Marco Sanudo, with eight galleys of his own, had set sail from Venice in the beginning of April. Many noblemen had followed him with their own vessels.

This was the vaunted privately funded campaign, aimed at subjugating the Aegean Islands, which had already submitted, except for perhaps two or three, before the fleet from Venice arrived in the Aegean archipelago.

It was around dawn when a skiff approached Sanudo's flagship.

"Who are you?" asked the sentinel.

"We are raftsmen," replied the voice of the steerer.

"What do you want?"

"Is Mavros here?"

"Sleeping."

"We have a letter for the boss."

"From whom?"

"From a boat that arrived today."

"Whom is the letter from?"

"I don't know whom it is from because I did not open it to read it. But it carries the seal of Saint Mark."

The sentinel whistled thrice to the boatswain, who was sleeping in the forecastle, and woke him up.

"What do you want?" he asked, rubbing his eyes.

"Is Mavros sleeping?"

"I don't know if he is sleeping because he is not in my dreams… Wake him up and leave me alone."

The sentinel went aft and whistled again, a different tune.

"What is it?" asked a half-dressed and barefoot cabin boy who leaped onto the deck.

"Where is your boss?"

"My boss who?"

"Mavros."

"Aw, is Mavros my boss, huh?" said the cabin boy coyly.

"Your boss or whatever the hell he is, what is he doing? Sleeping?"

"No, he is alive," said the cabin boy.

And screaming his lungs out:

"Mavros! Mavros! They are looking for you."

Mavros ascended to the deck. He was glum, and it did not seem like ordinary grumpiness merely due to having been awakened.

"Who is calling me?" he asked.

The boy, having snuggled under an old sail used to cover the narrow trapdoor from which the chains are raised, was unseen. Nobody else was visible on the deck except the sentinel.

"I didn't call you, boss," he said, "but I was the one looking for you."

"Then who was it that yelled so loudly, as if I was two miles away?" grumbled Mavros.

"This lad," said the sentinel.

"He told me you are my boss," the boy was heard saying.

"Where in the devil is he?" said Mavros.

The sentinel's eyes indicated the place where the cabin boy was hidden, and Mavros, grabbing one end of a tarred rope, got ready to beat him. But the boy, feeling Mavros' movements and foreseeing the results, jumped into the hull and landed on the ballast sand without hurting himself. And he called out loudly:

"Mavros! Mavros! I see you."

It was impossible for Mavros to reach him where he had snuck. He swallowed his rage and restrained himself.

"Tell me. Who is looking for me?" he asked the sentinel.

"They are asking for you from a skiff, boss. It's over there at the bow."

Mavros headed for the bow.

"What do you want?" he asked the men on the skiff.

"I have a letter for the chief, boss."

"And who are you?"

"I am a messenger to His Excellency."

"From whom?"

"The letter explains."

"Where are you coming from?"

"From Patmos."

"Come here. Now the chief will wake up."

The skiff approached the gangway and the man who had been talking to Mavros climbed on the deck.

By the time the messenger got on the deck, Marco Sanudo had long been awakened by the commotion all over the ship. He figured something was going on and called Mavros.

"What is it, Mavros?"

"Someone brought a letter for Your Excellency," said Mavros disinterestedly.

"Let him come in."

Mavros turned his back and returned to the deck. The look in his eyes spoke more of hatred than affection. He did not like Sanudo anymore. His old expression of blithe deceitfulness and snide carelessness had vanished; his eyes, cruel and awful, were colored with bile and blood. Yet Sanudo continued to trust him. Not out of goodwill or wont. He too sensed that Mavros was shaking him off. But in the emptiness forming around him he needed something tangible, a footing, some kind of handle or crutch. This was his lot. There were moments when he would feel genuine affection for Mavros, who had served him and continued to serve him. Sanudo considered himself grateful. He loved him like the tyrant loves the hangman, the executioner of his commands. These were the moments of peaceful suffering, of his solitude and his soul searching. But these moments yielded to agony, rage, madness. Then he hated Mavros, again like the tyrant despises and curses the hangman, the instrument of his cruelty.

In vain would we attempt to interpret the motives that initially made Mavros attach himself to Sanudo. Was he avaricious? Was he ambitious? Not really. Was he a thrill seeker? A romantic African? Did he long for adventurous and maverick living? Perhaps. Sanudo had long been looking for such a person. He needed a man who had both the devotion and the impudence of a dog. He wanted him to be like himself, απλόκυνα και ψευδόκυνα, true dog and false cynic[22]. Thus, nature, having anticipated this desire of his, had created Mavros. And these two souls found themselves in an orderly arranged marriage. Yet these well-arranged marriages are sometimes the ones closest to divorce. Truth be told, Mavros had not benefited from this arrangement, while Sanudo had reaped, it seemed, all the profit. Love, passion, orgies, retributions, brutalities; Mavros had served Sanudo in them all. But what about him, poor man? What had he enjoyed? Had Sanudo served Mavros in any way? Had he interceded in a love interest of his? Love? But Mavros did not like white women. He felt aversion and antipathy toward them. Fortunately there were many Ethiopians in Venice. Otherwise, Mavros would have been forced to abstain from the knowledge of good and evil and would have been transformed into a eunuch guarding Sanudo's harem. And to what purpose would he have applied this ignorance? Where would he have devoted it? To Allah? But Allah not only does not recommend abstinence to his pious followers, but he graciously sanctions polygamy. Besides, Mavros had nothing to do with Allah. He relied on himself for everything and had accepted neither Allah's nor Sanudo's assistance. Sanudo had promised reciprocity, but Mavros had soon enough understood that he should be content with the promise alone because the man who had given it encouraged him to distrust promises. And that was fine, for Mavros did not demand any form of compensation.

Unfortunately, he had long ago discovered a different form of payment from this man: ingratitude. Not merely ungratefulness, like a dry fruit hanging from a blossoming tree, seemingly ripe yet turning to dust when touched, but expressive ingratitude, armored, uproarious, accompanied by jeers and insults. Ah, spite had started taking root, like a fungus, in Mirchan's heart. The humidity of the spilling bile was feeding this fungus. Its fruit was not yet ripe. He had not yet formed a plan for revenge. But he was considering it and justifying it through his resentfulness. He did not care for vindication in the eyes of others. He did not elicit any form of advocacy. He disdained all of humanity from some innermost instinct.

As far as Sanudo was concerned, he was far unhappier than Mavros, who had at least found comfort and harmony within—an ally in himself. But Sanudo? Neither Mavros nor his own self were allies to him anymore. And Mavros did not have to suffer from a remorseful conscience; for everything he had done had been as a blind instrument, without a will of his own. He had sacrificed his freedom on Sanudo's altar; he had subjugated his will to him. And he had done all that like those who surrender to the supernatural, which may not be understood or investigated.

In the absence of the supernatural, Mavros had submitted to Sanudo, not because he failed to understand him, but because he did not want to find out about him. Sanudo's astonishing and almost sublime mania had from the very beginning made a deep impression upon him. Mavros was of fervid nature; he disdained good and was startled by evil. In his eyes, Sanudo had assumed colossal dimensions, like a phantasmic vision, similar to those that used to appear in front of him when he was a child and his mother brought him up with legends of dark giants seeking to dethrone Muhammad. When Sanudo assured him that he did not believe in any god, Mavros thought he had discovered the uncharted, solved the mystery of the ideal. Because he had earnestly longed to find another creature, human or not, living on this earth or elsewhere, that did not advocate what is commonly accepted, but substituted it instead with its own thoughts. But this unknown had since been charted, and the ideal thoroughly investigated, vaporized, and scattered, as all ideals are. Then Mavros became mistrustful, intransigent, an experimenter. He admitted to himself that after the studies of all these years, he was as ignorant today as he had been when he had first left the desert atop the camel that had brought him so far away from his homeland. He renounced all dogma, ostracized all prejudice, and recognized the need to start over from scratch.

In the meantime, the man who had brought the letter descended into the cabin and handed it to Sanudo, who opened it and read:

"My dearest Count,

I am writing this letter to you aboard my ship, sailing along the coast of Asia Minor a few miles from the island of Patmos from which I departed today.

I disembarked in Patmos to look for news regarding the person you know about. I had learned that this person was in Patmos.

I visited the Monastery of Saint John, an ancient and famed institution. These monks boast that they are autonomous. This is wrong. Having, as I have heard, sailed with such a mighty fleet, how much longer will you allow them, my dear Count, to enjoy this autonomy of theirs? Forgive this digression of mine. I shall return below to the person this letter is about. Is it fair for monks to rule an island in the East as civil authorities? And what good are the armies and fleets of Venice when the coast and the islands of the Mediterranean have some other lord? And how can we be the masters of the seas when we do not rule the islands and the coasts? Have you talked about this to the benevolent Pietro Ziani? What did he tell you? I am curious to know. What is the point of this new campaign then, if you are to grant rights here and there, especially rights to the monks of the Greek Church? Transport a few hundred Benedictine monks from the Adriatic Islands and sow them in the Aegean. This would be good. Otherwise, force these bearded goats of the East to cite the Pope in their ceremonies. And if they don't acquiesce, abolish this bizarre republic of cassocks that has strangely germinated on the curb of the Aegean Archipelago. Don't we have enough oddities and paradoxes, all those that will forever remain unexplained, to deal with? Besides, do we really need this bizarre republic of monks? But enough of this.

Returning to the issue at hand, I must inform you that I did not find her, as I had hoped I would. Instead of her, I met a monk who had known her. He informed me thus, that two years ago she had indeed been in Patmos and had joined the monastic order. But suddenly, one morning, she put on her civil clothes again and left Patmos. He learned, the monk said, that she reached the interior of Asia Minor, some village, the name of which he does not know, where some say she still resides, or, according to others, and this is the most likely possibility, she passed away. Therefore, if this is true, forgive her, my friend, and do not worry about her anymore. And I cannot find it in me to offer you my condolences. Friends and lovers come and go, my friend, and the remembrances they leave behind pile on our memory, like the bones in a cemetery, covering and adding to each other. I don't know if there is sufficient order and organization in your memory, such that you can tell remembrance from remembrance, and string them together. As far as I am concerned, I am grateful to nature that it did not bestow on me sufficient memory. I believe that a good memory must be a good crucible, like a stomach, which receives all kinds of foods without keeping track of them. This is the consolation I can offer you.

I will anticipate your letter in Patmos, where I will return in a few days. I intend to proselytize its residents, to convince them to mutiny against the monks! A fervent desire has gotten hold of me to conquer this island. Or I am good for nothing.

Kissing your two beautiful eyes.
Cecilia"

As the reader can see, the woman who had written this letter had only written and shown that other message to the nun Aghapi as lure and pretext, with no intention of sending it. She had instead composed this new, much longer letter and sent this to Marco Sanudo.

After going through it twice, with keen attention, he remained deep in thought for some time.

He then raised his eyes to the courier.

"Who gave you this letter, my friend?" he asked.

"Ms. Cecilia, Your Excellency."

"In person?"

"In person."

Sanudo became pensive again.

"And she asked you to bring it to me?"

"Yes, Your Excellency."

"Which ship did you come with?"

"With Ms. Cecilia's sloop."

"How many ships does she have?"

"Two. Her galley and the sloop I came with."

"How did you know I was in Santorini?"

"I concluded that this would naturally be the way of Your Excellency."

"And what orders did Cecilia give you?"

"To await Your Excellency's orders."

"Well," said Sanudo after a brief pause. "Stay in this harbor today, and tomorrow perhaps I may give you orders."

The courier bowed and exited.

Sanudo read the letter a third time, wholly absorbed in a certain thought. He walked three or four times around the spacious cabin of his galley, which had been majestically furnished. Large sumptuous sofas, made of red silken fabric, had been placed along each of the four walls. A round table stood in the middle, with a black ebony column ascending from its center to support the ceiling. Brightly lit silver lamps hung from it, one mimicking a seven-headed snake, another the lion of Saint Mark, a third a crooked sword, and another a Siren with protruding breasts. Several statuettes were set on the table: Aphrodite ecstatic in front of the mirror, Psyche unconscious in Eros' arms, Saint Mark writing the Gospel, and Enrico Dandolo, Sanudo's uncle. Sanudo's bed, on display behind double cloth-of-gold screens, resembled a cave with silver stalactites hanging from the ceiling.

Sanudo went on the deck and walked about, completely lost in the thought that concerned him.

"Come over, Mirchan," he said suddenly, addressing Mavros.

Mavros approached with his dour countenance.

"You do have the gift of auguring sometimes," Sanudo told him. "Read this letter and tell me what you think."

He handed him Cecilia's letter.

Mavros read it.

"So, what does it look like to you?" Sanudo asked him.

"This woman is lying," said Mavros.

"How do you know?"

"I am not a black man if I don't know."

"Yes, but how do you reach the conclusion that she is lying?"

"I cannot put it into words exactly, but she is not telling the truth. She is twisting her words and saying too much, both signs of lying. It seems to me that she found the woman alive, in Patmos, and to prevent you from suspecting it she invented and told you these other stories."

"I concur," said Sanudo. "This letter has too many preambles and epilogues. And that long digression, like ash thrown into the reader's eyes. But I will also ask my friend Provvidenza when she wakes up."

"Ask your friend, Provvidenza," muttered Mavros, as he withdrew dragging his steps.

Sanudo descended to his cabin. He opened a door and entered a hidden bedroom, where a woman slept.

"Are you sleeping, Provvidenza?" asked Sanudo, shaking her.

The woman awoke.

"Rub your eyes well, my friend, and read this letter. Then tell me your impressions."

"Fine."

Sanudo left. Provvidenza closed her eyes again. She thought that Sanudo's appearance had been a dream and tried to continue her sleep.

Provvidenza had invited herself to Sanudo's campaign and he hadn't dared expel her.

Fortuna, however, sleeping in another bedroom on the same galley, had been invited aboard by Sanudo, who had named his galley after her. Thus, the unfortunate Provvidenza, who had until recently considered herself impregnable to the passion of jealousy, found that she had been mistaken. And she became a co-travelling observer of her own failure, ripped apart by her rival's nails.

Sanudo returned again to the deck, where another skiff had approached his galley. It had come from Quirini's squadron, which was campaigning with Sanudo and had arrived in Thera a few hours after him.

What did Venice want sending these fleets to the Aegean? The same as what the slaughterer wants from his victim: its flesh, to satisfy his hunger. Why these private campaigns with the stamps and insignia of Saint Mark? Why so many contractors for these auctioned invasions? Venice designated herself a republic, and her sons were tyrants. She gave them her blessing and sent them off to conquer the world. Such is the genealogy of politics, contiguous and true to its ancestry: Sloth bore poverty. Poverty begot hunger. Hunger produced appetite. Appetite bore lawlessness. Lawlessness bore banditry. Banditry bore politics. This is the true origin of this monster. Those days and now, always the same. Those days by means of violence. Now by means of trickery… and violence. Unchanged these rope-dancers, these gypsies, these jester-monkeys (this is how I call the so-called politicians). Dark blacksmiths in the dismal gloom of their eternal shop, forging shackles for the peoples of the world…

7. CARTACCI

From the skiff that had approached the flagship, a man came out whom Sanudo recognized. He approached and handed him some documents on Quirini's behalf.

"Is it you, Cartacci?" said Sanudo smiling. "What do you want here? Or haven't I paid you for your idling yet?"

"No, chief, but I come on behalf of Count Quirini."

"Are you his man then?"

"I was forced to become, against my will."

"How so?"

"His sailors got me drunk and loaded me on his galley without my consent."

"But I see that you are his confidant now, since you are carrying his documents. You didn't do that without your consent."

"No, once I followed him, I did my best to satisfy him."

Sanudo opened the documents and read them.

"Go now," he told Cartacci. "Convey my kisses to the count and in the afternoon I will visit him on his galleys."

Cartacci took two or three steps, then seemed to hesitate.

"Why are you lingering?" asked Sanudo.

"Chief," said Cartacci in a low voice. "There is something I want to tell you."

"What now? Do you want to sell me your services?"

"No, not this time. But I have something to tell you that may be of interest to you."

Sanudo noticed an expression in Cartacci's eyes and nodded for him to follow astern. He sat on a stool and stared at him.

"It has been a long time," said Cartacci, "that I have wanted to tell you this, but unfortunately we didn't manage to catch up to you on the way here. Today I asked the chief to do me a favor and send me, if he had any documents for you on behalf of the Republic."

"Speak, Cartacci."

"In Venice, a few days before we departed, I met an old acquaintance of mine, a man called Minas."

"What kind of man was this?"

"Greek."

"How do you know him?"

"From *that time*," said Cartacci stressing these words with a glance and a certain grimace.

"What time?" said Sanudo, not allowing such familiarity.

"That time, when the Genoese captured us, myself and Your Excellency."

"So?"

"This Minas was a loyal and devoted friend of Yiannis Mouchras."

Sanudo, upon hearing this name, even though he had been expecting it, became visibly pale.

"And what about him? Didn't you tell me that he was in Venice?"

"Yes, and I told you the truth."

"What have you learned about him since?"

"I know nothing of him. I never saw him again."

"Now, back to the other one, this Minas. What about him?"

"It was the second time Minas came to Venice. The first time he came, I hadn't yet seen Mouchras or heard about him. Never saw them together either. And when by chance I saw Mouchras, Minas had already gone. When I saw Minas again for the last time, Mouchras had disappeared. The first time Minas had told me that he had a friend, named Vendikis, who was apparently Venetian. This Vendikis I never saw. But before Minas returned, I heard that some Vendikis had fallen ill and was being treated by a woman called Forkina in her house. Well, when Minas returned, the first person he ran into, in Kokkinou's tavern where he frequented, was me. He asked me if I had heard any news of Vendikis. I told him that I had never met this Vendikis but had learned that he was ill and was staying at Forkina's. As soon as I said it, he took a deep breath and left without saying goodbye. The next day I saw him again. 'Hey, did you find this Vendikis of yours?' I asked him. 'I found him,' he said, 'and we are departing together.' 'Has he recovered?' 'He is in excellent health.' 'And where to?' 'To Patmos.' 'Farewell.' And that was all."

Sanudo listened to him attentively and fell deep in thought.

After a few moments, he raised his eyes toward Cartacci and asked him.

"And what conclusions do you draw from all this?"

"Me? I conclude nothing."

"Then how did you know that I would be interested in listening to this story?"

"I expect Your Excellency to draw conclusions first, and then I will see if we agree."

"I say this Minas was probably not as close to Mouchras as you think. Did he ever talk to you about it?"

"He told me that he was his friend but did not know where he was or whether he was alive. This is what he told me the first time, before I saw Mouchras myself in Venice. 'Why?' I asked. 'I thought you were a man of Yiannis

Mouchras, his companion when he used to chase pirates, weren't you?' 'Yes,' he told me, 'but he fell on hard times, and I don't know what happened to him.' When I found him the second time, I remembered to tell him: 'I saw your old boss one day, here in Venice.' 'Which boss?' 'Yiannis Mouchras.' 'Really?' 'Really. I am not sure, perhaps it was him.' 'And is he still here?' 'I don't know,' I told him."

"So you see, they had severed their ties."

"I don't believe any of this," said Cartacci.

"Of course."

"It seems to me that this Vendikis, whom I never happened to see, must have been the same as Yiannis Mouchras."

Sanudo paled.

"Impossible," he said.

"Why impossible?" asked Cartacci.

"Impossible I tell you."

Cartacci shrugged.

"I am telling you this is my opinion, chief, and excuse me for insisting."

"Your opinion that it is him? And that he departed with Minas to Patmos?"

"Yes."

"Do dead men travel?"

"Did he die then?"

"Yes."

"Who? Mouchras?"

"Yes."

"How do you know?"

"I have information that he died."

"Perhaps I am mistaken then," said Cartacci shaken.

"Wait. Tell me the dates. Do you remember when you last saw Minas?"

"I remember. It was between the twenty-fifth and the twenty-eighth of March."

"And he told you that he was departing with Vendikis."

"Yes."

"To Patmos?"

"Yes."

"Well, Mouchras has not been alive since the twenty-third of March."

"Are you sure?"

"Yes."

Instantly Sanudo turned pensive again.

"And you said that this Vendikis was being treated?"

"Yes."

"Between the twenty-fifth and twenty-eighth of March?"

"Yes."

"Was he ill or wounded?"

"I don't know."

Sanudo smacked his knee with his palm.

"Who knows? Destiny!" he whispered.

"You see then?" said Cartacci.

"We don't know anything with certainty," said Sanudo.

And grabbing some change from his pocket, he handed it to Cartacci.

"Take it to drink, and go."

Sanudo rose and circumambulated the deck two or three times.

He called Mavros.

"Call for the man who brought me Cecilia's letter this morning. And while you're at it, order the crew to prepare for departure."

Shortly, the courier of that letter arrived and stood waiting. In the meantime, Sanudo returned to his desk and wrote the following:

"My dearest Cecilia,

I received your delightful letter, conveying your compassionate consolations and your precious advice.

The monk who talked to you about Augusta deceived you too cheaply. I have good reasons to believe that she is alive and resides in Patmos.

Furthermore, I have received information that two men, who are probably looking for the same woman I am interested in, are on their way to Patmos and perhaps already there. From these two men, one, the younger and least important to me, is named Minas. The other is called Vendikis or he may have taken another name. The first is Greek, the second may present himself as Venetian or as Greek, or as Greek-Venetian. These two men are bothersome to me because they are working against my plans.

With the present letter I give you the unequivocal and explicit command, certified by the seal of Saint Mark, to arrest the two aforementioned men, wherever you may find them.

Regarding Augusta, you must search the island more carefully and thoroughly. And if you find her, by persuasion or force, take her on your ship and bring her to me. To this end, make use of the military force under your command and heed not the republic of the monks.

Kissing the two dimples that mark your sweet smile, dearest Cecilia.

Count Marco Sanudo"

When he was done with the letter, a new idea occurred to him and he called for Mavros.

"Mavros! Mirchan! Come here."

Mavros appeared immediately.

"Is Cartacci gone?" asked Sanudo.

"Who's Cartacci?"

"The man who brought me the documents on behalf of Quirini a few moments ago."

"I can check if he is gone."

Mavros left then came right back.

"Here he is," he said.

Cartacci appeared behind him.

"Ah, here you are," said Sanudo. "You are an invaluable man. You have the instinct of an intelligent animal. You smell, like a dog, and you understand what goes on. I will ask Quirini to grant you to me as a favor."

Cartacci bowed showing his teeth with a cunning grin.

"Describe to me," Sanudo went on, "the features of these two men."

"Of whom?"

"Of Minas and Vendikis. Isn't this what you called him?"

"But as I told you I never saw Vendikis myself."

"So be it; Minas then."

"Minas is tall, blond, with a thin mustache, small eyes, and thick red lips. The sun and the sea winds have turned him red through and through."

"Good."

Sanudo added the following postscript to the letter he had written.

"P.S.: The features of the two men, whom I am ordering you to arrest for the benefit of the Republic of Saint Mark, are these: Minas is of tall stature, blond, with small eyes, thin mustache, thick red lips, and a completely red face…"

"Now tell me," said Sanudo to Cartacci, "the features of Mouchras at least, since you cannot remember Vendikis."

"Not that I cannot remember," replied Cartacci, "but I don't know Vendikis."

"So be it; speak."

"But what do you mean to say?" said Cartacci. "Do you suspect me of hiding the truth from you?"

"No, you fool; I forgot. I have too many worries. But tell me quickly the features of this Mouchras."

"But it seems to me Your Excellency knows him better than I do."

"I cannot remember him anymore. So many years have passed since I saw him," said Sanudo with a trembling voice. "Besides, after all these years he must have changed a lot."

Cartacci dictated and Sanudo added the following to the postscript of his letter.

"... The second one, the one called Vendikis, is of medium stature, dark, the hair on his head has started turning grey, and he has a long beard, if he has not shaved it. He is simple-minded, boorish, dour, and has a unique character that makes him discernible among thousands. He has an intense and deep tone in his voice, although he seldom speaks. His clothing is unkempt and he looks like a Jew moneychanger gone broke, a rare thing, and therefore remarkable, or like a vampire who has returned from his grave to find his wife, whose trace, it appears, he has lost."

With that, Sanudo put the letter in an envelope.

"Go now," he told Cartacci.

Cartacci left quickly, considering that he had another master.

"Mavros," said Sanudo, "if Cecilia's messenger is here, tell him to come over."

Mavros complied and the messenger appeared.

Sanudo sealed the letter and handed it to him.

"Take this letter and cast off immediately, without delay, to Patmos, and give it to Ms. Cecilia. Go."

The messenger bowed and exited.

It was the content of the aforementioned letter that led to the events in the port of Patmos that we detailed earlier.

Sanudo, after giving the letter, went to find his friend Fortuna, who was still asleep. Under her bed, the dog Augustos was lying, tasked by Sanudo with guarding the lady's sleep. These two heirlooms had been brought by Sanudo, each to take care of the other, when he had set sail from Venice.

And he wouldn't have left in such a hurry, but the Doge, Pietro Ziani, who knew Sanudo all too well, upon receiving his promise, made sure to also send him the urgent order to campaign promptly, an order Sanudo received on that same night when he—as the readers remember—was hosting his friends. This is because the Doge and the Council of Ten were worried that Sanudo may forget himself amidst his orgies and postpone his campaign indefinitely. And the Venetian authorities knew of the injuries Sanudo had suffered on a certain night, and thought that the sea breeze and abstinence from orgies would be the best medicine.

8. THE ESCAPE

In a cell of the Monastery of Saint Kosmas in Naxos, around the fifth hour of the night, a feverish woman lay on a bed. Next to her, sitting with a book on her knees, another woman was reading in a lowered voice. A large black cross of the crucified Jesus Christ hung above the bed, and a nearby table held a lantern on top of it. There was no other furniture in the room. The faces of the two women were lit dimly by the weak glow of the lantern. The woman on the bed had her eyes closed. She seemed young, with a pale complexion and deep circles around her eyes. A melancholic expression, sign of sadness and remorse, exuded from her closed eyes, paling, as we said, her eyelids and brows. There was a vertical wrinkle between her eyebrows, like a seal, a symbolic signature of her pain and sorrows. She seemed to have struggled with passion, strived to find peace, but failed. One could say that she was looking to repent but wouldn't dare to. Such was the mixed and diffuse feeling evoked by the totality of this woman's features. Her eyes were closed and it was unclear if she was asleep or awake. If she was awake, she was probably daydreaming.

The other woman, sitting on a stool by the bed and reading, was of course not reading for her own benefit; but her voice was so low and nasal that phonemes would be indistinguishable to the lying woman even if she was not sleeping. The reader's age was incommensurate with the duty she was assuming at this moment. Her hair was white under her scarf, but smooth as silk and shining in the light. It would seem to those unaware of this woman's profession that she did not color her hair out of a sense of superiority instead of common vanity, because the skin on her face was white, smooth, and florid. This woman was perhaps in her sixties. But she could still tempt a man. She looked only forty, sitting there, but if one saw her walking, he would be surprised how harmoniously she moved her body, which was completely symmetric and curvy with majestic stature. But let us finally say that this woman was the abbess of the Monastery of Saint Kosmas and had no need for the usual exhibitions of female vanity. Yet all of her style professed prurience and emanated desire.

In time, the bedridden woman opened her eyes momentarily.

"What time is it, Mother?" she asked.

"Nearing midnight," answered the abbess.

"And nobody has come?"

"Nobody, my daughter, but you must be patient at this time."

"But he promised he would come."

"Tomorrow he certainly will."

"Tomorrow? After all these days?"

"Tomorrow, or today, it's the same. In the eyes of the Lord a thousand years are like a day that has already passed. Why shouldn't we be patient when life is so short? In the end, the destination of our hopes is one and the same. We will not be staying here long, but we seek the future life. Our polity is in the sky."

"I have read these things many times, Mother," said the young woman.

"You have read them, but they haven't registered. You should have marked them down where they cannot be forgotten."

"And why do we anticipate, Mother, if we don't know what we anticipate?"

"Say rather, why would we anticipate, if we knew what to anticipate? The unknown is the lure that made so many thousands of people sacrifice themselves. The unknown made the martyrs, the saints, the ascetics. It is the unknown that to this very day manages to tame and subdue all these herds of people."

"Alas, not even the unknown can lure me anymore," lamented the young woman.

"Because you thought for a moment that you found it. Because you pinned your life to a passion, my daughter."

"I have no passion…"

"Of course, one eventually degenerates to having no passion, once all the means of passion have been exhausted. Then the passion fragments, dissolves, seeps, and leaves emptiness in the soul."

That moment, a bell was heard ringing from atop the monastery walls. It rang sorrowfully, sweetly, mysteriously, amidst the night's silence. When it stopped, it left a muted echo descending like a sigh of the wind upon the ears of the two women. The abbess crossed herself. The other woman remained silent for a while and felt a shiver of piety running through her veins.

"Is it time for the mass already?" she asked.

"Of course, my daughter."

The abbess stood.

"Are you going to the church then?"

"It is my duty. And are you sleeping?"

"I won't be able to sleep."

"You will do well to come with me to the morning prayers."

"I am cold."

"Cold? In July?"

"I am ill."

"Sleep then."

"Perhaps I will come to the church later, if I don't sleep."

"You will do well. This is the source of all comfort."

And the abbess exited saying: "Be brave, my child Augusta."

Having been left alone, Augusta closed her eyes again and tried to fall asleep, but in vain. She plunged into daydreaming and tried to find a corner in her conscience where she might enjoy a bit of peace and serenity. But it was always the same suffering: searching for consolation in her daydreams, in the end she found only agony. And this is what happened again. Always deluding herself, never learning. The daydream excited her imagination, exacerbated her senses, and raised the blood to her head. Enraged, Augusta discarded the sheet that had covered her, got up, and donned her garments. What was her plan? She did not know herself, but she did not want to go to the temple of course. She turned to the Crucified and smote her breasts. She kissed Jesus' feet.

"Christ," she said, "You, who console so many, why can't you console me? But what am I saying? Why would you console me? For my misfortunes? No, for my sins. But please forgive me."

She exited the cell without taking a light, and proceeded with careful steps, feeling the wall in the dark corridor. She imagined a gaping pit or a chasm right under her feet, even though she knew well that the floor was paved and sturdy. She turned the corner of the row of cells, arrived at the staircase, and in the dim glow from the skylight above, she saw her surroundings and slowly descended the stairs. She reached the yard of the monastery opposite the temple sanctuary. Psalms were audible and reverberated in her ears. She hesitated for a few moments and considered entering the church, but in vain. The force that had taken hold of her was pushing her elsewhere. She turned to the gate of the monastery and knocked on the door of the gatekeeper.

"Xenovia," she called.

Mother Xenovia was awake. She was standing with her rosary in her hands, reciting her canon. When she heard the voice calling her, she approached her door.

"Who is it?"

"Didn't you go to the morning prayers, Xenovia?" Augusta asked.

"The abbess has given me her blessing to say my canon in my own cell," answered the nun.

"The abbess did very well. Because if you had been in church, I wouldn't have found you here."

"Why do you need me?"

Augusta hesitated for a moment, conscious of the unseemliness of the request she planned to submit to the nun.

"Speak up. What do you need me for?" she repeated.

"I must ask you for a favor, Xenovia."

"What favor?"

"To open the service door for me."

"The door?"

"Yes!"

"Why?"

"So I can exit."

"Are you mad?"

"No."

"Alone? At this hour?"

"Exactly."

"And where are you going?"

"Why do you care?"

"You made me curious."

"Will you open the door?"

"No, I cannot."

"Please, Xenovia."

"Did you at least get the abbess's blessing?

"What blessing?"

"Her permission, in the secular."

"I did," said Augusta.

"You are lying."

"How do you know?"

"Because she would have stopped you."

"And how do you know that it is not her sending me?"

"Then wait for a moment, so I can go get the abbess's permission."

Augusta was growing impatient.

"What permission? Open the door for me. I am not a prisoner, nor do I depend on the abbess."

"No, I will go."

"But didn't the abbess tell you that you are to open the door today, no matter what time it be knocked?"

"Yes, she told me, but someone was to come from the outside, whose name she has given me, and nobody else."

"So it is the same thing."

"How is it the same?"

"It is the same; when I'm telling you to open for me, it is as if someone is knocking from the outside."

"This is not how I understand it," said Xenovia. "But we will find out if the abbess told you to exit. Just wait a minute."

Xenovia grabbed her cowl and left her cell to go to the temple.

Augusta had no more power to resist. Yet she was seeing her plans being foiled. There was no chance the abbess would grant permission for her to leave. But as soon as Xenovia walked away, and Augusta's distraught eyes—wandering left and right—fell on Xenovia's shrine, which was lit by a small lantern, she saw the gate keys hanging from a nail on the wall next to the holy icons. Xenovia had thought of everything, except to take the keys with her. When Augusta saw the keys, she immediately rushed and grabbed them, without taking the time to think, or decide, as if she were afraid that they might vanish in an instant, like a magical vision. She took a candle from the shrine, lit it from the lantern, and hurried to the gate, where she fitted the smallest of the keys into the lock of the service door, turned it forcefully, pulled up the heavy iron levers, opened it, stooped down, coiled her back, and exited. At the same time, Xenovia had just entered the temple and was performing the appropriate bows to the holy icons. After receiving a negative response from the surprised abbess, she returned to her cell where she found neither Augusta nor her keys. The cell had been left alone and in the dark, because Augusta, in her rush to get the keys and disappear before Xenovia's return, had turned off the lantern when she had lit her candle. Thus, the cell of the sister gatekeeper was in tangible darkness, not unlike that, which Xenovia suspected may exist in Hell, but was too afraid to imagine.

9. WHERE IS SHE GOING?

While Augusta was surreptitiously leaving the Monastery of Saint Kosmas and taking the path to the beach (for the monastery was two thousand steps from the beach), a small boat had anchored in the very cove, also known by the name "Saint Kosmas", that this sleepwalker was headed for. A skiff detached from the boat, approached land, and two men disembarked. The beach was empty. The Venetian fleet had reached the island several days ago and anchored next to the port of Neochorio, two or three stades[23] from the Cove of Saint Kosmas, but hidden behind a small promontory with sharp cliffs, on top of which owls and seagulls chattered and feuded for rights to nesting space at an edge between sea and land. The mocking thuds of the heavy seas could be heard there joining the wailful caws of the wild birds and the distant howling of the winds. A sarcastic silence reigned, as if to challenge the rambunctious day to a fight saying: "*Stand up* if you dare!" That night held something exceptionally mysterious and mournful. It seemed to enclose a prophecy or a riddle, soon to be explained.

Augusta wrapped herself in her shawl and descended with quick steps to the beach. She prepared to enter the path that would take her to the main port and away from the wilderness of that location. Where was she going? According to a poet, the creek would answer this question as follows: "My thoughts are winsome and childish, and they push me forward, where to I know not." If this is true about the winsome thoughts of children, what can one say about the melancholic thoughts of adults, especially women? That personified creek adds the following according to the same poet, "Whoever summoned me from the boulder, this is who my guide must be." So somebody summoned the creek from the boulder. But who summoned this woman from the sanctuary where she had betaken herself to seek peace? … And if the creek speaks thus, how does the torrent speak, when it pullulates in winter? And how about the waterfall, that lashes out with audacious splatter from the height of a steep cliff and pours into the valley, on the land, and into the underground? They both reply in their own languages, the former by its uninterrupted, monotonous cry, the latter by its stupendous, ineffable thundering. The human tongue cannot translate into words what they say.

While Augusta got ready to take the way that would bring her to Neochorio, she heard the splash of oars from the skiff that had approached the shore. She turned and stood on the tips of her toes to see above a bush that hid the beach. She saw the skiff and told herself:

"That's good. Since a skiff is here, I can charter it to take me to my destination, so I don't have to walk all the way."

And she called:

"Hey, you from the skiff!"

The two men, as we said, had already disembarked.

The skiff was getting ready to return to its boat.

"Where are we going to now, master," asked one of the two men.

"You seem tired, Minas," replied the other. "Hold out, and we will find a place for you to sleep."

"It would have been better to sleep on the boat, master," said Minas. "And in the morning, we would have had plenty of time to come out."

"Haven't you gotten tired of sleeping on the boat all this time, Minas?"

"I have, but this would have been the last time."

"Be patient. You will sleep."

"Besides," insisted Minas, "it is unsafe coming out this hour of the night, in a place where there is a war between the Venetians and the Genoese."

"This is none of our concern, Minas. We are neither mercenaries of Venice, nor spies of the Genoese."

"Then why can't we stay on our boat?"

"You almost said it; why come at all?"

"That's not what I am saying."

"Ah Minas, Minas. It is so joyful and so terrible for me to return to this land after all these years. Remember, Minas? Here was the paradise of happiness for me. Alas! The paradise has transformed into a cemetery."

"Don't chagrin, master; this world is futile. Whoever expects happiness here is a fool."

"Minas, don't say this to me. Perhaps happiness is not to be expected. But honor! To me, my honor was my happiness. What happened? My happiness melted, seeped out, and carried my honor along."

And in the midst of the silence and loneliness of that night, a deep, mournful, and heart-wrenching sob was heard, much akin to the groan of a lonesome vulture. It was the eloquent voice of that night. It was as if the many mysterious sounds: the splashing of the waves, the whooshing of the breeze, the rustling of the leaves, the distant echoing cackle of a night bird, had met and joined to form that one sound, one voice, one whistle, the one that roughly translated into that piercing and sharp sob.

Poor Minas was forced again to ignore his exhaustion and renounce his philosophy. He was looking for something to say but couldn't find it. He fell silent.

In the meantime, after these two men had disembarked, the raftsmen were about to leave the waterfront. It was at this moment that Augusta noticed their presence and called for them to wait.

Minas and his companion, Yiannis Vendikis, had moved a few steps in the opposite direction from where this woman was standing. They were exchanging the words transcribed above. However, Augusta's voice was heard by Minas, immediately following the moment when Vendikis had given off that sob, the one that had resounded so mournfully in the silence of the night.

"Did you hear?" asked Minas shaking Vendikis' arm.

"What is it, Minas?" he asked, as if suddenly awakened.

"That voice," said Minas.

"What voice?"

"The voice of a woman."

"Which woman?"

"I don't know. There she is, emerging from the bushes."

And he pointed at Augusta, whose graceful shape was traceable in the dark.

Those in the skiff heard the voice of the young woman and stopped.

"Who is it?" asked one of the raftsmen.

The woman sped up her stride and soon reached the coast. Then she noticed the two men who had moved away from the beach and had now come to a halt. They seemed to have turned toward her. Augusta did not realize that they had heard her voice. There was no moon, but the starlight was so bright that one could discern things at a distance of several feet.

Augusta spoke in a lowered voice to the two raftsmen.

"Which boat are you from?"

"We are from some boat," they answered.

"From the Venetian fleet?"

"No."

"From a merchant ship?"

"Yes."

"Can you do me a favor?"

"What?"

"Take me with your skiff?"

"Where to?"

"I will tell you."

"Tell us now."

"Take me to the flagship."

"To the flagship?"

"Yes, to the flagship of the Venetian fleet."

The two men looked at each other in bewilderment and one of them said:

"Impossible."

But the other said:

"On what terms?"

"I will give you all the money I have on my person, two golden rings, a golden buckle, my earrings, all of my jewelry," replied the woman quickly and willingly.

Hearing this offer, the second of the two raftsmen did not hesitate.

"Come in," he said.

But the first one objected.

"Wait. What are you saying, Nassos? Do you want to get arrested by the Venetians and handed over to Count Sanudo gift-wrapped? Don't you know that he will not thank us but hang us? Because he won't know what else to do with us."

The raftsman pronounced these words aloud, such that they reached the ears of the two men standing on the far side of the beach.

The other raftsman replied:

"Don't yell so much, Krampis, and don't be such a fool. I don't believe he will hang us that easily if our cargo is nothing but a woman."

"Don't worry about anything," said the young woman. "As far as this is concerned, I assure you, you will be put in no danger."

One of the two men, the one who had been convinced, started pulling one of the oars to bring the skiff ashore, but the other remained indecisive.

In the meantime, Yiannis Vendikis had observed the gait of that woman and it had made an impression on him. He had heard the voice of Krampis resisting his companion, and he had only marked down the words *Count Sanudo!*

"Sanudo!" repeated Vendikis mechanically. "This name again! But who is this woman?"

"This woman," whispered Minas like a hollow echo.

"Who is she?" repeated Yiannis.

"Who is she?" said Minas as well.

"This gait! I know it."

"You know it?"

"Where is this woman going?"

"At this hour of the night?"

"My God! Have mercy."

"Did you hear her voice?" said Minas.

"No."

"I heard her."

"And how was it?"

"I cannot reenact it."

The skiff had approached the shore and the woman was about to board.

"Come in, madam," said Nassos, "if you are to give us the golden jewelry you promised."

"I will give it to you," replied the woman.

Nassos extended his arm and the woman boarded the skiff.

"Get going now," said the woman, directing an uneasy glance toward Minas and Vendikis.

"We will get there in half an hour, madam," said Nassos.

"Who are they?" she asked, pointing at the two men.

"They are good men, madam," said Nassos. "They travelled with us and they just disembarked."

"Why are they coming toward us?"

"I don't know; it seems like they saw you and got curious."

"Why get curious?" said Augusta. "But you are right, and you must be curious too. Seeing me here in the middle of the night. But my home is nearby and I have a brother on the flagship who, I've learned, is sick. I have to go. I have no other."

"That must certainly be it, madam," said Nassos, "but we did not ask."

Vendikis and Minas had indeed turned around and approached the beach, while the skiff was withdrawing.

"I am trembling, Minas," said Yiannis.

"What is it, my master?"

"Curse!"

"What is it?"

"It is her."

"Who is her?"

"It is her, Minas."

"How do you know?"

"Who else can it be?"

"Let's call Nassos back," said Minas, "shall we?"

"No, Minas, it is pointless."

"Why?"

"We shouldn't."

"But you are falling apart, master, for no good reason. At least make sure it is her!"

"I am certain, Minas."

"And where is she going?"

"To the place of misery, most certainly. Yes, this is my ultimate devastation. I have never suffered as much before. And I thought I had emptied the whole glass. I couldn't have foreseen the unhappiness of this night."

"What are you saying?"

"Yes, there is nothing to fear anymore. What was written has been fulfilled. Nothing else remains but death."

"Yet, perhaps we can prevent a misfortune here," said Minas. "If we approached that woman. If we met her!"

"No, no. Remember what I told you: observe but not outrun. So we will follow! Come with me, Minas."

The skiff, gliding along the seashore, was about to turn the corner on its way to the second harbor where the fleet was anchored. Vendikis and Minas had taken the coastal route and were walking on the sand in pursuit of the skiff. Eventually, they reached a spot where the rocks became treacherous and the bank steep.

"How can we continue here, master?" asked Minas.

"Come this way, Minas," said Vendikis. "I know this place well. But it seems you have forgotten it."

They entered a trail that led to the harbor across the promontory.

In the meantime, the young woman observed her surveillance by these two men with concern.

"Why are these two following us?" she asked the raftsmen.

"Their curiosity has been roused, madam," replied Nassos. "But look; now they have taken another path. They are not following us anymore. They must have run into some impassable rocks."

When Minas and Vendikis arrived at the harbor, and saw across from them the outline of the high rigging of the Venetian galleys along the deep blue, starry sky, the skiff had not yet appeared. Some time passed, that seemed too long to both of them, and the skiff had still not shown up. It had to go all the way to the cape and turn around, so the delay was justifiable, but Vendikis and Minas were getting impatient.

The latter expressed a suspicion.

"I was right to say that we could have prevented a misfortune. Who knows what happened in the skiff, between two men and one woman?"

"No, Minas, do not worry about this. Besides, nothing is worse than reality."

This could be translated to: "No misfortune is greater than the one that has already struck me."

By and by, the time came when the skiff appeared. Augusta was crouching in the stern, wrapped in her shawl, and the two men were rowing.

What was this woman thinking at that moment? A suspicion was troubling her mind. One of these two men, who were following the skiff, could be her husband. It seemed unlikely, but not impossible. This idea came to her like an unexpected ghost, like a memory buried long ago. Was there in the ruins of her heart room for her husband? Aw yes, so much is hidden in ruins! Besides, under the ruins of her heart, there was the dark cavern of her conscience. The cavern, where a certain echo lived. An echo, that no matter how suppressed, how choked, always speaks out and can rarely be muzzled. That cavern—alas!—was in the depths of this woman's chest. Where was this woman headed and what was her purpose? Is there a step more slippery than this? Is there a steeper cliff? But Augusta had already assessed that cliff and was not afraid of it. She had learned to despise herself and easily throw a veil on her conscience.

Was there anything natural about Augusta's love? I don't know. In those days, it could have been considered the product of spells, the work of sorcery or witchcraft, and such it was considered. And it would be convenient if this interpretation were also possible for us today. But obviously some inexplicable disturbance had taken place in her imagination. Before she met the Venetian, she had lived in peace and had never asked herself if she had been happy. She had only been married for two years. Her husband was by all accounts a congenial man. He was brave and virtuous. He was five years older than her, her being eighteen at their wedding. As a man he was good-looking; his features were not common: flashing eyes and dark skin. He ruled over his home and was ruled by his wife. He loved her as he could love her, with respectful love. And she was an honest woman. She was compassionate, tender, prudent, and benevolent. Impossible for her to misbehave. In ancient times, one would have thought of her as the only daughter of the goddess Hestia, conceived with some lucky mortal. Who could seduce her? One night her husband brought a stranger in the house. The stranger saw her walk by, and without knowing with certainty who she was, followed her. He climbed behind her to an ancient tower of fantastic infamy. It was around midnight, the time of ghosts and loves; he saw her; he caused her terror; he made her like him. He lusted for her. He conceived a plan to kidnap her. He executed that plan. He kidnapped her without being confident of her love. He only knew that he desired her passionately. Who could have believed that she, despite having been kidnapped through trickery, would fall in love, instead of being repelled by him? And yet she was in love with him. Aren't these mysteries? But no, they are not mysteries. Because this is the eternal tendency of the human heart, to love all that is abhorrent. Don't protest this blasphemy, for it is not blasphemy. It is the truth. Look into yourselves. Nobody believes anything you say with your mouth. What you say to yourselves, that is the truth. Who loves virtue? No one. You all love wickedness. Not only do you love it, you admire it. Not only do you admire it, you pray to it. So be it. No worries. This is none of our concern. Besides, it suffices that we all have reason enough to admire ourselves.

The age of self-adoration has come and all other religions have been abolished. Everyone is content feeding his own passions and aren't all other words for naught?

However, the unfortunate Augusta neither harbored nor fed such passions. She was innocent. What kind of bewitching fate put that Venetian in front of her eyes? He conquered her by onslaught, took her unconditionally. He captured her without accepting ransom. She buried all remembrances, silenced every regret, and she was content to stay with him. But she soon realized that she couldn't fill the void of a heart floating out of control in immensity. She understood that he was unfaithful, that he did not love, that he wandered everywhere. Hence she couldn't stay with him, but she couldn't return to her husband either. Where could she find refuge? All doors had been shut to her. But there was in those days a gate, a room of endless dimensions, wide and welcoming to all.

It was the monastery. She went there, in hopes that she would forget the world and find happiness in her solitude. This hope was in vain. Poor Augusta was destined to be a victim of her two contrasting memories, one of which threatened her, and the other, which tortured her. One was a tyrant, the other a persecutor. She struggled, resisted, tormented, and martyred herself. In vain. Augusta exhausted all means. Where could she find refuge then, after the asylum of faith had become inadequate for her?

Then a major upheaval happened in the soul of this woman. Like a migration of reason, like a temporary death. She decided to consider herself provisionally dead, awaiting complete necrosis. Yet for all her inner shake-up, she continued to be no less alive, and life takes place in real space; so, unable to endure the narrowness of the monastery, where she had found refuge as if in a temporary grave, unable to tolerate living in it any longer, she thought—no, didn't think, she instinctively felt—to look for refuge… where? Exactly there, where all of her misery had originated. And awakening in the middle of that night—because the night is the dark and awful advisor of the wretched, for it is then that imagination is amplified and reason travels to the land of dreams—that night when she could no longer tolerate herself, she got up, I tell you, and went to meet *him*. Like the Prodigal of the Parable who "left for a faraway land". But no, Augusta did not go to a faraway place. On the contrary, she went to a place nearby. But alas, Augusta had long ago left. And she did not need a long voyage to distance herself from the place where she had been. Indeed, she had returned completely to the land that had borne witness to her old happiness and her fateful desertion. But she had left, the wretched Augusta, left for a faraway land.

Alas! Upon returning to that island, to the scene of such innocent and blissful conduct, what pathos gripped Augusta then? What anguish did she feel inside? Alas, on that island, each rock had been a silent spectator of her unadulterated happiness. On that beach, each wave had been an audible witness of that venerable innocence. How could Augusta apologize to these speechless witnesses? How could she stay silent to these whispering indicters? What could she rebut? Nothing; she remained silent. And because she stayed silent and wouldn't dare speak, it was natural that this explosion would happen. This explosion was unavoidable. And this explosion did happen.

Thus, Augusta was no longer concerned about anything. Suffice it to say she had been condemned to live, dragging the burden of her life, like a victim she was looking to bury, to a place not seen by sunlight. Because she had "no fate under the sun", as the proverb says.

10. HISTORICAL

Count Sanudo had arrived at Naxos one day during the month of June.

Almost all of the islands in the Aegean had submitted. Besides, they were looking for nothing better than to find someone to submit to. It seems slavery is always preferable to anarchy, just like leprosy is preferable to the plague. Nobody had been left ruling these islands. Because all of the lands in the East had fallen into the hands of whoever had lucked out. Constantinople had for some time belonged to the Franks. And the Venetians were their co-rulers. There was in Constantinople a Frank king and a commissioner of the Doge of Venice. It is unclear how all this was reconciled. There was in it an Orthodox Patriarch, another who was half-Orthodox and half-Latin, a purely papal one, and a fourth one appointed by Venice, Thomas Morosini if I am not mistaken, such that these four arch-shepherds would suffice to pastor not only the sheep and the kids, but also the chicken and geese. Apparently the city of Constantine the Great fed all four of these kinds of animals in those times, just like today the dogs are in the majority, enjoying blissful privileges and honored as saints by the

Muslims. And it was a stroke of luck that the Muslims showed up and finally conquered this city, since it had been proven that the previous owners had been divided into four different camps representing four different animals. And if we were to add to these the lion of Saint Mark, an all-powerful beast that roared mightily for five to six centuries, until it perished and four or five states formed from its skin, then these animals that emitted various voices were akin to the *bleating Gods*[24] mentioned by Milton, which vanished when Christianity arrived. Thus, the Turks came after this long and fruitless competition in the arena of the East. But today, if the bulldog is to expire, we cannot see anyone else winning the battle of the world other than the red boar, because it may perhaps come to a peaceful compromise with the magpie, which speaks many languages and plays various instruments. But we return to the matter at hand.

Many noblemen had followed Sanudo in this campaign. They were: Marino Dandolo, Leonardo Foskolo, Jacobo Barozzi, Yiannis Quirini, Filocalo Navigajoso, Andrea Ghizi, his brother Geremia, and others. Like we said, most of the islands had submitted without resistance, as was to be expected, since none of the inhabitants were in a position to put together and coordinate a resistance. But in Naxos, the Genoese, these benign pirates who governed the Mediterranean by default, had garrisoned the fort, one of the few built by the Byzantines. So Sanudo met resistance there. And it seemed to him like a trick of destiny, an involuntary revenge of that land, to which he was tied—or rather repelled—by a crime…

The Genoese were powerful. They had foreseen this occasion and had prepared themselves with extensive fortifications. They had supplies sufficient for two or three months. Sanudo understood right away that, barring a betrayal or a reckless move of some sort, he would never come to control the fort. But this resistance excited his bellicose mania. His companions had become demoralized.

Some of them had cooled completely and were willing to capitulate. Foskolo and Navigajoso had already made overtures to this effect. But Sanudo intended to persist. Besides, he cared little about the cooling of the others. Aside from Quirini and the Ghizi brothers, no one had contributed anything to the campaign other than a few mercenaries. These three had three galleys, one each, and Sanudo had eight galleys and over five hundred mercenaries by himself; he was gambling his fortune and his destiny.

Every day, during the morning report, he would hear complaints from his partners. But to Sanudo's ears, these were like the breeze of the wind. He was completely indifferent to whether his partners were unhappy. It sufficed that he succeeded in his campaign. He had been disgusted, instead of pleased, by the ease with which so many islands had been conquered extempore. He needed a victory to get intoxicated. Those trivial daily Venetian orgies had irritated him. He required a different type of orgy to rejoice. An expensive victory, a bloody triumph, a day or a night red from blood; a red sun or a red moon, as he would call it, could breathe new life into him. He thought the blood he would spill would be transfused into his own veins and restore his youth, which he had so inordinately embezzled. Every day he concocted strategic plans, one more bizarre and queer than the next, and after he bore them, he rejected them as abortions and hoped to devise something even more reckless.

On the morning of the day on which we found Augusta in the Monastery of Saint Kosmas, Sanudo had woken up very early.

A few days prior, he had rediscovered Augusta, who had only conceded to a single hearing and had come to Naxos without herself knowing what she was looking for. Sanudo had sent her fifteen letters, to which she would not respond. He had asked Abbess Filikiti to advocate on his behalf to Augusta, promising to take care of the salvation of his soul and to award tax-exempt status to the produce from the estate of the Monastery of Saint Kosmas once he became ruler of the island. Filikiti served him; she applied all of her diplomatic skills toward both Sanudo and Augusta. This woman was so artful at everything that no one could ever catch her in the act of lying. She managed to satisfy both parties. She would tell Augusta that she needed to take care of her repentance, to secure the afterlife, and to free herself through a heroic decision as to the vanity of the world. On the other hand, she would assure Sanudo that the present life is plenty profitable, as long as one knows how to make the best of it. In the end, Filikiti had not promoted Augusta's liking of Sanudo in the slightest. But Augusta did not need any encouragement anyway; it would have been wasted on her. After resisting temptation for many days, by her own strength perhaps, or due to Filikiti's exhortations, finally, on the morning on the aforementioned day, she wrote a letter to Sanudo asking him to come, if he was available, within the day.

She told herself that she intended to demand and obtain his apologies, nothing more. In that regard she assured Filikiti, who did not believe her. She was in such a psychological state that she needed to assure others to convince herself. Yet she achieved neither.

Despite all expectations, Sanudo did not come all day; that day happened to be the day of all the inspections, accounting, payments, and arrangements in the army and the fleet. Sanudo spent the whole day with these duties. He called Mavros and asked him to send a letter to the abbess, letting her know that he was going to go to Saint Kosmas at night. But Mavros neglected—or perhaps did not want—to attend to it. Besides, we know that he was feeling rather tepid toward Sanudo.

Nevertheless, Augusta waited until late at night and she had asked the abbess to request from the gatekeeper that the doors be opened for Sanudo, at whatever hour of the night he might will to arrive.

Sanudo stayed on his flagship for seven hours. In the afternoon, he returned to his quarters. He called for Mavros and asked him:

"Did you send to Saint Kosmas to notify them like I told you?"

"I did," replied Mavros, lying offhand.

And lowering his nebulous countenance, he moved as if to exit. But Sanudo, who seemed possessed by a resolute thought, told him:

"Stay."

And Mavros stayed.

"Listen, Mavros," said Sanudo, "I have something very important to tell you."

"Very important?" said Mavros, dilating his lips.

Sanudo, watching intently, noticed it, and knew to recognize it as a sign of sarcasm. In order to show surprise or admiration, Mavros used to dilate his eyes, not his lips.

"I see that you are not convinced," said Sanudo.

Mavros did not respond.

"There is something I want to tell you," repeated Sanudo. "It is true that you are unhappy with me, and perhaps you are plenty right. But I want to give you opportunities to indulge, and this is one of those occasions. I want to uproot your resentment. If I wanted to hurt you, I am still the stronger of the two of us, and whenever I decide, I could order to have you hanged, if you irritate me. But I will never do that. I prefer to give you opportunities to act in such ways as to find pleasure, my friend Mirchan. And if you continue to dislike me, that's fine too. But I hope you will have better sense than to wish me harm."

Mavros stayed silent.

"Therefore, I am giving you this chance to test me, Mirchan," continued Sanudo. "Because of course you may complain that I have never allowed you to test me, and you have formed whatever opinion about me on your own. But you are as mistaken in this opinion of yours, as I am correct about you because I have tested you and you have not."

Mavros did not seem persuaded.

"What do you have to say about all this?" asked Sanudo.

"I don't want to lie," replied Mavros.

"Good. I am happy you are honest with me. To this quality of yours I owe bigger gratitude than to all of your other services to me."

"Thank you," said Mavros.

"Well then, tell me, are you ready to do as I say?"

"First tell me what it is."

"It is something that of course will be a service to me, but at the same time a great honor to you if you accomplish it."

This time Mavros showed a slight dilation around the eyes. Sanudo was pleased with this observation.

"Tell me, do you have men who are intelligent and deft, capable of a feat?"

"What feat?"

"I will tell you."

"I have Cartacci."

"I know him. Anyone else?"

"I have Skiachti."

"Who is this Skiachti?"

"He is the man who brought us that corpse in Venice."

"Ah! … yes, but that corpse was not the one we were looking for."

"Irrelevant. It was something suitable to the situation."

"And proof of greater ability," said Sanudo.

"Certainly."

"Do you have anyone else?"

"Do I need many?"

"Probably five or six."

"I will find them."

"Where will you find them?"

"Cartacci and Skiachti have them."

"Tell me, Mavros, how did Skiachti end up coming with us?"

"I recruited him."

"And is he brave?"

"Most fearless and tough."

"Good, go on then. What were you saying?"

"I was saying that Cartacci and Skiachti have an entire gang. It is a company most honorable by all accounts. They drink a devil, but their works are terrifying. Very entertaining company. Occasionally I spend my time with them."

"Tonight then, when it gets dark, you will meet them," said Sanudo.

"Very well."

"And prepare them for an urgent job past midnight."

"Past midnight?"

"Yes."

"Where?"

"I will tell you now."

"Good."

"Don't let them drink too much."

"Of course."

"A daring job, but not too difficult, I think."

"Good."

"In the evening, make sure to request, in my name, all the guards to abandon the ships."

"To abandon the ships?!"

"Yes."

"I don't understand."

"Everyone should sleep on their mats in the land camp."

"Why?"

"I will tell you; not a soul is to remain on the galleys."

"But will they listen to me?"

"Here, take this."

And Sanudo gave Mavros a parchment carrying the official seal of Venice.

"With this they will assent to you."

"I know," said Mavros, folding the document and placing it in his pocket.

"And nobody should remain on the galleys, I said, except if you have any enemies."

"I don't have any," said Mavros.

"And make sure you prepare the incendiary material early."

"Incendiary material?"

"Yes. Torches, tar, asphalt, resin, and whatever else you find."

"Yes."

"And hide all of it in a place known to yourself, and yourself alone."

"Very well."

"And don't tell anyone what this is about."

"Of course."

"Only say, on my behalf, that I ordered you so, and that it will be a great service to me."

"Rest assured."

"And you can promise any payment on my behalf, up to five hundred ducats."

"Very well."

"I give you full authorization."

"Yes."

"After you make sure that they are moderately drunk, tell them to wait for you and leave them in a tavern around midnight."

"Leave them?"

"Yes. And come to meet me."

"Here?"

"No."

"Where?"

"In the monastery."

"Which monastery?"

"Saint Kosmas."

"Your Excellency will go there?"

"Yes. Didn't I tell you I am going there tonight?"

"Yes, I forgot."

"Come and meet me there. Knock on the door and they will open if you say my name."

"Good."

"I will probably be in the church. Because that is the time the nuns pray. You will come in and find me."

"Certainly."

"And I will give you further orders."

"Very well."

"In the meantime, your men should be waiting for you in the tavern."

"Of course."

"I will give you orders, you will return, find them, and execute my orders."

"Sure."

"Agreed?"

"Completely."

"Go recruit your men."

"On my way."

Mavros exited and Sanudo was left alone. He walked around the cabin rubbing his hands and talking aloud to himself.

"Ah, so you want to leave, Quirini? You want to desert, Barozzi? We will see if you want to jump into the sea and swim back, both you and Navigajoso and Foskolo and the rest of you. I did not build the galleys for you to run away, but to follow me. And as for Quirini and the two Ghizis, I can pay them for their three galleys if they are worth something. But spare them I will not, because three galleys are enough to carry eight or ten Venetian nobleman ready for retreat. Mavros will take care of this. And his services will have never been more valuable, except from that infamous and special night. But which night do I mean? There were two nights, or rather there have been innumerable such nights. Every year has three hundred sixty-five. What a shame one cannot have three hundred and sixty-five lovers, one for each night. But what am I talking about? I am raving. For me these days have passed. Now something braver must be done, so that Sanudo does not leave this world completely unnoticed. And in the meantime, I will take care of the smaller matters. But let me go find them."

And he left to look for his noblemen companions.

11. SKIACHTI

At an advanced hour of the night, we find Mavros in a tavern by the beach in the company of our good friend Skiachti, whom we have not met for some time. Mavros had ordered four wine bottles from the taverner, who had been fasting involuntarily twice a day for seven years because of the lack of customers, and had not even been able to use his unsold wine as vinegar because he had no delicacies to flavor with it. But he had finally lucked out on the occasion of the Venetian campaign, for the Venetians seemed very thirsty and in twenty days had consumed more wine than he might have otherwise sold in twenty years.

Skiachti seemed very content with his life and was much more jovial than the first time we met him. He was portly, rosy, robust, and his features had tamed and humanized after the murder of Morozzi. Proof that unless one commits a crime, he may not improve his fortune in this world.

However, Skiachti had not benefited as much as he had hoped from that venture; had he been satisfied, he would not have taken part in the present campaign. Old Kokkinou had gobbled two-thirds of his proceeds from that makeshift trade he had attempted, with the corpse of Morozzi as merchandise. That old woman was very wily; she had dug out old ledgers that Skiachti had paid twice or maybe thrice already, such that in the end nearly nothing was left to Skiachti from his earnings. Hence, he was forced to undertake a new venture and was recruited by Mavros in hopes of kinder luck. Kokkinou smelled what had happened between Morozzi and Skiachti and promised to keep her suspicions to herself, as long as he gave her part or all of his profits. Otherwise, she threatened to inform everyone in her tavern about it. If not for that, it would have been easy for Skiachti to convince everyone that the absence of Morozzi was due to travel, or disease, or sudden death. But Old Kokkinou was not a harmless woman. None of the drunkards congregating around the tables of her tavern understood, suspected, or imagined that Skiachti would ever have been capable of murdering his closest friend, Morozzi, in order to sell his corpse. But Kokkinou, both as a woman and as a taverner, was replete with sobriety and cunning. Nobody could trick her easily and nothing seemed too strange to her.

Poor Skiachti was forced to recognize that although he had improvised everything with all possible composure and skill, when faced with the cunning of that old shrew, he was no more than an infant. After seemingly having deceived Sanudo and Mavros, and after almost deceiving himself, he nevertheless failed to evade the unsleeping eyes of that devious woman. He indeed fooled himself because the real danger came where he didn't expect it. Skiachti had improvised everything wonderfully, but who could have guessed that as soon as he came to possess the fifty ducats, Kokkinou would show up with demands, like an investor expecting profits without any capital invested in the business? Skiachti had worked alone. He was the one who was offered the job and agreed to it with Mavros; the one who invited Morozzi as a partner and who suggested that midnight excursion with the skiff and the torches for the underwater search. He was the one who came up with the idea of murdering Morozzi in order to obtain the corpse in question. And he executed his idea by himself. He provided for a safe place to hide the corpse of his beloved friend, not only to secure it from all kinds of hungry sea monsters and seals, but to ensure it stayed for multiple days in the seawater, such that it was both maintained and disfigured sufficiently to not be identifiable by anybody. Finally, he chose to deliver this present to Sanudo on that night, when he knew that Sanudo's intoxication and orgies would prevent him from recognizing it or suspecting anything. And this was an even more major and impressive endeavor than the job itself, because he had to enter the mansion of a Venetian patrician after midnight bringing a corpse with him, putting his life at risk and making himself a candidate for the Bridge of Sighs, notorious among its kind, the bridge from which one safely travelled from this world to eternity. Nobody but Skiachti could have conceived and executed this. Yet Skiachti fell victim to Old Kokkinou!

Thence, Skiachti regressed to gloomy thoughts regarding human affairs. He became pessimistic and despaired for the future of mankind. And he would have completely given up, if Mavros, who had understood the game Skiachti had played, hadn't formed a high opinion of him and hadn't become his protector. But Mavros had more of a reputation and honor than the taverner woman and did not deign to demand a share of Skiachti's profits. That would have been beneath his dignity, so he did not even utter a word about his suspicions, which was certainly very tactful of him.

However, this evening, upon receiving Sanudo's request, Mavros decided to look for Skiachti and question him as a psychological ploy. He first found Cartacci, whom he asked to meet him at a certain hour of the night in the tavern, after enlisting four other daring men. Then he went to the tavern to find Skiachti. He shared with him a lavish dinner, and after the second bottle of wine, started unbosoming.

"My friend Skiachti," he told him, "do you know that I really like you?"

"Your Highness honors me," said Skiachti.

"I like you so much, you cannot even suspect it."

"That's possible."

"I have decided to help you make it big."

"I believe it."

"Tonight we have a job to do."

"What kind of job?"

"Tonight I will test you."

"What must I do?"

"I will tell you. But I don't know yet."

"Then what are you talking about?"

"I will find out soon."

"Good."

"But it's a risky job."

"Risky?"

"Yes. Are you quailing?"

"Me? The devil knows."

"So I will see you then."

"You will see me."

"From that night," said Mavros winking, "I have held you in high regard."

"I deserve it," said Skiachti.

"That night you entered my heart," said Mavros. "You seemed like a superhuman being to me."

"Which night?" asked Skiachti.

"That night, when you brought us a dead man," said Mavros.

"Aw, yes," said Skiachti, "truth be told, I am a formidable diver."

"Forget about that; you have other qualities."

"I am trustworthy to my friends," said Skiachti.

"Certainly, since you are able to sell their very skin."

Skiachti showed no sign of trepidation, but seemed confused, unable to understand Mavros' last words.

"What are you saying, Mavros?" he asked. "Speak clearly. I don't understand what you mean to say."

"Aw yes," replied Mavros, "and this is yet another quality."

"Which quality?"

"The ability not to understand."

"I don't get it. Am I drunk perhaps?" said Skiachti bringing his hand to his forehead.

"I can't imagine you are."

"What the devil! Did you bring me here to get me drunk?"

"I am not worthy," said Mavros.

"Are you speaking in another tongue?" said Skiachti. "Because up to now, I knew our tongue. But I see now that I don't understand a word."

"And you are doing well."

"So don't make me torture and kill my mind then, Mavros."

"Ah, and you don't want to kill it, do you? Because if you had to kill it, it would be dead already. Besides, you don't know how to kill."

"What are you saying, Mavros?"

This time Skiachti did not hold back. He stood up, his eyes casting lightning, ready to seize Mavros by the neck.

"Calm down," said Mavros unperturbed, "I am not interfering with your secrets. After all, what business is it of mine if you killed Morozzi or not? You were doing your job. Everybody needs to take care of themselves and not worry about others. This is my opinion. Besides, even if you did kill him, he is not coming back, is he? And either way, if he was to die, just like we all are, it is better for him that he went by the hands of a friend, who meant him no harm. If I knew I was about to die sometime soon, I would prefer to be undone by a friend of mine with a single stab than to be hanged by the hangman of Venice. Because my trial would have to go through the Council of Ten, and until my sentence was confirmed by His Serenity the Doge, I would have rotten from torture."

Mavros threw these words like a fire extinguisher at Skiachti's burning rage.

Skiachti took the time to recover and realized that if Mavros had meant him harm, he could have hurt him long ago since he had harbored suspicions. So Skiachti lowered his face, twiddled his mustache, and sat by the table again. He poured wine into both glasses.

"Drink, my friend Mavros. Your Highness and I should be drinking. But what can I tell you? You already know all of it."

And he emptied his glass without a breath.

"There are many things, my friend Mavros," he continued, "that are best implied and not spoken of. See, how do I say it? We know each other. We are friends. Assume for a moment a third one comes, some other devil, and tells me, as we are drinking our wine, and tells me… And Kokkinou was not kidding, she chewed us to the bone; the hag. All this time I used to work for her. Work, work, like a dog. And I drank everything I made. I could see that while I was drinking Kokkinou's wine, Kokkinou was devouring me flesh and bone. I had never considered getting ahead. Except maybe once in a while, when a little fly would come to my head and I would say to myself, me Skiachti, to the same Skiachti, I would say: 'Why you, Skiachti, don't you know, you wretch, what you are doing? Why do you work? Do you know why you work? For you drink all of it, and find yourself in a deep hole. And it is not a wine barrel you are in, but it is Old Kokkinou's drawer. And you work, you wretch, for what? For Kokkinou takes all of your money and you are left in debt.'

With such fingernails, I used to scratch my head now and then. But I should have been knocking it on the wall, not scratching it. I'd say these things, but then nothing would be done. Because right after I'd say: 'Why worry?

Isn't it better to think of nothing? What good is it for a man to be thinking? And if I cannot fix myself, why do I care? It is better for a man to be forever drunk, such that he has no time left to think about himself.' During one of those moments, as I was sitting in the tavern with my friend Morozzi, Your Highness came in, Mr. Mavros. And you told me this, you told me that you will give us fifty gold ducats, to me and Morozzi, if we fish out of the bottom of the sea a man drowned or killed, I don't remember. So I took Morozzi and we went to the sea that night. And throughout the way I was telling myself, without having come to a decision or a plan yet, I was telling myself throughout the way:

'—Fifty ducats! With fifty ducats I can purchase a trawl net, I can settle, I can become an upstanding citizen.' This is what I was saying throughout the way. And Morozzi was drinking in the skiff and singing. And I was talking to myself like a madman. There, I don't know how it came to me, when Morozzi dove first, to find the corpse, which did not exist… and I knew it too well, that we would not find anything, dead nor alive, down there in the bottom of the sea. For the job you assigned me, Mavros, was such as to arouse the desire for money but offer no sure way of getting it. I would see it there, with my imagination, in the deep waters: fifty gold ducats, beautiful, shiny, round, glowing in the bottom of the sea. But who could dive to get them? They were illusory, like the nocturnal glimmer of the waves. Elusive; no one could get to them. Because to fish out a drowned or a killed man from the sea, you must first drown or kill him. The sea is very big, and no matter how skillful a diver you are, you cannot compete with your betters, the seal and the swordfish. And not just with those two but also with the little fish. What could I do? The fifty ducats were eluding me. I couldn't get to them. I thought that if I could not share them with my beloved friend Morozzi, because we could never have gotten them together, I should at least get them myself. And there was no other way, but to keep my friend Morozzi in the dark regarding my method, and not let him ever wake up, so I could get the fifty ducats, with the intention that in the next life, when I meet him and owe him twenty-five, I could give them to him then, if he should ask. So I don't believe I did wrong because I could have done worse. A terrible trance came over me; I couldn't think; I was pushed in by luck and I couldn't hold on. I didn't know what I was doing, and I was drunk too, more from fate than from wine. And after, after, listen to me, Mavros," repeated Skiachti suddenly fuming, and with a grim, wild look in his eyes, "you think I care about all this you are telling me? You think I sweat it? You believe I am afraid of you and whether you threaten to turn me in? I—and listen well to what I will tell you—I know that this world is put together such that men will thieve and kill. And those who act as masters have stolen and killed much more. I don't care if I have stolen or killed. Because it is for this reason that the master God has made this world and separated light from darkness. And light is in the daytime and darkness is at night. He made the day to thieve and the night to kill. It is me who is telling you this, and worry not, nothing more. Now let's drink!" And Skiachti poured wine into his glass and drank to wet his throat. And he was right to do this, because all orators, as is well known, need a drink to wet their mouths so they don't run out of saliva.

Mavros listened to the oration carefully, even though he seemed absorbed by his own image on the deep purple in his glass. But perhaps he felt forced to lower his eyes under the strong pressure of Skiachti's radiating glance.

"It means nothing, my friend Skiachti," he told him once he was done. "Understand that I am not snooping, just curious. I brought our discussion to this matter, not to upset you, but because I like you. You have nothing to fear from me."

"I am not afraid of anyone," replied Skiachti, emptying another glass.

"This is how I like you, my friend. I like fearless men."

"I care little, whether you like me or not," said Skiachti.

Mavros was forced to admit to himself that Skiachti was stronger. Skiachti had demonstrated such skill and aplomb during this interrogation that Mavros genuinely admired him. Nevertheless, his African instinct compelled him not to recognize superiority and not to capitulate easily.

"And I care just as much myself," said Mavros. "You think you are dealing with a male old hag? I am not from Venice. I am from Africa."

"And I have no idea where I'm from," responded Skiachti.

"You have lost your mind then," said Mavros.

"It is you who's lost it, Mavros," said Skiachti darting an irate glance.

After some consideration, Mavros realized that this argument could perhaps get out of hand, and worried this would put the venture, for which he had recruited Skiachti, at risk. So he decided to give an example of placidity.

"We did not come here to argue, Skiachti," he said smiling. "You understand, if it wasn't for an important matter, I wouldn't have called on you."

"So?" said Skiachti staring at him intently.

"I will leave you for a little bit. Wait for me here."

"Where are you going?"

"I am going to find the chief, Count Sanudo."

"Far from here?"

"Not too far. Besides, I told you earlier that I was going to leave you alone for a while."

"I don't remember."

"And if in the meantime, Cartacci comes with another two or three men, tell them to wait and I will be back here."

"Fine."

"In the meantime drink, but not too much. I told you we have an important job to do. Your luck will turn tonight."

"Go to Hell!" mumbled Skiachti sneakily.

Mavros stood up and was getting ready to leave. Suddenly, Skiachti moved violently and grabbed Mavros' shoulder tightly.

"Mavros, did you bring me here to investigate me and go betray me to Sanudo? Who knows what reward you will get for your betrayal."

"Are you crazy, Skiachti?" replied Mavros. "If I wanted to betray you, I wouldn't have told you I am going to find Sanudo. Besides, Sanudo knows about you more or less."

"He knows?" asked Skiachti despondent.

"Don't worry, he knows some but not much, and he doesn't mean you harm."

"Is that so?" said Skiachti.

"And as far as the reward goes, I told you I think: Mavros is not one to sell his secrets for money."

Skiachti released Mavros who then exited.

12. IN THE TEMPLE

Augusta had thought that Sanudo would enter the precinct of the Monastery of Saint Kosmas from the main gate, in accordance with the abbess's order that the gatekeeper open it for him at any hour of the night. But he had somehow obtained a key to a smaller side door, whether by the abbess's grace or by some other means, and he was able to enter the monastery at will. Besides, two days ago he had settled his two friends, Fortuna and Provvidenza, there. This was unknown to Augusta, since he had strictly forbidden Filikiti from mentioning this sensitive situation to her.

Thus, around midnight, when Sanudo left Quirini, the two Ghizis, and Navigajoso, who had repeatedly proclaimed that they planned to leave him alone in the siege of the fort, a hopeless situation according to them, Sanudo took that small key and made his way to the monastery. He was followed by a single armed guard at a distance of a hundred steps, whom he had ordered to withdraw upon seeing him approach the monastery walls.

Sanudo turned his key in the lock and the door opened. He entered and headed for the temple because the bell had properly signalled the morning prayers and because he had requested that Mavros find him there.

When, at that late hour of the night, Augusta deceitfully opened the service door of the monastery gate and escaped, as we saw, through the sacred precinct, Sanudo had already entered the temple. But how could she have known about Sanudo's presence, since she was no prophet to guess? Mother Filikiti could have certainly told her, but Sanudo, who was in no rush because he was preoccupied with other worries, had forbidden the abbess from announcing his arrival.

Upon entering the temple he stayed on one side, under a marble column by the choir. When the abbess saw him, she hastened to him.

"So you came," she said.

"I came."

"Should I announce your arrival to Augusta?"

"Not yet."

"What? Are you perhaps looking for Fortuna?" said the abbess with a wry smile.

At that moment, the psalmody was being read in the choir. There was darkness in the temple, as the wicks of the candles, worn out, barely glimmered. Discernible in this feeble light were faint glints of holy icons, blessing hands, winged angels, silver crowns. On the chairs along the walls[25], human bodies—nuns—could be seen on both sides, motionless like statues, with their cowls lowered to their eyes; breathless, without vision, without signs of life. And yet who knows what sorrows and passions were hiding under those cowls?

The old priest, who served as chaplain in the monastery, had just started reading the psalmody in a low voice, when Sanudo entered and the abbess approached him. His voice was serious, monotonous, melancholic, and rang like the swashing of a brook amidst complete silence and tranquility.

As the confidential conversation between Sanudo and Filikiti began, the voice of the old priest recited the following devout verses[26]:

"I am faint and severely bruised.
I have groaned by reason of the anguish of my heart.
Lord, all my desire is before you.
My groaning is not hidden from you.
My heart throbs. My strength fails me.
As for the light of my eyes, it has also left me.
My lovers and my friends stand aloof from my plague.
My kinsmen stand far away.
They also who seek after my life lay snares…"

Simultaneously, the private conversation between the abbess and Sanudo continued:

"No," he answered to the abbess's question, "I am not looking for Fortuna, even though she is very dear to me; I've come for Augusta with whom I have a long history."

"Then why don't you go directly upstairs to the cells to find her? She shouldn't be asleep yet. She has been waiting for you all day today."

"I haven't gone yet because I am waiting for someone here."

"Waiting for someone?"

"Yes, for an important matter."

"And he is coming now?"

"Certainly. I told him to say my name to your gatekeeper."

"Don't worry about it then. She will open, as long as he uses your name."

"And how is Augusta doing?" asked Sanudo.

"I cannot tell you that she is well. This woman is suffering."

"What is she suffering from?"

"Ah, she has, she has… has many pains."

"What type of pains?"

"I am a nun and I don't know," said Filikiti, "but it would seem that it is no small matter for a woman to leave her husband. Pangs of conscience are a greater torment than any of those invented by tyrants, which torture only the flesh. But people invent by themselves the most certain means for their own torture."

"So she has pangs of conscience!" said Sanudo questioning the abbess's honesty.

"What else?" said she.

Meanwhile, the voice of the old priest continued with a psalm's verses[27]:

"My soul thirsts for you.
My flesh longs for you,
in a dry and weary land, where there is no water.
So I have seen you in the sanctuary,
watching your power and your glory.
Because your loving kindness is better than life,
my lips shall praise you.
So I will bless you while I live.
I will lift up my hands in your name.
My soul shall be satisfied as with the richest food.
My mouth shall praise you with joyful lips,
when I remember you on my bed,
and think about you in the night watches.
For you have been my help.
I will rejoice in the shadow of your wings.
My soul stays close to you.
Your right hand holds me up."

This voice could be heard, with phonemes only just discernible, while the whispering between Filikiti and Sanudo continued.

"So, thus is Augusta suffering?" asked Sanudo.

"She is suffering; won't you visit her?"

"Right after, after the man I am awaiting comes."

"She will be very happy to see you."

"I won't deny her that happiness."

At that moment, someone entered the church. The abbess noticed him, understood that he was the man Sanudo was waiting for, and withdrew with silent steps, inaudible on the slabs on the floor.

That man was Mavros. He entered looking neither at the shrine, nor at the dome, nor at the floor, only with eyes wandering on the chairs, seeking Sanudo, who raised his arm in the shadow behind the column where he was standing, and signalled for Mavros to approach.

"Are you here?" said Mavros.

"Speak lower," said Sanudo. "This is a church."

"Of course it is a church," said Mavros, "but why did you invite me in the church? Do you want me to pray perhaps? Don't you know that I have never prayed, not even in a mosque?"

"It doesn't hurt; I won't force you to pray. But don't shout. You see that I can hear you."

Some of the nuns, upon hearing Mavros' sarcastic and crystal clear voice, had momentarily turned to see. But the abbess nodded to them to refocus their attention on the liturgy.

"Speak then. What is it?" said Mavros.

"Mavros, Mavros," said Sanudo, "I see that you have had a good time with your friend Cartacci."

"Why are you saying this?"

"You seem very vibrant."

"And you think I am drunk?"

"That is not what I am saying, but it seems you have emptied a couple of bottles."

"Don't worry," said Mavros coldly.

"I am not worried, but I don't want this business I am about to assign you to fail."

"Have any of your businesses ever failed because of me?"

"No, I have a lot of faith in you. But make sure they don't get too drunk, or it is all for naught."

"I guarantee it."

"So listen."

That moment, the voice of the old priest, who was reading very slowly, pronounced the following verses[28]:

"I have called on you daily, Yahweh.
I have spread out my hands to you.
Do you show wonders to the dead?
Do the departed spirits rise up and praise you?
Is loving kindness declared in the grave?
Or your faithfulness in Destruction?
Are your wonders made known in the dark?
Or your righteousness in the land of forgetfulness?
But to you, Yahweh, I have cried.
In the morning, my prayer comes before you.
Yahweh, why do you reject my soul?
Why do you hide your face from me?
I am afflicted and ready to die from my youth up.
While I suffer your terrors, I am distracted.
Your fierce wrath has gone over me.
Your terrors have cut me off.
They came around me like water all day long.
They completely engulfed me.
You have put lover and friend far from me,
and my friends into darkness.

Yahweh, the God of my salvation,
I have cried day and night before you.
Let my prayer enter into your presence.
Turn your ear to my cry."

And Sanudo's conversation with Mavros continued.

"Is everything ready like I told you?" asked Sanudo.

"Ready."

"Have they all left the ships?"

"They have left."

"Nobody is aboard?"

"Nobody."

"Have you prepared the incendiary material?"

"I have."

"Is it enough?"

"Enough to burn down this monastery, and ten more."

"Do you know if anything valuable has been left on the flagship?"

"I know that we moved everything to your headquarters long ago."

"Everything without exception?"

"There is a locked armoire, the contents of which are unknown to me, and the key must be with one of the two women."

"Ah, Fortuna's toys! Don't worry about it."

"I am not worried about anything."

"So listen. Do you know what to do?"

"Tell me."

"You will take your five men, board them on a felucca with the incendiary material, and set the ships on fire."

"Now?"

"Immediately. This is the right time."

"Very well. Anything else?"

"No. But I see that you don't seem impressed by what I told you."

"What kind of impression did you want to make?"

"It seems that you knew about it."

"I had guessed Your Excellency's plan long ago," said Mavros coldly.

"He is terrifying," said Sanudo to himself. "I was expecting him to be surprised, and instead he forces me to be surprised."

"So, can I go?" asked Mavros.

"Go, and be discreet and deft. I want my ships burned down completely."

"Rest assured, we won't even leave the ashes."

"Because these little men are suffocating me; they want to make me release the siege, and to leave the fort to the Genoese."

"I am going," said Mavros.

"Go. I will head up to the monastery attic and open the window. I want to see if you will light a big fire."

"It will be such that the fish will roast and the sea will boil," said Mavros.

"In one hour I want the job finished."

"I promise."

And Mavros disappeared.

13. THE TWO FORTUNAS

Sanudo stood contemplative for a few moments. He thought that he should be very satisfied, because of his decision to act in a way that could universally be regarded as heroic, while at the same time Venice would probably compensate him for burning the galleys by allotting him comprehensive taxation authority over the Aegean archipelago.

Indeed, the campaign had reached such a state that there may have been some logic to Sanudo's audacious decision. Quirini, the Ghizis, Navigajoso, and the rest, after bothering him daily demanding for the dissolution of the siege, had finally decided to cast off with their partners, leaving him alone with his two hundred soldiers and his eight galleys. With such a small regiment, Sanudo would never overrun the fort, and he considered it a disgrace to be forced to leave it in the hands of the Genoese, his bitter enemies. Unable to prevail over the headache of that hydra, his partners, he decided to remove their means of escape and force them to cooperate. He couldn't find a better way. Besides, the thirst for the absurd and the grotesque that possessed him, that internal urge for bold deeds together with his manic ambition, contributed much to this decision.

When Mavros left, Sanudo grew excited and eager to watch the incineration of his fleet with his own eyes:

"Let me go wake up my friend Fortuna now, so that she can see my galleys burn. I will tell her that I couldn't handle two Fortunas and had to sacrifice one for the other. Augusta should be asleep by now. I will see her in the morning. Besides, poor thing, she is suffering."

And he left the temple.

The abbess thought he was going to Augusta and remained quiet.

Only a few moments passed, before Xenovia the gatekeeper came to tell her about Augusta's unreasonable demands, as we have seen. It was at that exact instant when she escaped, without the slightest suspicion regarding Marco Sanudo's presence in the monastery.

Hearing these demands, Mother Filikiti told Xenovia:

"Tell her not to go anywhere. Sanudo is here. He just left the church to look for her in her cell. Tell her to go upstairs to catch him."

"Sanudo who?" said Xenovia.

"Count Sanudo," answered Filikiti.

"And how did Count Sanudo come in if I didn't open for him?"

"I don't know how he came in, but this is not relevant right now. Do as you are told."

Xenovia turned her back and left. But after a few moments, she returned bringing the strange news that Augusta had disappeared and the gate of the monastery had been violated.

"What is going on?" asked the abbess.

"I don't know myself."

"And the keys?"

"I felt around in the dark and found them in the lock of the service door."

"Let us go check."

And they both left the temple. Thus, Filikiti witnessed the violation of the gate.

For a moment, she thought that maybe Sanudo and Augusta had in the meantime met and left together. But immediately this idea seemed absurd to her. First of all, Sanudo had his own key and would not resort to stealing the keychain from Xenovia's cell. Besides, where would he go, and for what? Then, Filikiti understood that Augusta had left on her own, and the abbess was split between two opinions: to run after Augusta, catch up to her, and recall her by informing her that Count Sanudo was in the monastery; or to look for the count in the monastery and send him in pursuit of her, if he wished to go. This second opinion prevailed and she went upstairs to the cells, expecting to find Sanudo there (Or perhaps Augusta herself. Who knows? Perhaps Xenovia had been dreaming, or she had been sleepwalking and opened the service door involuntarily on her own, or perhaps someone else opened it). But she found neither Sanudo nor Augusta. What to do? She returned to her former opinion and suspected that they had left together. But no, impossible; if Augusta had met Sanudo, she would have rather stayed, not leave, since it was him she was looking for, and because she couldn't find him, she left, most likely. So what happened then?

"Ah, I know," said the abbess, remembering Fortuna and Provvidenza, these two vestal virgins of Venice who had found accommodation in the monastery.

"Let me go look for him; this is where the count must be."

She headed for the attic where they were both housed. After climbing four or five stairs, she reached and knocked on Fortuna's door, but very timidly. Nobody answered. Perhaps she hadn't been heard. Yet she could see light from the skylight in Fortuna's lodging. She knocked on Provvidenza's door. Nobody. She thought: "What should I do? Become obtrusive? Besides, what does Sanudo need now? Augusta is gone. He can't catch up to her. And if he loves her so much that he prefers Fortuna to her, how willing will he really be to chase her in the middle of the night in the wilderness? And he has been in the monastery for two hours already and hasn't shown much interest in visiting her. I will leave things as they are. What business is it of mine?" And she returned to the temple to complete her prayers.

Meanwhile, Mavros had returned to the tavern and found the men waiting for him: Skiachti, Cartacci, and two or three other companions.

"Have you drunk enough, lads?" he asked.

"I am soaked," replied Skiachti.

"And you, Cartacci?"

"I will stay sober," answered Cartacci, "until I find out what this is about. I don't like hearing stories when I am drunk and then get treated like a yoked ox."

"I will tell you what we will do," said Mavros. "But I hope you won't find it strange."

"No."

"Here, all of you, take a look."

"What is this?"

"Is this the seal of Saint Mark?"

He showed them the parchment Sanudo had given him.

"It is," said the five men, some of whom could barely see their own noses in their stupor.

"Is this the signature of Count Sanudo?"

"We don't know about signatures," said Skiachti.

"I do," said Cartacci.

Mavros opened the parchment and showed him Count Sanudo's signature.

"This is indeed his signature," said Cartacci.

"Well then," continued Mavros, "if you like, go ahead and read the text in this document to see what it says."

"What is this Mavros telling us?" said Skiachti impatiently. "Does he want to teach us how to read now?"

"I don't want to teach you how to read," replied Mavros. "But it is necessary that you are aware of the orders so that you are not in the dark."

"We believe you," said Skiachti. "Tell us what is going on and that's enough."

The prescient Mavros had thought that if he were to tell them the entire truth, namely that Sanudo had decided to burn his fleet and chosen them as executors of this decision, the affair would have been regarded as monstrous and completely chimerical, and his words would have been difficult to believe. So, he considered it prudent to find a middle road to present his plans and he told them the following:

"Listen. Count Sanudo, my master, has faith in all of you and commanded me to invite you to take part if you will, in the glorious deed that he is sending me to execute tonight. Aside from his gratitude, which my master, Count Sanudo, will owe you, he ordered me to promise you monetary compensation, up to fifty or seventy ducats each, and allowed me to offer you an advance."

And taking a wallet out of his pocket, he counted fifty ducats and handed ten to each of the five companions, who were sweetened up. Drool flooded their mouths, and they couldn't believe their eyes or their hands.

"He is not joking, I see, Mavros," noted Cartacci.

"Mavros pays well," said Skiachti. "If only it wasn't for that Kokkinou," he muttered with a barely audible voice.

"Now," continued Mavros, "this is the job we will carry out tonight in two words; but don't be surprised no matter what it is, and don't be scared of anything. We all have Count Sanudo's guarantee against the whole world. And he told me to promise you that nothing will happen to us, and not to be afraid, as he takes it upon himself. Don't worry at all; he is there for you."

"We are afraid of nothing," replied Skiachti.

"Speak," said Cartacci.

"In a few words: tonight we are to burn the three galleys that don't belong to Count Sanudo; that is, the one of Quirini and the two of the Ghizi brothers. These three galleys we are going to set ablaze and burn down right now. What do you think? Do you have the heart for it?"

The five men had certainly been expecting from the beginning to hear Mavros suggest a reckless plan, and indeed Cartacci, who was the shrewdest of them all, had already partly understood what it was about, from Mavros' preparations to which he had seen him devote his day. Nonetheless, and even though they were in between intoxication and sobriety, Mavros' announcement caused some surprise.

"It is nothing really and worry not," said Mavros. "I told you that Count Sanudo guarantees that nothing will happen to us. I have prepared today all the incendiary material: plenty of tar and asphalt, torches, and resin. We will go and stick the fire to three ships and go and sleep peacefully; indeed, we will have some fun tonight. This is a theatrical play, the kind that is not easy to find."

"But what about the men who are in the galleys?" asked one of Cartacci's three recruits, who was called Fiammis.

"There are no men inside," answered Mavros. "This, of course, I took care of today, following the count's instructions to empty the ships of people, not just the three that we are to burn, but the other eight that belong to Count Sanudo as well. We will not have a human soul on our conscience. All we will burn is wood and ropes, which are made to burn. This will be a fun game. Imagine the fire climbing with thuds to the rigging and the masts; imagine the light brightening the bottom of the sea, the smoke rising to the sky to turn off the stars! And when Quirini and the two Ghizis wake up tomorrow, they will think that the sea ate their galleys. They will rub their eyes and won't be able to understand how such a miracle took place."

"But tell me, Mavros," said Cartacci, "how does your boss benefit from setting these three galleys on fire?"

"That, I don't know myself," answered Mavros. "But it seems that these three comrades of his are making things difficult for him, looking to leave him and take their mercenaries. And so that they don't leave and become a bad example for the entire army, the count decided to burn their galleys."

"That could be it," said Cartacci.

Mavros looked at him and winked, a sign that he wanted to tell him something privately.

"Let's go then," said Cartacci.

"Let's go," said Mavros.

And the other four stood up and followed them.

When they exited, Mavros held Cartacci by the arm and stayed with him a few steps behind the others.

"Do you understand what is going on?" said Mavros lowering his voice. "I didn't dare tell everything to the others so as to not bewilder them."

"What is it?" asked Cartacci.

"We are not just burning the three galleys."

"But?"

"But all eleven."

"All eleven?"

"Yes."

"Sanudo's galleys?"

"Yes."

"The entire fleet?"

"Yes."

"Impossible."

"Exactly like I am telling you."

"For what reason?"

"For the reason that nobody should be able to leave until the fort surrenders."

"And this order was given to you directly by Sanudo?"

"Indeed."

"Truly?"

"In all honesty."

"It seems strange."

"Not to me."

"I am losing my mind."

"Don't because you will repent."

"Are you mocking me, Mavros?"

"No, in the name of Allah."

"You believe what you are saying?"

"Solidly and steadfastly."

"And we are going to do this right now?"

"It seems. But listen, Sanudo has confidence in you. He told me a lot about you; I am not trying to flatter you. Indeed, he told me he will give you a lot of money, as long as the job is successful."

"Aw, devil!"

"But look now, when we start burning, if the others present difficulties, you need to help me."

"Help you how?"

"It will certainly seem strange to them when they see me set fire to *Fortuna*, Sanudo's flagship. This is where I need you. We must convince them that it is fine."

"Don't worry. I will try."

"Here. Take this," said Mavros.

And he gave him his wallet, which Cartacci quickly hid in his pocket. Then they sped up and reached Skiachti and the other three recruits who were leading the way.

14. THE FAREWELL

Sitting on a rock at the beach, Yiannis Vendikis and Minas watched the skiff carrying Augusta approach Count Sanudo's flagship. They saw the woman climb the stairs and disappear behind the tall gunwale of the galley, as the skiff with the two raftsmen detached and headed back to the schooner to which it belonged, following the same curved route. The water was deep in the harbor, and the flagship, just like the rest of the ships, was no more than seven fathoms from the shore. Under the glint of the stars and the galaxy, which glowed brilliantly that night, Vendikis and his companion could easily make things out.

Yiannis Vendikis' soul seemed to have relocated to his eyes. Minas stared at him sideways and would not dare to address him.

Yiannis and Minas had arrived in Naxos that night. They would have certainly made the trip long ago, but our readers may remember the complication that occurred when they were preparing to depart from Patmos. And although they had gotten rid of that queer woman, who had been chasing them on Sanudo's orders, they had both received injuries in the scuffle and had needed treatment. However, this alone would not have been enough to delay their departure, because they had already chartered a boat, but another obstacle arose. The representative of the monks of Saint John, a monk himself who resided at the port, found out about the incident and invited Yiannis and Minas for questioning. He ordered them to stay under safe protection until he could present the events to the so-called *judicial*, a higher officer of the executive authorities in the autonomous state of the monks of Patmos. The *judicial* came the next day and examined them as well. Meanwhile, Cecilia and her soldiers had disappeared from the moorage they had previously found next to a deserted beach. Yiannis and Minas had nothing to reveal to the interrogating monks, except some likely conclusions they had reached. In the end, these formalities lasted a few days, during which Yiannis and Minas treated their injuries and enjoyed the willing assistance of the residents. After this, they were granted their freedom and they cast off from Patmos. But due to the lack of winds, their sail lasted many days.

During his stay in Patmos, Yiannis managed to find out—albeit with anguish in his heart—a lot of information about Augusta. He met Brother Nehemiah, who used to serve her, and he met Father Amun, her confessor. From the former he learned about the physical affliction from which she suffered, and from the latter about the moral illness that tormented her. Yiannis Vendikis did not present himself as the former husband to these two monks, but as a distant relative of this woman. Neither of them disbelieved him, and they told him a large part of the full truth. Father Amun declared categorically that this woman suffered from intense mania and that she was the toy of the most cunning and audacious demon from Hell, one who, having found no hay to graze in the other world, had smashed the gates of his jail and leaped decisively onto the present world, to find refuge in the body of a woman; because it is in them, according to Father Amun, where all kinds of cunning demons find comfortable abode. On the other hand, Brother Nehemiah would cross himself with an automatic motion upon remembering that woman, the likes of whom he had never seen before. He talked to Yiannis Vendikis about one night when he had seen a bizarre vision while sleeping in his cell. He seemed to be in the vestibule of the temple of Saint John the Evangelist, praying by himself devoutly in an inaudible voice. On the wall in front of him, the image of Hades was drawn in the shape of a gluttonous beast devouring the sinful souls thrown into his open mouth. Suddenly, Nehemiah noticed that the shape of the beast changed; it took human form with the face of a beautiful but infernal woman, whose features resembled remarkably Sister Aghapi. The mouth lost all heinousness and monstrousness and became the beautiful mouth of a young woman, who stopped being gluttonous, and wasn't devouring the sinful anymore, but on the contrary it was praising, praising constantly. And it wasn't praising men, but (and this surprised Nehemiah, who understood in terror that Hell transforms the sinful into demons) praising demons—demons unsightly, with horns and tails, resembling various animals. And this vision contributed indeed to the deliverance of Nehemiah from the influence of the demon of lust (a demon very mighty and dangerous, who has such a multitude of horns that he can gore almost all of the human race), because since then, and this consequence of his vision was stranger than the vision itself, he no longer saw Sister Aghapi with her beauteous and very attractive shape, but she seemed like an old, wrinkly, repulsive woman. Thus, through this supernatural miracle, he had forever been freed from the incitements of that cunning and unclean demon. And he had become capable of serving this wretched sinner, who had been seduced from the way of truth, purely out of philanthropy; and of helping her comfort her impermanent body without himself being subjected to the dangers that continually besiege this clay vessel; without fear of the snares that the angel Satan has laid at the feet of the anchorites of this vain world.

This is the information that Yiannis Vendikis managed to obtain during his stay in Patmos. Eventually, he left this island and arrived with his heart torn apart in Naxos, where that villa—the cause of his misery—was; the one he had sworn never to see again. And yet, alas! Destiny! This nocturnal sail of the woman, whom he had run into when he disembarked, led his steps exactly there, where he had no intention of going, because his villa was opposite the rock on which he stood, spying the movement of the skiff that was carrying Augusta. And these three witnesses found themselves facing one another, seemingly beholding one another, even though one was by nature mute, and the other two were by circumstances speechless; them being: Mouchras' villa, Mouchras himself, and Mouchras' wife.

Regarding Augusta, she had climbed, as we have already said, on the deck of Sanudo's flagship. The two raftsmen who had transported her there had been surprised that no sentinel had addressed them when they had reached the fleet to ask them who they were. Nor had anyone shown up to try to prevent them from approaching. There was complete silence, not a soul seen, not a sound heard. And another thing had also surprised them: the galleys seemed to be anchored very close to one another, so close that they touched. This was the work of Mavros' foresight. He had neared all eleven of them that evening, to facilitate the planned incineration. The two raftsmen were pleased that nobody had shown up to try to prevent them and that they had not run into some other hitch. And this surprise caused them no trouble. Augusta was so well fortified in her shawl, she hadn't even noticed that they had already approached the fleet. Her head was bent, hiding her face, and she could see nothing.

When she climbed on the flagship, and the skiff distanced itself on the way to the other anchorage from where it had come, Augusta wondered about the deathly silence that prevailed on the ship. She headed astern and descended with an intensely beating heart into the cabin. Solitude reigned there, and nakedness. There was no furniture or mattresses. Everything was gone. Fortunately there was a light, but it only shone on nakedness and emptiness. It was the candle burning in front of the icon of Saint Mark, left there by Mavros, who thought that if the flagship was to burn, it wouldn't hurt if the icon of Saint Mark, patron saint of Venice, burned as well. Augusta found an iron bed frame, sat on it, because she was trembling all over, and cried out:

"Where are you? Isn't anybody here?"

No one answered. She called repeatedly:

"Is there nobody here? Come!"

No voice and no sound. She called again.

"Count Sanudo! Marco! Marco!"

But there was no Marco other than Saint Mark, as we mentioned.

Then Augusta started worrying, fearing, trembling. What had happened? Why had they abandoned this ship? So many soldiers, the crew, what happened to them? Where was Sanudo? She got scared and returned again to the deck. She wanted to call the raftsmen to come back with their skiff and pick her up. But it was too late. The skiff was gone; it had turned around the cape and returned to its anchorage. Augusta couldn't see anyone. She felt abandoned. She looked around. Not a soul in sight. She called with a timid voice to the other ships, those by the flagship.

"Isn't anybody here? People, where are you?"

No response. Besides, she did not dare to call louder; she was afraid of the echo of her own voice. Then, turning west, toward the rock across from her, she saw two dark shadows that resembled people, and if they were people, they seemed to be looking at her. What were they? Augusta wanted to call to them but wouldn't dare. A strange idea came to her. Maybe it was him… her husband? Was it him, whom she thought she recognized a short time ago on the beach and whom she observed following her during her sail along the coast? But no, it couldn't be her husband; it was probably the shadow of her husband. Because Augusta did not know whether he was still alive. She had often wanted to ask for information about him and hadn't dared. She had been waiting for someone to offer that information voluntarily. But other people similarly, and even more so, wouldn't dare mention the name of her husband in her presence. No, it was certainly not him. It was his shadow. A shadow sorrowful and groaning that had escaped from the underworld and was wandering the earth followed by its guardian angel, or rather guided by him, to the places that it was tied to with memories of unhappiness. The shadow had seen her, it seemed, in the act of this excursion of questionable purpose, and it had recognized her. And not only had it not turned its face away from her, but it had followed her with patience and forbearance, both attributes of those departed from this world. Because such superhuman forbearance cannot possibly exist in the hearts of the living!

Augusta, unable to face this shadow anymore descended to the cabin. The candle of Saint Mark still glowed, but aside from this, there was no other comfort for this wretched woman.

She started considering what she should do. This deserted galley seemed like a grave to her, a grave where she would find her end after all her travels in this world. This was to be the last word in her story, this symbol of desolation and disaster; the solution to the enigma proffered by her destiny. It was there like an awful irony of her fate; it was a trap arresting her finally and not letting her go. Gripping her like a pillory, it seemed to be saying mysteriously: *"I hold you"*.

For a moment, Augusta denied all egoism and was forced to admit that if she were to be lost there that night, if she were to meet death, this would finally be long-delayed justice. She wrapped herself in her shawl, lay on the iron bed frame, and tried to go and welcome death; that is, to fall asleep. Unable to think, without enough courage to face her position, she sank into a state worse than consciousness or sleep, in between daydreaming and slumber.

But suddenly she awoke from this condition, abruptly and terrifyingly. An eerie and awful crash resounded in the silence of the night, while ample and effulgent light flared. Augusta rose with trembling movements, let out a scream, and rushed to the deck.

15. THE HOLOCAUST

Mavros and his gang walked down to the beach. They entered the dockyard and carried the tar, the torch, the asphalt, and the resin, to the felucca and boarded it. They untied the ropes and oared in the direction of the fleet…

They reached the flagship. Mavros prepared the grate with the incendiary material and lit it. He raised his arm and attached the fire to the side of Sanudo's flagship. Fiammis observed this with bewilderment, just like the other companions, except for Cartacci, and protested strongly:

"What are you doing, Mavros?" he shouted. "This is Count Sanudo's flagship! Do you mean to burn it?"

"You are mistaken, my friend Fiammis," said Mavros sternly. "This is Quirini's galley."

"No, you are mistaken," countered Fiammis. "This is *Fortuna*, the flagship!"

"You are drunk, my friend Fiammis," said Mavros full of innocence.

"Calm down, Fiammis," said Cartacci in a low voice. "You have my guarantee. Don't worry about anything."

"And they don't even ask us?" mumbled Skiachti, who barely understood what was going on.

"It is enough that you are present here," said Cartacci.

"Don't complain, my friend Skiachti," said Mavros. "We are all in agreement to do what must be done."

During the discussion, the fire spread to the tarred planks on the side of *Fortuna*, and it was starting to roar and blare. Meanwhile, with two or three pulls of the oars, the felucca reached the other side of the galley and Mavros attached his fire-bearing grate to it. Within a few moments, the flagship, having been freshly tarred, was engirded by terrible flames. Mavros and his companions did not waste time. They moved with their felucca to the rest of the ships, and the moans of Skiachti and the complaints of Fiammis were drowned by the fiery waterfall that engulfed and overflowed all of the wooden ships. The flagship, having been the first to be set ablaze, quickly turned into a bright pyramid, illuminating everything around it: the sea, the land, and the sky. The slithering monster had permeated everywhere in no time, having apparently found a victim that, due to the extended summer drought, had been preordained for a long time. In a few moments, it conquered the planks, the rafts, the ships, the reefing ropes, the rigging. The fiery snake was whistling, coiling, branching, rising, and falling, and was not going to let its prey escape. No salvation was possible for these ships anymore, except if the sea would rise to the top of the rigging and force the ships to surrender, all the way to its bottom. But nothing was falling into the sea's authority other than some broken and burning ropes, scantling, and masts, which crashed unheard in the midst of the horrifying tumult of the fire, sinking and extinguishing in the waves; and the chains, which fell ablaze as soon as the gates and bores, on which they were tied, burned down. A hodgepodge of thunderous roaring detonations rose in the air, and a black tornado of smoke, traversed by brilliant sparks that lit up and went off like shooting stars, covered the horizon. The fire took shape and soul and it tongued, breathed, raged, and shuddered. The sea was almost boiling, just like Mavros had boasted. Amidst this apocalyptic volcano, amidst this cyclopean whirlwind, under the roar of that underworld thunder, in front of the horror of the cleaved aroused water, who could have discerned, or guessed, or imagined, that there lay the heart-wrenching agony of a human soul?…

Only one. When the felucca approached, and Mavros attached the first torch to the flagship, Yiannis Vendikis saw, understood, and unable to hold back any longer, cried:

"Don't burn it yet! There is someone in there!"

But the wind, at that late hour of the night, around the final morning prayers, had started blowing from the land, and the voice of Yiannis Vendikis was drowned, unheard, dragged to the open sea, to the north, while the fleet was to the east. Minas jumped into the sea and Yiannis did not attempt to prevent him. Eventually he too, forgetting his dark theory regarding fate, sunk to his waist in the sea and started swimming, hoping that he could manage to save Augusta's life. But in vain. There was no time. The flames had immediately surrounded the ship. When the poor woman recovered from her slumber, the forerunner of her death, and heard the terrible crashing of the fire, and saw the flames slithering and engulfing everything on the ship, she had no time to do anything, other than to climb on the deck and look around in search of a lifeline. But there was no such thing; the one she had sought refuge in was on fire…

At that moment, she noticed Yiannis Vendikis standing in the waves by the beach, getting ready to swim. The resplendence of the fire that burned her shone on Yiannis Vendikis' face, and she recognized him as her husband. She stepped on the gunwale, held herself up from some rope, and, in the middle of the besieging flames, stood. Her stature seemed majestic in her impending doom, and her face was illuminated at last from that fateful glow. She waved with her right hand in a gesture of goodbye and supplication to him, who was swimming toward her, and cried out hoping that she could be heard:

"Yiannis, my husband, forgive me!"

"I forgive you with all of my heart," replied Yiannis, understanding her signal.

And the flames surrounded her, burned her golden hair, her arms, entered her flesh, and transformed this beautiful body to a black smoldering ruin of arson.

A ruin in no way distinguishable among so many ruins.

Yiannis, trembling from pain and emotion, saw her horrible agony and forgave the poor creature, who was by nature good, but sinned and was punished.

....

Within two hours, the fire completed its work of disaster. When the aurora dawned, coloring the horizon with a rosy hue, there was nothing to shine upon in the harbor of Naxos, other than land and sea.

....

Around noon, Cartacci met Mavros by the shore.

"Have you heard?" he told him, "Count Sanudo washes his hands."

"I've heard," said Mavros.

"He never stops with his usual politics."

"His politics?" said Mavros. "Is this politics, ordering me to burn the fleet and then telling Quirini and Ghizi that I did it all on my own?"

And as he was leaving, he said to himself:

"I don't know who to swear to, but I swear I will take revenge!..."

EPILOGUE

Two years later, Count Sanudo, the lord of Naxos and many other islands, who had forced the Genoese out of their last refuge, was hosting his friends in the same villa of Yiannis Mouchras, in which the present story started.

Around midnight, Sanudo went to the familiar Tower of Pragotsis and gazed at the sky and the stars.

Mavros had followed him unobserved.

Sanudo reminisced about that first scene with Augusta, when he had met her atop this very tower. He sighed and whispered.

"Where are you, poor woman! I hurt you too much."

"There is someone else here," said Mavros sarcastically.

"What do you want?" asked Sanudo.

Mavros grabbed him by the throat.

"Two years ago," he told him, "I swore revenge. I have waited long enough. I will strangle you."

With his throat pressured by Mavros, Sanudo couldn't speak. He tried to escape. But Mavros was stronger.

"And after I strangle you," he repeated, "I will throw you from this cliff to find your grave in the waves."

And he did as he said. Mavros clamped powerfully on Sanudo's throat and strangled him. Having done that, he pushed him from the edge of the cliff.

....

As for Yiannis Mouchras, it is known from the manuscript found in that monastery, and given to the publisher for the copying and publication of the present tale, that he became a monk, having no better options. It seems that it was he who was the writer of the aforementioned manuscript, and he did well to document it.

....

It is mentioned in some other unpublished chronicles, different from that manuscript, that Minas armed some galley and was fighting in the Aegean against the Venetians for a long time. It is also mentioned there that he adopted Yiannis Mouchras' idea of taking revenge against Sanudo and that he besieged the villa on the very night that Mavros had murdered him. And that Mavros, hoping to receive amnesty from Minas, confessed that he had murdered Sanudo, but despite all expectations, Minas ordered to have him hanged from the boom of the front mast of his galley. And the executioner of this sentence, overstepping Minas' orders, tied the noose not only around his neck, but both around his neck and his right armpit, very tightly, such that for many hours he dangled and wobbled in the wind, like a spider hanging from its net, tortured but unable to die. But it seems to me the information in these chronicles is extremely unlikely to be true.

....

I did not manage to gather any information regarding Skiachti and the other people in this story.

END

TRANSLATOR'S NOTES

1. The last name "Mouchras" (Μούχρας) evokes the word "mouchros" (μουχρός), meaning dim or dusk.

2. "Augusta" (Αυγούστα) derives from "august", that is, respected and impressive.

3. "Filikiti" (Φηλικίτη) is the Greek version of the name "Felicity".

4. "Pirachtis" (Πειράχτης) translates to "Teaser".

5. "Mavros" (Μαύρος) translates to "Black man". It is the nickname used to refer to Mirchan throughout the story.

6. Married women were commonly called by the husband's first name. Manos' wife becomes "Mano".

7. "The state of the Romans" is nowadays known as the Byzantine Empire.

8. "Fate", Μοίρα in the original: any of the three goddesses of Greek mythology who control the thread of life.

9. The name "Skiachti" is derived from the verb "σκιάζω" (scare).

10. The name "Kokkinou" (Κοκκινού) evokes red wine (κοκκινέλι).

11. In Greek mythology, "Moros" personifies doom.

12. The Gorgons are female sea demons of Greek mythology. Medusa is the most famous of these.

13. "Forkides" ("daughters of Forkys"): two or three sea spirits of Greek mythology who personified the white foam of the sea; old women from birth who had one tooth and one eye, which they shared among themselves.

14. "Aghapi" (Αγάπη): Love.

15. "Aidos" personifies shame, modesty, and humility in Greek mythology.

16. The "Νεαραί", or "Novellae Constitutiones", are one of the four major units of Roman law initiated by Emperor Justinian I (AD 527-565).

17. "Spirit of Python": Spirit of divination.

18. "Greco-Romans": The Byzantines.

19. Echo (Ηχώ) is a nymph of Greek mythology condemned to repeat the words of others.

20. Ritual food used in the Greek Orthodox Church.

21. "Thera" is better known as "Santorini".

22. "True dog and false cynic" is how Brutus called Marcus Favonius in chapter XXXIV of "Life of Brutus" by Plutarch.

23. One stade is 600 ft.

24. English in the original.

25. Greek Orthodox churches do not have seats or pews. Instead, they have stacidia (στασίδια) along the walls. These high-armed chairs allow a person to use the arms for support when standing.

26. Excerpt from Psalm 38, World English Bible.

27. Excerpt from Psalm 63, World English Bible.

28. Excerpt from Psalm 88, World English Bible. Note: In Papadiamantis' original, "Kyrie" (Κύριε) is used in place of "Yahweh".

Made in United States
North Haven, CT
12 April 2023